YOUR BODY OF WATER

YOUR BODY OF WATER

A novel by Siouxzi Connor

Published by Repeater Books

An imprint of Watkins Media Ltd

Unit 11 Shepperton House

89-93 Shepperton Road

London

N1 3DF

United Kingdom

www.repeaterbooks.com

A Repeater Books paperback original 2025

1

Distributed in the United States by Random House, Inc., New York.

Copyright Siouxzi Connor © 2025

Siouxzi Connor asserts the moral right to be identified as the author of this work.

ISBN: 9781915672858

Ebook ISBN: 9781915672865

The manufacturer's authorised representative in the EU for product safety is: eucomply OÜ - Pärnu mnt 139b-14, 11317 Tallinn, Estonia, hello@eucompliancepartner.com, www.eucompliancepartner.com

Printed and bound by CPI Group (UK) Ltd, Croydon, CR0 4YY

"There are tides in the body."

– *Virginia Woolf*

This book is dedicated to the rivers that flow through it:

The Yandhai (Nepean), the Spree, the Tagus, the Styx, and the Barwon.

It is also dedicated to the ancestors who generously shared their stories across time, and the loved ones in my life now and in the past who also haunt these pages.

PROLOGUE

This is a mythology of love and rivers.

It is all true in the shape of its emotional landscapes, and in its psychogeographies.

It is partially true in the shape of the narrative it takes, especially in its moments of wishful thinking: things that would have been better said and done the first time around; and in the things that should exist on these plains we wade.

And it is true in exactly the way you want it to be, while you meander its many mythological tributaries.

The story navigates the pleasure that comes through knowing that we are all more fluid beings than we are fixed. It empathises with the pain that comes from loving what is slippery — what drips through our fingers — when we are craving something graspable. It traverses those landscapes of desire, tensed between buoyancy and drowning, that will forever keep us divining for deep connections wherever we go.

Ultimately, I hope the story will bring you to the banks of that thriving feeling of being seen and known through a kinship with all the bodies of water on this planet of ours.

PART ONE

SAPPHO

"You burn me."

– Sappho.

"…
… nor …
… desire …
… but all at once …
… blossom …
… desire …
… took delight …"

– Sappho

CHAPTER I

It was what I could see on the horizon that was causing my blood to pump this hard, this hot. The beauty of *feeling towards* this something *moving towards*.

The moonlight was cresting from behind, and the very last exhalations of the sun were ambering the tender place where the ocean and sky meet.

Toes curled, I felt my way through the nerve endings of my feet to the absolute cliff edge. A churn to my stomach unbalanced me: a fear of falling, along with a more complex fear that maybe I didn't mind falling?

A body moved by a body of water. Your body.

Light fading, my eyes strained harder to understand the language of this naked female form in the distance, and what she was doing swimming out there in the ocean. There was a fire to her, motioning towards me in heat waves, from hundreds of metres below. I could feel the chemistry between us.

Your salt-sunken body, swelling in me, sweltering me.

My eyes squinted for details of her in the creeping darkness, inwardly burning with anticipation, while my skin shivered in the wind. I was dressed only in the white silk kimono that I had found in the wardrobe of my hotel room. I had fled the hotel directly after showering off another day of filming, aching for one more sunset and sea-spit breeze; another chance to play Sappho on the clifftop in my billowing robe.

Now I had gotten what I had craved, and then some. I had spotted her moving towards my clifftop just as I had been ready to head back to my room.

I was drawn to this particular cove each night because I had learned it was drenched in tales, some as ancient or even more so than Sappho herself. It is a place known as Galazio (the Greek form of Galatian — presumably where the Galatians attempted to invade). But what fascinated me was knowing that underneath the surface of the waters I gazed upon, glinting in all the shades of lapis lazuli — the very meaning of Sappho's name — was a deep underwater stream that crossed underneath the island and flowed all the way across the sea to a river's mouth near the town of Parga on the mainland. That mainland river was said to be the real-world version of the River Styx, the waterway transporting the dead to the underworld.

Tell me, what is it that you love?

A wave surged and lifted her into the clarity of moonlight: all flailing limbs, with a torso like Venus marble; her hair a midnight tryst.

Is that your warmth I smell, swelling closer?

Something like love wound its way warm through my veins and wormed its way into my guts.

The swimmer had almost reached the foamy crescent of sand below me when she turned over and revealed herself to the dark sky, and to my magnetised eyes. The muscled form. The waiting thighs. Her long hair obscured her face like she had been caught in an affair with the ocean.

Then a huge wave came and rolled her face down. I startled—

And then the next wave came and washed her to shore.

She wasn't swimming, she wasn't in control. The waves had taken their control and had their way with her. She was fleshy driftwood. Washed up to the surface and dumped on the sand.

All at once the body became no longer a she but an it. A body that the sea had used as it saw fit. And it saw fit, this night, to wash the body ashore right when and where I was watching. I rushed through the brambles from my clifftop down to the beach, holding my breath.

Face down, naked on the sand, the body could have been almost anyone. But as I ventured to turn it over and saw her face for the first time, I realised she was only one particular "someone."

And that "someone" looked almost identical to me.

CHAPTER II

I took the overgrown goat track back up the cliff, not looking back, just surreptitiously slipping my left hand inside my kimono pocket a few times during the climb.

Instinctively, I'd taken the ring from the body's left middle finger. My act shocked me, and I was hit with waves of nausea as I climbed. Why had I done that? And why had I run from the body? To get help, I tried to convince myself, but I knew the deeper answer. To get help *for myself.*

I would grotto you, I would cavern you...

Poetic debris was surfacing in my mind as I hurried through thorns, no doubt leaving my bloody DNA everywhere. The urge to run and dive under the weighty hotel linen and never emerge kept me scrambling up those cliffs.

Through the twisted olive branches, I could finally see the warm lights of the hotel ahead and hear the nightly chaos of clinking glasses, like cats treading the high notes of an untuned piano, along with "cheers" and "yamas" yowled into the night.

Pausing for a moment to think, I pressed my back up against the ancient comfort of an olive tree, feeling my knotted spine against its knotted trunk. It was still warm from the last of the summer sun. I drew the ring from my pocket and turned it this way and that, brass glinting in the hotel lights. It looked almost identical to the heirloom I had once worn on my middle finger before I lost it, except that this one was tarnished from the sea.

The idea pressed on me to pretend to be horribly drunk and tell them about the body in a slurred, vague rush. A way to tread water in a moment that threatened to pull me under.

I slipped the warmed ring onto my right middle index finger, like a talisman, and staggered forwards into the camaraderie of the hotel terrace, filled with the ragged bunch I'd lived with here these past weeks.

Picking up an empty wine glass, stained a little red, I approached David, one of the permanently drunk cast members, as he downed what seemed to be one of a succession of Mastika shots. I leaned in so close that my lips grazed his hairy ear.

"Maybe I'm just really drunk, David, but I—"

David shivered from the contact my lips made with his ear. Taking me by the shoulders he gave me a once-over at arms' length.

"There she is, our disappearing directress," David chuckled. "Pale as a ghost, you are."

He embraced me in the way he used to after every good take, like a proud grandfather, back when we were shooting the series pilot.

The Circle. Even the title had become ironic. There was no escaping it.

I'd written the script for the pilot a decade or so ago when I first moved to Berlin. Rather than getting picked up in the Berlinale film market, as I'd dreamed, it instead gained the attention of a big streaming service. The version I'd written featured Ophelia connecting with a medium from beyond the grave to finally get to tell that well-trodden tale in her own words. The studio bought the general idea and the name, but not the script, and asked me to completely rewrite it using more "activated" subjects like Hitler, the Zodiac Killer, Alexander the Great, King Henry VIII, and other pop-mass murderers... The nerd in me was kept occupied, meticulously researching mediumship and early twentieth-century Spiritualism and the lives of these antiheroes, but the remainder of my character was slowly killed off by enabling this glorification. But the golden formula had been set: each episode revolved around the savvy young medium bringing back the most notorious villains from the dead, letting them run riot in the modern day, then fighting to contain them once more with an almost imperceptible moralistic nod in the last scene "It's just my foot in the door," I kept telling myself as I signed on to each new season. Until I was well and truly through a door that didn't seem to ever want to close.

Fast forward more than ten years, and I became known for *The Circle* and only *The Circle*. For a long time I luxuriated in this spotlight and in the fact that streams of the series were still through the roof. But then I threatened to walk after the producers forced me to write an episode bringing back Jeffrey Dahmer from the dead and unleashing him in a present-day gay nightclub, and they finally waved me an olive branch. They let me go off to Lisbon to research a season led by Lady of Shallot episodes, then after all that went into chaos during my COVID burnout, their next olive branch was to let me shoot here on Paxos Island, Greece, so I could create an uncensored Sappho episode to spearhead this whole season we were shooting now.

"My love," dear old David slurred, "tell me what we're covering tomorrow? Is it when I finally tell the medium how I knew her father?" He had been cast as the medium's mentor every season since the beginning.

If *I* wasn't actually drunk, David most definitely was. He chewed a little on the overgrown edges of his moustache. The sides had yellowed long ago, but now with his absent chewing he was staining them an obscene shade of scarlet. I could see it was going to be no mean feat to try to steer the conversation towards what I needed to tell him.

He was a slight man, with immaculate, always-on-stage posture. When he wasn't in costume, he lived in the same threadbare white shirt and plaid pants for the entire shoot, both three sizes too big. Over the shirt and pants he had thrown on a beige peacoat that gave him the air of authority of a detective inspector.

Being in such close proximity to him, I remembered, from those early pilot days, his signature odour of damp couch.

"David, I have to tell you something — I think I found —"

David put his tobacco-stained fingers on my lips and whispered conspiratorially into my ear:

"I think we should suspend the revelation as long as possible, don't you think, kiddo? Really draw out the tension so he only tells her about her father at the very last minute of the scene..."

He paused dramatically, eyes sparkling in the hotel terrace fairy lights, red-stained moustache arched upwards vampirically.

Police sirens blazed into earshot before he could finish. My stomach knotted instinctively. My muscles tensed into flight mode.

The whole cast and crew on the terrace fell silent. Then came the inevitable gasps: the what-happeneds, the what-the-hell's-going-ons, and the what-the-fucks rippled through as the sirens grew louder.

Hair with too much product turned this way and that, searching for answers, and wind that was beginning to smell like summer's end came up from the cliffs, rustling through the olive groves and jostling its way around the old hotel and the thirty-odd of us out there on that tiny Greek island that only the Ancients and goat herders care about.

"Showtime!" David chuckled and threw his wine glass over his shoulder.

The shattering silenced everyone.

"Who called the police?" demanded the first assistant director, Aini, in her clipped Finnish accent.

Stomach knotted, I clambered up onto one of the sun-roughened wooden outdoor tables and tapped a teaspoon against my empty wine glass. I swayed for effect, still wearing that flimsy white kimono. Blushing and trembling, to add colour to my picture of inebriation, I shouted over the oncoming sirens:

"Um, hi, everyone. I don't know who called the police. But I do know that I saw something down at the beach about an hour ago." I paused and fumbled with the ring on my finger.

David and the rest of the cast were used to taking direction from me, and they met my eyes with the thrill of the drama unfolding. The grips and gaffers were too weathered and jaded to care, and were already smoking and cracking jokes. The producer was eyeing me with disgust while texting at such speed her thumbs blurred. Hair and Makeup were stroking my legs in a show of support with their perfectly manicured hands. The sound team were bemused and already recording the whole thing. Aini looked as though she were plotting ways to kill me, and Stuart, the endlessly patient principal director of photography (and Aini's fiancé), was plying her with more white wine.

"By *something* down at the beach..." Aini's voice was cracking, and she hit send on an email as she continued, "you actually mean you found a...?"

"Body" was left unsaid.

The sirens reached their peak, and for a moment I felt as though I were DJing a rave as the staccato red and blue of the police lights illuminated all the upturned faces.

A moment later, the lights shut off and the sirens cut out.

CHAPTER III

"In every act of beauty, there must be an element of horror..."

The booming delivery of the logline from *The Circle* preceded him into the room. I was unable to tell from his delivery whether he was being facetious or trying to flatter me.

"That's the one," I stammered regretfully. "Did you watch it?"

He was a towering, physically intimidating man with a patchily shaved head. Dark circles under his eyes and unseasonably pale skin told me he wasn't one for beachside leisure. As he offered me a thick Greek coffee in a cracked espresso cup, I noticed he had let his fingernails grow over the tips of his fingers, and something dark had stained them. He sat himself down on the edge of his desk, sighing loudly and massaging his shadowed eyes with those fingernails as I sipped the coffee with both shaking hands.

There were more forest fires and drunken man-overboards than serious crimes on Paxos, so their fire department received better funding and far more staff than the police department. Tonight, despite a dead body being found on the beach, they had me perched on this little metal chair in the office of the police inspector who doubled as head of the fire department. The overhead fluorescents were mercifully broken, so we sat in the dim green glow of his desk lamp — an aspirational brass and green plastic banker's lamp, fashioned to look antique. The rest of the department was decked out in genuine antiques, including their computer system, stuck in about 1995.

We sat in silence in exactly these positions — he towering over me on the edge of his desk, and me on the edge of the cold metal chair, clutching my coffee — until the office door soundlessly swung open.

She was silhouetted, motionless, in the doorway; we remained frozen in place, wide-eyed. The stale air of the office was gradually bathed in her fragrance — at first there was a sweetness, like citrus and fig trees in late summer, but then, beneath it, the burn of things no longer alive.

From her sleek, poised shoulders, clad in a fitted leather jacket, to her gunmetal-grey manicured fingernails, to her shiny, high-ponytailed head, she was uncannily, disarmingly beautiful.

She moved behind the desk and lowered herself into the inspector's chair, impossibly slowly, her flickering golden eyes fixed on me.

Without breaking her gaze, she slid a recording device out of her black leather handbag and placed it in the centre of the desk, shunting the inspector's clutter out of the way as she did so. She drew one serpentine hand up slowly underneath her chin, and, with the other, placed an expensive-looking pen in between her lips, which she moistened with her tongue.

"Coroner Pythia," she murmured.

I nodded to her, feeling as if I might catch fire. *Pythia?* I wondered, trembling.

"How was the trip over?" The inspector asked her loudly. It startled me: I had forgotten for a moment that he was even in the room. After a few seconds without a response, he opened his desk drawer and started pouring some shots of Mastika from a half-empty bottle.

"How about a welcome drink?"

The coroner barely bothered to mask her disgust and continued without missing a beat.

"Tell us about your big discovery tonight, then." She clicked the record button on her device and pointed it my direction.

I stammered a little then fell back into silence. Unblinking, the coroner scratched grooves into her slicked-back hair with her too-long nails as I tried to find the words, any words.

Her patience wearing thin, she prompted me with an attempt at human warmth: "So you're here making your famous horror series and now you find a real horror story of your own? That it?"

The coroner arched her lips into what was meant to be a smile. After more of my stammering, which must have seemed like an indication of guilt by now, she cocked her dark, slick head sharply skywards and looked at something only she seemed able to see.

After a moment, the coroner inhaled sharply and continued, slowly, softening her tone as if I was a missing child who had just been rescued in the woods.

"Start by telling us about the body, *Sophie*." I blushed at the sound of my name in her mouth. "How you found it, what state it was in. Whether you know who it is."

I returned her gaze, then, for the first time.

Swimming in the fierce glow of her eyes, I finally allowed the attention she was directing at me to warm me, to bolster me. As I held onto this smouldering gaze for dear life, I let myself float backwards with the current of my thoughts, down, down, back, deeper...

PART TWO

OPHELIA

Yandhai: "Walking in the path of the past and the present," as defined by the Dharug, traditional owners of the Yandhai riverlands

"I see you everywhere, in the stars, in the river, to me you're everything that exists; the reality of everything."
— Virginia Woolf, *Night and Day*

CHAPTER IV

It was all a matter of consent, with you and me.

(So I thought in the beginning.)

Me with all my assumptions and hesitations; you, a current, electric.

Cold, and it made blood rush from my extremities, directly to my softest parts, my softest hard. Heart.

Hot made all of me lull, slow... and I would lie back amongst the reeds and let your current take me where it would.

I imagined that, from above, we looked like a crime scene.

The spiralling, reedy depths of you, overgrown with secrets. Me sprawled over you, into you, all teenaged bones and sex-tangled hair. I'd open my eyes and try to stay as motionless as the dead. I'd see the sky above, doomed to another outburst, and then look to you to see how you saw the sky, in that dappled rhythmic language all your own.

You speak like a green girl
You speak like a green girl...

Once we had tired of this game of going nowhere, I would lift myself off of you and sit by your side, bare ass on the wet earth. With my mind's eye, now returned, I would watch your every languid move. And with those troublesome, bong-bleary eyes inside my skull, I would keep busy by weaving a flower crown for you. This, of course, was a very long time before the days when flower crowns had landed on the heads of chemical girls and white saviours.

Larded with sweet flowers...

Each time, I would carefully weave only those friends which spoke to me of you: rosemary for remembrance, pansies for thoughts, fennel and columbines for the day we sink each other's ships. For my own crown it will always be crow-flowers, nettles, daisies, and long-purples. All thick with the scents of drama, (especially after rain), woven into everything you.

I made you wear the crown. You didn't protest. But if I looked away, the crown would be gone. Later I would find it miles downstream, half shadowed into mud.

Which time she chanted snatches of old tunes,
As one incapable of her own distress...

Did crowns remind you of how I tried to be unfaithful? When I thought myself capable of wearing the heavier crown of another? Primrose path dalliances. How could I ever promise myself to that kind of anthropocentrism when I could be betrothed to all that is you: suckling the trees, seeping beauty back into everything that beholds you?

Larded with sweet flowers...

***

There's a moment, every sundown, just before the sky bursts into flames, when you grow warmer and the air gasps cooler above me in response; an exhalation to my perspiration.

I watch this ripple your surface, making waves that reflect in the deeper-burning sky, and these synchronised movements towards me, here, knee-deep on your moist bank. And it feels like a beckoning.

I want so badly to believe my feeling is accurate — that your undulations are beckoning me into you, to let your waters devour me whole — yet I know you more deeply now. I've seen, excruciatingly, that beneath this surface synchronicity of yours is a watery chaos just as unpredictable as fire. You are as likely to be beckoning me with your liquid lilts and lulls as a flame has a preconceived intention of bursting that one special seedpod in a eucalyptus forest into fertility. The truth is that no seedpod is singularly blessed. It will burst open like all the others in the unfocused rage of the flames.

Deep down here, I convince myself that I feel your love as surely as I feel your current wrenching my body around like a car crash. Then, just as I have almost gulped too much of you, your liquid love buoys me back up to the surface (saving me?). Cruel optimism in the way you coil yourself around my fingers, my hands, my fighting arms, to keep me from drowning.

Do these new waves of yours prove that I captured your attention, that I move you? That I cause you chaos in return? As I keep swimming, I imagine that my moving thighs make waves like sound waves, the shape of which is a language you can hear and understand.

Then suddenly the fire in the sky is out and you blush back at this sense of melodrama, intrigue, overblown romance (but I feel you swell around me all the same). Your secret inner romantic lifts me to your surface and balances me on this dusk meniscus before your current continues flowing onwards, reminding me that neither my skin nor anyone else's will ever experience the same river twice.

Never consistent.
Never stagnant.
Never graspable.
Never possessable.
You, the landscape of pure pleasure, pure pain.

***

Black feathers, large and slick with the prime of life, float downstream to my perch back on the muddy shore.

Resigned now, in the dark, to my river's running away, I welcome the distraction of the feathers and pluck one from the water, holding it dripping up to the moon. I blow on it absently. The other feathers float into a nest around my legs — either entrapping me or cocooning me, or both at once.

There's a faint smell of fresh blood on the rising wind.

Keeping that single black feather clutched in my palm, now trembling a little, I step out of the river and let her drain down my legs to the dying grass at my feet. The grass clearly needs her nourishment as much as I do.

***

So I had thought what was keeping you so distant was all about the lack of consent between us.

Until the day you flooded, violently, and I came to understand there was something else entirely.

You were ripping, limb by limb, from the leafy companions you had long held dear, by your side, keeping you whole. Now you devoured them like live bait. You were fucking angry.

Was it that I was still nothing more than human? That blood still flowed through me, sweat still poured out of me? I was crippled with shame at remaining a culpable part of this Anthropocene. I wanted an out from my species and my out was you. Your ripples lingered on my fingertips.

There were bloated cow corpses now surfing your rapids, along with the broken limbs of your former companions — eucalyptus and pines, mostly — along with all else that couldn't be seen in the depths of your new filth. I was huddled up as high as possible from your flooded force, camped out in my rejection-of-humanity cave. I'd settled myself out here, with my university texts on ecofeminism, and declared my new more-than-human kingdom with you. I had never felt more alive.

At night I'd gaze sickly at the moon, not even needing to seek you out in the distance from my cave because I could still smell you. The smell of cow carcasses rotting inside the waters I used to drink so needily into my skin. I could smell your fury, forcing all matter from its origins along your banks, and bidding it to decompose and recompose in your unmade bed. I could smell your ruthlessness making all matter your own by transmuting it into entirely new forms, then feeding on what you had created. The power and will of your body of water. It fed my love for you like a virus. The host-destroying kind.

I did a seance one night, during the flood. So lost was I that I thought we would more clearly communicate with one another through a medium generally reserved for the living to reach out to the dead. Yet I was the dead one reaching out to you.

I fashioned a Ouija board from the covers of my textbooks. I used a stone I'd stolen from your banks as the planchette. I was so convinced that this method would translate this river tongue of yours into concrete words and letters — so graspable and convenient – that I boldly formulated a question: "Do you love me back?"

I did all I could to divine you, to quash all of your slippery, drenched language into the binary notions of my flesh — white knuckles knotted over the river stone ready on the board to point to "yes," "no," or otherwise.

In this loud, stinking silence of yours, it became clear to me that you had indeed communicated your will and desires to me, along with anything else in your path. It wasn't at all just a matter of me, in this human body, imposing my desires and will upon an unspeaking body of water, supposedly incapable of expressing or imposing any desire or will in return.

You speak like a green girl.
You speak like a green girl.

Eyes closed, I released the planchette from my grip. My ego dropped all of its white noise from its usual roar to a low hiss. I could finally hear you.

Your electrified current, running hot and cold, fast and slow, light and dark, the push and pull of you, the fire and ice, the highs and lows — all of the tides of you in my body, and the flood of everything not-body, beyond body, this flood — this was all just me reflecting back at myself this whole time. An imbalance, a one-way flow. You had been trying to tell me this all along.

You speak like a green girl.
You speak like a green girl.

This was not a matter of consent. This was an emotional echo chamber. Just old-fashioned unrequited love.

***

After this flood of truth, I would sometimes get in these moods where I wanted us to be half-shadows of each other. That is, if we would just muse enough about how your reeds trickle the sunshine like the waves of my hair as I swim in you... or how your wet mud, slow-drying on my toes and ankles as I wade in you, is our voluptuous shared skin... or how the tricks of the light in the exhaling sun on your surface wink at me, the visualisation of trilling bells, and I whistle back, a holiday tune caught in me since a childhood summer road trip to Dubbo. The birds of your banks whistle in harmony, and because I know you so well now, I can sense your orchestration of them, weaving their music with your currents of water and air. I forego a moment of clarity about the unrequited nature of our love and shimmer right back to my soft, mirroring heart. I spent my days composing river poetry as if Donna Haraway and Ursula Le Guin had had a Pre-Raphaelite love child. Urgh. My human stink.

And how could I not? Anyone would, when they gazed upon you, my conductor of songbirds — letting them lilt and flow, feeding and breeding always with song, letting them feel as if these were acts of their free will, but I can hear your majesty over them. The dusk music of my river, beating my heart.

Their wings hummed, your songbirds, as you exhaled that last warm breath up from your surface to the sky exploding crimson. The birds felt it in unison and, as a murmuration, fled upwards as an extinguished flame.

***

You and I have always been more than.

More than friends, more than kin, more than human. Definitely more than a rebound.

Your brown-green made me happy on those warm, fat days you just lolled by, with the crickets chorusing you. And your sick-green made me excited on those rushing days of flood and algae. The army-green made me excited on grey days hung with storms when I was ready to go to battle for you against the world. Any battle at all. Teenage angst is a great motivator. And your pink-green made me swoon every dusk when I would plunge into you, skin welted by ravenous mosquitoes, and give you little drops of my blood as I swam.

I finally realised I never wanted you to be anything other than exactly yourself, in constant flux and continuous unpredictability. Your self built precisely upon unreliability and unpindownability. I never asked you to change a thing because you change everything on your own literally all. the. time.

The way you let the wild grasses from your banks caress you one day and the next you wrench them out by the roots. The way you smooth the stones and give them mosses to adorn themselves for one season and the next you suck them dry and let the sun corrode them to dry husks of themselves. The way you make your surface look so glassy and inviting, beckoning me into you, but below that gloss and glow is a deep turbulence with the force to drown me at your whim. Is that what you want? Another floater to add to your collection?

Some days, as I would sit with my toes gingerly testing your mood from the safety of the rock shelf, I wondered if I was just a control freak. What's the worst that could happen if I let myself be carried along, utterly, by you? Yes, I could be smashed upon the rocks of your gorge, and maybe rot away downstream in your wilderness before anyone would ever find me, but wouldn't that be the ultimate act of love? Is there a word for self-immolation by water? And I don't mean drowning, I mean allowing my body to be subsumed by the power and rage of a river? My price to pay for so blatantly anthropomorphising you?

Why hold onto this human body, this humanness, when I could be as resplendent and transcendent as you?

I cannot tell anyone else on earth what I can tell you. Not my mother, not Will. They would see it as suicide, as a rejection of life, and more personally, a rejection of the love I shared with them as humans, in all its limitations: safety, earthiness, solid ground. But I can speak to you without fear of your judgement at my estrangement.

There's one thing, specifically, I can't admit to anyone, have never admitted: it hurts to have sex with him. With Will. It hurts physically and it hurts my soul, if that makes any sense at all. I either cry or hold back tears almost every time.

But I also hold back tears when I think of the alternative — that if I don't do it, and don't do it in the ways he wants to, I will lose him and lose our entire future.

The religion of my childhood was the one that taught me that a dunk in the divine water as a baby would save me. But it's the same religion that has me living by a credo that life, especially "love life," is all about suffering. And the more *earthly suffering I endure now, the greater the reward will be when life ends.*

I've been taught, since baptism, since that holy water was dripped on my baby head, that to suffer is divine. The more pain you get through, the better a human you are. That I can only have nice things, and a measure of happiness if I'm also prepared to endure more of a measure of pain and suffering.

So what's wrong with me?

My body speaks to me, tries to be heard, when my "soulmate" is enjoying himself doing what is most natural, what our bodies were made for. My body speaks to me in sensations of nausea, sickness, pain, tension, fear, wanting to flee, and freezing up until my increasingly elaborate sexual fantasies take over, and they have taken me to the darkest parts of me I didn't know existed and that I can only speak of to you.

The fantasies are all about rape; being raped by someone more physically powerful than I am so that I have to relinquish myself for any hope of survival. In my fantasies, my body is being enjoyed fully by others while I'm completely dissociating from it, even abandoning it. I have to go to these extremes in my mind to be able to protect my body; the only way out is to orgasm, to show enjoyment, otherwise it keeps going or I'm dismissed as "damaged goods."

But there is also power in it. The submissive power gained from relinquishing control. The sexual pleasure in being dominated, even if it involves physical pain — or rather, especially if it involves physical pain. It's the way I found to feel power and pleasure within the pain, and even to give it all a purpose: all this suffering will be rewarded, somehow, in the end.

But being here with you, river, I feel right. I feel whole, complete, soft, safe. I can be wholly in my body, next to or even within your body of water. This safety and pleasure and relief reaches me deep in my blood, in my bones. My comfort zone. And when I'm feeling comforted like this it opens up a

*crack in me wide enough for the question to trickle in, drip
by drip:*

Is there another way?

*This hoped-for transmutation could take place in your liminal
zone, swanning the edges of earth and water — your swampy
banks, with your mud all the way up to my thighs — this would
be the new reality of us as compatible bodies / bodily waters
intertwixt. How to disappear completely.*

CHAPTER V

Sophie had been on her ecofeminist rejection-of-humanity kick for about a month by the time Will tracked her down. It was in his nature to let others work themselves out, not to play boss or think he knew best. But after two weeks without any word, or even a short return to gather new supplies or fresh water, Will had reached his breaking point.

Frustrated, disappointed, and just slightly (and secretly) in awe of what she was doing, he had decided — grumbling to her mother that muggy late summer morning — that he would pack a bag with enough goodies to keep the two of them alive for the weekend, and get himself through the bush, out to her encampment.

He muttered some phrases he had rehearsed as he forced his feet into his Docs, still sticky with beer and dented from the mosh pit of the night before. No time to style his spikes this morning, he clamped a Chicago Bulls cap over his bleached hair, swung the backpack on his sunburned shoulders and slammed Sophie's parents' front door. He had assured her mother that he wouldn't return empty-handed. He would end this death-throe of teen angst once and for all and bring her daughter home.

Coming of age in Sydney's punk scene, around a lot of straight-edge vegan kids who'd never smoked, drunk, done drugs, or eaten meat, Will was accustomed to strong willpower, especially for a higher cause. He'd had plenty of friends and bandmates who'd chained themselves to trees, laid in the paths of bulldozers, or set factory-farmed animals free in the dead of night. He even knew a lot of crust punks who chose valiantly to shoplift from the chain liquor stores instead of the mum-and-dad corner stores. But to have his own girlfriend — who couldn't stick to veganism because of her cheese addiction and wasn't even a punk or an anarchist — go to such an extreme had come as a bit of a shock. Add to this the fact that she had not only abandoned her cult-level-close family, but had effectively abandoned *him* as well — that really cut deep. They were supposed to be best friends. They were supposed to be soulmates. They were supposed to be getting married.

She was the middle child, the easy daughter. Sure, she was the black sheep of the family, but she was always the soft, tiptoeing one, known to get a bit wild at raves but otherwise compliant, polite, eager to please. She had confessed to him that her ultimate dream was to live on a warm island with everyone she loved and a hundred rescue animals, all happy, peaceful, and in harmony. That kind of sappy idealism made him question their whole connection if he was really honest. And yet here the sap was, now being the ultimate troublemaker, renouncing her family and her fiancé, as well as her own species and their entire way of existing, to go live by the river and retrace the steps of some long-lost ancestors.

Sophie had written in her scathing (albeit very beautifully composed) note that the human race made her increasingly sick, physically, and to the depths of her soul, and she could no longer, in good conscience, continue living in the current system. That she had to go back to her roots and uncover certain truths. That still didn't soften the blow to his ego.

It took him a few hours to tramp his way, grumbling, to her solo encampment.

He knew exactly where she would be since she had rattled on about the place since they met — trying to coax him to come with her to the spot along the river she and her siblings had clambered to as kids. Sophie had complained to him a few times how she had tried in vain to find out the local Indigenous name and the history of the place — checking local libraries, online, asking local organisations — and had come up with nothing but a thin, self-published volume that one long-time resident had donated to the small gallery nearby. It would be decades before she found any depth of research, before there were any resources put into the stories to be told of that land. In the meantime, Sophie had explained, she would have to rely on the scant stories that were told to her about the ancestors, along with the knowledge she felt from the place in her bones, and she really wanted him to experience that, too.

Its name, since the white invasion, was the Narrows.

Sophie had explained that one of the reasons that the Narrows felt so special to her was that it marked the furthest extent of where they were allowed to venture as kids. Their childhood threshold. It was a good hour-long walk through snake- and spider-infested scrub, clambering over moss-covered rocks and logs, and even required scaling a small cliff edge over the river. With rocks, rivers, even snakes, Sophie and her siblings were allowed to run wild. And yet when it had come to trusting their children around other people — particularly those of the opposite sex — Sophie's parents took a very different tack. Perhaps there was something in the family bloodline, at least on her mother's side, which understood the instinct to "go bush," to run away. Her great-aunt Eliza had it. Even Eliza's mother had it, but she was just far better at hiding it. If Sophie's mother had it too, she had become the family expert in repression.

The place looked like the stones had all gathered around to discuss something very important back in the last ice age and never reached an agreement. When you clambered past this meeting place of stones, you were greeted with a rushing current of water coming all the way down from the highest elevations of the Blue Mountains. It was mountain-cooled and clear, perfect for wading through and splashing cheeks hot with all that clambering along the riverbank to get here. Over untold thousands of years, the water had worn twists and turns into the stone, revealing dramatic sandstone cliffs on the eastern side and bushland stretching wild westwards into the gorge and the vast wilderness of the Blue Mountains beyond. On summer days, the cicadas were so loud that you had to stay in the stream, away from the trees, for fear of their singing deafening you.

By the time Will got there, stripped down to a loose basketball singlet, long Carhartt shorts, and with the Docs off and tied by the laces to his backpack, he was snorting raw anger from both nostrils. He was sore, he was hot, and he was very much not a hiker. He didn't mind sitting with a nice view and a good book, or sitting outside with the window open and a great record playing, but hiking like this in the fuckcluster of summer with mosquitoes and snakes and thorns and neck-breaking cliff edges — this was not his idea of fun.

"Sophie!!" he called over the sandstone cliffs. "Soph!"

He already knew she was down there. He could hear her reciting that damn Ophelia monologue he had helped her memorise for school last summer. He'd memorised the whole scene by osmosis.

"Quoth she, 'Before you tumbled me,
You promis'd me to wed.'"

Her voice lilted up to him from the water below.

He called back to her, in his raw Australian accent:

"'So would I 'a done, by yonder sun,
An thou hadst not come to my bed."

"Oh it's you!" Sophie called back. She giggled nervously.

There was a silence filled only by the song of the cicadas. Then Sophie laughed again, sounding closer now. She called sheepishly: *"Where is the beauteous Majesty of Denmark?"*

Will had only been there with her once before but he had golden memories of their swimming together in that wide natural pool, cooled by the mountain shade in the mornings and warmed by the long fiery sunsets in the afternoons. The memories softened his anger a little and he started down the cliff towards her now with a smile on his face and a willingness to make peace.

"Fare you well, my dove?" he asked as he edged down the last sandstone ledge and landed on the sand by the rockpool, feeling a fool as the words slipped out of his mouth. He burned bright red as he stood before her on the sand.

"Sorry, that was lame," he muttered, then handed her a crushed packet of Cheezels.

CHAPTER VI

"We don't need a special board or anything," Sophie reassured Will as they smoothed out a spot in the sand by the waterhole.

The sun was disappearing and they were losing light fast. Sophie had only just managed to convince Will a half hour ago to go ahead with the séance, so they needed to rush their preparation before they were plunged into darkness.

"It was only just in that one room in the house that it happened?" Will asked Sophie as he drew the numbers and punctuation marks for their makeshift ouija board. They fashioned it with the letters and numbers around the edges of the "board" with the planchette in the centre. Sophie had destroyed the last one she used in a rage after the river had turned her down, so they needed to improvise.

"Yes it was just that one room in your parents' house," Sophie answered as she drew the numbers, carefully looping each one with her stick in the sand, "but I still don't think it had anything to do with the room itself, I think it's actually attached to me."

As the cockatoos screeched home to roost and the kookaburras laughed through the warm squeeze of the dusk air, their conversation had meandered back to the night terrors that Sophie had been getting every time that she slept in Will's parents' spare room.

Sophie was still forbidden to sleep over in Will's bedroom when she visited, even after they had been together for a year. She was relegated to the stuffy spare room on the opposite side of the house to all the other bedrooms. There was a desk with a computer from the early '90s in there, and some bags of old clothes stuffed in the built-in mirrored wardrobe, that someone kept neglecting to deliver to the charity bins.

Ever since the first night she'd stayed over, after the party where their mutual friend Ange had introduced them, Sophie had felt this oppressive air in that room, sometimes so thick and hot it was hard to breathe. It was easy to ignore in the daytime, especially when Sophie's stomach was in a whirlwind of butterflies over Will, her first love and the person she had already convinced herself was her soulmate. She was nineteen and he twenty-one, so she had looked up to him like a worldly, well-travelled, well-read mentor, not just a boyfriend.

Meanwhile, he was composing the first love song of his life, "You Make Me Pathetic," with his punk band. The song became a scene-hit for a few months for all the punks who liked their love stories nihilistic. Sophie remained oblivious for longer than she should have that his punk-styled profession of love was actually sincere. She didn't want to let herself believe it for fear of being wrong and feeling idiotic, especially in front of the infinitely cooler, always-inebriated band of girls that Will was close with — the kind who knew every Bikini Kill lyric, printed their own zines, knew how to screen print T-shirts, and had already seen Peaches play live. Then, one day, Will was driving her home after a music festival and he placed his hand on hers, wordlessly. After months of agonising ambiguity, this was the signal she was looking for that they were something more than friends — it wasn't just all in her head and scrawled in her journals.

They finished carving the letters and numbers into the sand, and Sophie drew a curved rectangular border around the whole thing. She went over to the water's edge and squatted there, palms against the bank, and closed her eyes. Her Uncle Peter had snapped a shot of her in this exact position when she was four years old, in blazing sunlight, on a summer camping trip with all the cousins. Somehow her instincts, even as a four-year-old, were to trust in the river, to sit by it, to spend time with it and in it. To listen to it and play with it. Now her body was back in that same reverent position, as night was falling. Her hands searched in the shallows for a flat, palm-sized river stone that could serve as the planchette. She'd tossed the last one as far away into the water as she could. This time, she thought she could feel the river's approval of one particularly smooth one. As she ran her fingers over it, her palms immediately tingled with a "Yes!", so she pulled it from the water and set it upon their makeshift board.

Will was busying himself by lighting tealights and setting them up around the board, leaving enough space for them both to sit facing each other. He was humming one of the new songs his band was working on and kept careening way out of tune on the high notes. She started humming along with him now, remembering the bare threads of the tune from hearing them rehearse over and over.

Another high humming, coming from up over their heads, started joining in. At first the sound seemed to mimic the tune they were both murmuring, but then it started wavering up and down notes rapidly, like a radio going between frequencies. Eventually the humming dipped to a low, deep sound, crackling a little, wavering in and out of earshot.

They sat in stunned silence for some moments as the low crackling sound continued and then faded out completely.

"But I hadn't even asked anything yet," Sophie whispered when the cocoon of nighttime river sounds returned.

"I guess that doesn't matter," Will whispered back. "It was already here. Whatever it is."

They sat for a few more moments with their hands over the stone. It remained motionless.

"Ow!" said Will suddenly and pulled his hands away.

"Yeah!" Sophie said, shaking out her hands. "I felt it too."

"Like a little static electric shock," Will grumbled, massaging his hands. "What the hell..."

Sophie cleared her throat and shook out her long, dusty hair. She had prepared something to say to kick off the ritual, but now everything had been mixed up. She had to improvise.

"OK, so ah, we are here to honour the history of this place," she began nervously, "the Dharug, and all the original custodians of this land, all the energies that have passed through here before, and the energies that remain... including my ancestor Eliza, and Nell too, if they are here..."

She looked over to Will and he nodded his approval, still cradling his hands to himself.

"Also... on another note," she stammered, "I welcome whatever energy might have attached itself to me to make itself known now, so that we might release you and help you move on."

Sophie moved to put her sweaty hands back on the riverstone and beckoned Will to do the same. She thought she caught sight of his eyes rolling in the dim light, and she realised again that he was doing this purely for her peace of mind.

As she reached for the stone, she realised the stone was not where it had been when they took their hands away. She looked up to Will and saw that he'd noticed too. They squinted in the candlelight to see where around the board the planchette had ended up.

It was sitting at the part of the board that simply said "No." Sophie squirmed and drew her hands back away from the stone. Will did the same and she could see that his hands were shaking.

"Soph, I don't know if this is such a good idea — you never know what you're inviting—"

Sophie's stomach dropped. Up until this point, she'd drawn some comfort from feeling that Will took it all with a grain of salt. That he was her anchor to 'reality' and common sense if she started feeling weird. But now he was clearly feeling weird as well, starting to feel less sure in his scepticism. It felt like her anchor had lost its hold and they were both now drifting together.

Sophie drew her knees to her chest. She could feel a constriction in her throat — like the lump you have when you're trying not to cry, but three times as big and three times as painful.

"Maybe all I'm inviting in is myself," Sophie said in a small voice.

"What do you mean?" Will asked, looking at her intently, his feet now buried protectively in the sand.

"I think that all these night terrors..." Sophie continued, her gaze fixed on one of the tealights, "and all this other weird stuff around me, is just me. Like I'm using it all as a way of avoiding the real me. Like I'm performing all these scary rituals and having all these scary things happen because I'm actually just afraid of my real self."

"Your real self?" Will interrupted, now fidgeting in the sand — picking up piles in his hands and letting the sand fall slowly back down. "I thought you said only *I* know your real self, that you could only be your real self around me?"

Sophie nodded, knees still hugged to her chest. She looked up to the sky and could see some lightness glowing up around the bushy sandstone cliff on the other side of the waterhole. She sighed.

"That's true, or it *was* true. It *has been* true."

Will raised his eyebrows now and passed a hand across his features. He shook his head and looked squarely at the sand shifting around in his hands.

"Sophie, you can be your real self around me, you know that," Will reassured her. "You can tell me, even these kinds of things about being, you know, forced, that I know you have."

There were countless times that sex with him caused her body and mind so much pain that she would often find herself sobbing afterwards, and that feeling definitely wasn't a turn on. But experiencing pain was just normal, wasn't it? That was just part of having an adult sex life, no? She didn't know any better, had never had a boyfriend or had sex with anyone before Will, and had assumed that these sorts of encounters and the pain was all just part of being in a relationship, something everyone had to accept.

Will was such a "nice guy," such a self-confessed feminist – pretty much everyone he knew thought that about him. She knew he was so much more knowledgeable of the world and the way it worked than she was. And he loved her so much — and she him — that anything he said felt to her like the ultimate truth. No matter how her body felt.

"Yes, I do know that," Sophie said, her voice getting smaller and quieter. "And I really appreciate that you accept that part of me and don't judge me. But you know that sometimes, or a lot of the time, my body really is in a lot of pain during sex — and not good pain... plus my head feels all mixed up... It gets really dark..."

This was so hard for her to say out loud. Her throat felt so constricted it was as if there were two hands strangling her.

"Yes, bu, Sophie, this is just that psychosomatic thing, you know? Like we were talking about. It's just a mental thing, and you can train yourself to relax and go with the flow, and then you won't feel pain anymore. And therapy can really help with that."

"OK, but I don't think all of it is just in my head—"

"You mean it's my fault?" Will snapped, then thought better of it and continued more softly. "You can tell me what to do to make sure it's more comfortable, you know. I can't read your mind..."

"Yeah, I know," Sophie said, voice now almost a whisper. She sighed and clamped her eyes shut for a few moments. *But what if I just don't want it?* She still couldn't say this aloud. When she opened her eyes and looked up, the glow over the cliffs had gotten brighter. Surely it wasn't so late that the sun was already coming up?

Sophie sighed again. She decided to try a different approach.

"OK, so I've got good news," she said, using all her strength to bring some brightness back into her voice. "Remember that film script I wrote?"

Will nodded, and started playing with one of the thick, heavy piercings in his ear. "Yep, I remember: the lesbian horror film."

"Well, this film centre in Berlin loved it, and they want me to come over for the fellowship program to make the film there!"

Will looked up at her sharply now. He was motionless for a moment.

Then he stretched his legs and his gaze out towards the river, beyond Sophie. He moved his feet in the sand, erasing the numbers and the letters of their makeshift board, then finally hugging his knees to his chest. At first he hunched his back over, then, with a sigh, eyes still on the water, he straightened up and sat tall.

"To Berlin? You're gonna move there?"

Sophie's throat was throbbing so badly she struggled to get the words out. "Well, yes," she squeaked. "But it's just for a few months, just to make the film, and then I'll be back."

Will lifted his feet from the sand, arms still wrapped around his legs, and balanced there for a few moments. He rocked himself backwards and slowly lay himself down on his back so Sophie couldn't see his face.

Will tried to keep his voice from cracking. "Well that's so great, congratulations," he said, still lying on the cold sand. "And I can come over to visit and come to the premiere screening?"

"Yes," cried Sophie nervously. Slowly, the strangled feeling in her throat was subsiding.

After a few moments, Sophie stood up from the bank and came to lie down next to Will on the sand. They lay like that, side by side but not quite touching, facing the glowing cliffs beyond.

"I'm really proud of you," Will said softly after a long time. "My girl, the filmmaker..."

Their eyes gazed skywards now, and some of Sophie's tension began to uncoil.

"You remember the story, right? This girl discovers she's a kind of medium and starts doing seances to contact all these famous dead people she admires, and one night she conjures Ophelia and..."

Will laughed, then, despite himself. "Yep, I remember... and Ophelia falls in love with the river and the river wants her too, and it starts trying to drag her into its waters one night to be able to keep her forever..."

"This could be really big, Will," Sophie gushed. Then she sighed again, keeping her eyes out ahead to the night sky, not daring to look at Will as she continued. "But you know... it came from my own subconscious, all this, even all the sexual parts, and it's really left me thinking..."

"That you might want to have an experience with another girl?"

Sophie was silent for a moment, not expecting him to make that leap just then. She looked down at their toes fumbling together as they lay there.

"Well, yes," she said shakily, "that's part of it but—"

"It's OK, I've thought for a while you might want something like this," Will interrupted. "I know you too well." He smiled at her then and drew her to his chest.

"I get it if you want to explore, especially while you're away in Berlin," Will continued. "Just don't go falling in love!"

Sophie didn't know how to feel at that point. Relieved, confused, annoyed that she hadn't finished saying the huge things that she desperately wanted to say, resigned...

They hugged for a very long time then, burying their faces into each other and shutting out the whole, huge, confusing world for a few moments.

"It's getting late," said Will, looking at his watch. "It's half-past midnight."

"Yeah, you're right," Sophie said, about to stand up and get ready for sleep, until something up above them caught her eye. She stayed sitting on the bank, head uplifted to the sky.

"What's that?" she whispered, pointing.

Will shifted his gaze to follow where she was pointing — to just above the clifftops where the glow in the sky had been earlier.

Arching upwards, from behind the clifftops, upwards into the night sky, was a series of lights shooting one after the next. The lights could have been mistaken for shooting stars, except that they were much bigger and were moving upwards into the sky, not falling down. There must have been about six of them, some shooting upwards together, and some alone. They were all the same circular shape and more or less the same diameter. They were all a pale yellow colour and each glowed as brightly as the moon.

The pair were struck silent as they watched them, their upturned faces aglow and in awe. After a few moments, they stopped and the night sky, with its stars and planets, returned to normal.

"What on earth...?" hissed Will. "That was..."

"Could they be Air Force? I think there's a base around here?" Sophie was stuttering rapidly.

"I don't know but I'm fucking exhausted," Will said, looking at his watch again. "It's definitely past my bedtime."

Will went to stand up, then promptly sat back down on the sand again. He looked at his watch again. "Hang on a second... didn't I say it was half past midnight before?"

Sophie yawned, also feeling lethargic and heavy. The thrill of the sighting dissipated once Will lost his enthusiasm for it. "Yeah."

"But now my watch says it's 4:30am. That can't be possible..."

Sophie rubbed her eyes, feeling like all she wanted to do was fall into a deep sleep. "You must have looked at the time wrong before?"

"Nah, you saw it too, right?" Will said, fear rising in his voice.

"I don't know, Will," she said softly, yawning despite the fear in her body. "I really don't know."

She let herself fall against his chest and moved with him as he eased backwards to lie on his back on the sand again. They had no energy to crawl to their tent, or even to grab a blanket to put over themselves. They were suddenly just so, so tired.

"I'm so sorry, Will," Sophie murmured, half-awake, half-asleep. "But I can never be who you want me to be... I'm so, so, sorry..."

But the river's distant lapping had already lulled Will into a deep, dreamless sleep.

CHAPTER VII

One sticky, overcast morning, a few days after Will had trudged back alone, Sophie's mother was next to scramble all the way through the bush to her encampment, convinced she would be the one to bring her daughter to her senses.

When she finally made it to the Narrows, Ellen immediately unravelled, panting, onto the sandy bank under a lone ghost gum — the spot where Will had assured her that her daughter was camping out. It looked like an Ancestral tree from ancient times, standing there all alone and protective. Ellen caught her breath there under its nurturing branches; her exhaustion soon swept away by the trill of the rushing water harmonised with the sound of a familiar little voice.

"'And will a not come again? And will a not come again?'"

Sophie's high-pitched warbles echoed from the sandstone cliffs as she emerged from her morning bath in the rockpool.

"You know it's just family legend, don't you?" Sophie's mother called sharply.

Sophie almost jumped out of her skin at the sight of her mother on the bank. Blushing deeply, both at her nakedness and the fact she was probably singing out of key in the presence of her classically trained mother, she raced to her pile of clothes on the bank and wrenched on a T-shirt and shorts.

Dressed but still dripping with river water, Sophie gave her mother a limp, one-armed hug. Her mother sighed, channelling the last dregs of her energy into her disapproving heavy breathing.

"My Aunt Eliza, whom I never met," she continued, rummaging around in her canvas shoulder bag, "ran away from home at your age, as a teenager, made her parents sick with worry, never came back. The end."

Sophie almost laughed, then stopped herself, seeing the worry rising in her mum's eyes. She smiled politely instead.

"Well, good morning to you too, Mum," she said, sitting down next to her in the sand. "Good to see you. Really."

Her mother rolled her eyes at this and rummaged around in her canvas shoulder bag until she found a couple of pieces of homemade date loaf. She unwrapped the cling wrap and handed them to Sophie.

"Here," she said firmly, "you look like you haven't eaten in weeks."

"Thanks Mum," Sophie smiled, batting a fly away, "I was getting a bit peckish."

A goanna, almost a metre long, was swimming past them downstream, his little head poking up earnestly above the cold water. Ellen kept her eyes firmly in the sand around her toes.

"Look, you might think that you're being very clever doing what you're doing, thinking you can run away from your own life to chase some big family mystery that you're wrapping up into an environmental crusade, but firstly, it's none of your business, and secondly, who even has time for it? Don't you think you're old enough to start living in reality?"

Sophie watched her mother's toes squirming into the sand as she spoke, realising how rarely she had even seen them. Even on the hottest days, her mother would keep her feet locked away in stockings and respectable leather shoes.

"This is my reality, Mum," Sophie said in a small voice, realising that from the approach her mother was taking,

Will had told her nothing of their discussions a few nights ago. "Or at least I'm trying to understand what my 'reality' might be."

Ellen kept on, now meeting Sophie's gaze with her signature steely squint that Sophie and her siblings had become giggling experts on behind closed bedroom doors.

"Maybe instead of being curious about someone who probably died fifty years ago," Ellen continued, "you could be more curious about daily life, productivity, getting things done?"

At this, Ellen now began unwrapping salmon sandwiches from the fridge-cooled tea towels, along with a little stack of freshly baked Anzac biscuits. Sophie tried a softer approach.

"Well, Mum, what do you *feel* when you come here to the river? Do you feel any special bond with the place because of the family history, or is it just another river to you?"

Ellen was munching hungrily on the sandwiches now, letting herself delay, at least for one more moment, some questions she'd been avoiding since her own childhood.

"Look," Ellen eventually said, in a tone that only usually emerged after a glass of white wine (which meant Sophie must be making headway). "My mother used to bring us to the river as kids, too. Down Mulgoa way, though on the other side and farther southwest by a few kilometres. I guess that's no coincidence, that my mother would travel all that way, alone, with five kids to look after. Every summer holiday, she would bring us down there to spend a week swimming in the river. I think my mother's mother had theories of her own, that it was that part of the river that Eliza and Nell ended up at, but I've always felt in my bones that they ended up right here, in this place..."

"Nell?"

Now Sophie's curiosity was officially piqued. She had never heard her mother give Nell the respect of calling her by her name before. She was always just the lost, anonymous Aboriginal girl, or at most, Eliza's "companion."

"Yes, Nell. That was the name on those diaries anyway." Sophie saw her mother's toes squirming deeper into the sand. She grabbed an Anzac biscuit and chewed while she deliberated on what to say next.

"But they could have been wrong," Ellen snapped suddenly. She was already closing up again.

"About what, Mum?" Sophie tried to press her softly.

"About any of it. They might have never made it as far as the mountains. They could have died on the Western Plains. Maybe Nell went back with her own mob... no one knows who she even was anyway. That's why they call it a family legend and not family history."

The silence now between them was filled with the cicadas, piercing the air like heat waves. Sophie lay back on the sandy bank, hair straggling out behind her, and sighed loudly. Why did it have to be so hard to talk to her own mother? She looked up past the twisted arms of the ghost gum to the sky above, now an endless magnetic black.

"What is it about this 'family legend' that makes you so tense, Mum? You know I'm old enough to handle anything..."

At this Ellen laughed, spraying some biscuit crumbs out as she did so – then blushing and covering her mouth just as quickly.

"You know it's not just about Aunt Eliza, don't you?" Ellen said darkly, once her laughing had subsided. She kept her eyes on the river beyond.

"There's something about all the women in our family, including me, including you. We either find a decent love, but we can't manage to keep ourselves still in one place long enough to make it work, or we marry someone like your father with ants in his pants who is set on abandoning us no matter how much love we give him. Us Fowler women, we just can't win either way."

Sophie kept silent as she let this new information sink in. She had never heard her mother talk this frankly. She picked at some grass and tried to form her thoughts into well-kneaded words. But then she jumped in breathlessly while the words were still raw.

"You mean like a kind of curse? A love curse?!"

As soon as Sophie said this aloud, Ellen turned pointedly away, her features hardening and her shoulders stiffening. Whatever response she was about to make was swallowed back down deeply inside her.

She wrapped up the remains of lunch into the tea towels and folded them away neatly into her bag. Drawing a freshly ironed handkerchief from her pants pocket, she dabbed at her lips, reapplied her lipstick, then brushed the remaining crumbs from her lap. She looked at her daughter steadily for the first time during this little talk by the river, and was overcome with a sinking feeling through her entire body.

"Yes, Sophie," she said sadly, "I guess you could call it a love curse, if you want."

"But, Mum—"

"And yes, Sophie, I don't think any of the relatives would mind if you use it for one of your movie scripts — I know what you're thinking. It's all just silly hearsay after all."

Ellen smiled at Sophie then with a tremble of fright at the edges of her mouth and handed her a second handkerchief. She waited until Sophie had also wiped her hands and face before taking the handkerchief from her and folding it back into her bag.

It was dark sooner than they imagined. The storm clouds had now completely swamped the sky. The only light from the sun was an otherworldly greenish haze, like the reversal of light during a solar eclipse — as if the light was moving backwards into the sun, not radiating down to earth.

A flock of cockatoos took off out of the trees in fright and made their way east along the river's path. Even the goanna was startled from the bush and scrambled back into the stream, going back the way he came.

"That's not good," Ellen muttered, looking around them, then checking her watch. "My watch says it's only 3 o'clock but the sun's already disappeared."

Sophie agreed, suddenly getting a little cold. She picked up her mother's well-stocked backpack and started towards the tree cover.

"Come on, Sophie," Ellen sighed, easing herself up to stand, looking out west to the tangled wilds. "Let's get you home." Her eyes went all misty for a moment, as if some part of her wondered if Eliza and Nell might be still hiding in those very trees, listening to them. "It'll be dark soon."

As soon as she said this, the black sky opened up into chaos. Thunder, lightning, and a wild wind echoed high above them, suspended for just a moment — then crashed down on them seconds later with lashes of sleet and sand whipped up from the river's shore.

They squealed like girls at their school formal.

Throwing jackets over their heads and clutching the bag, the picnic blanket, and everything else they could carry from Sophie's flimsy tent, they tore over the bank and towards the cover of trees.

In the understory, they scrambled through the whipping ghost gums, skin tearing on blackberry bushes and lantana, until they reached the base of the sandstone rock face. This marked the entrance to the river's gorge and the wilderness beyond. Sophie had never been this far into the bush, beyond the Narrows. And her mother definitely hadn't either, judging by the lost look on her face, drenched by the lashing rain and sleet. They huddled under a narrow rock ledge to catch their breath.

"I hate storms," wailed Ellen, dabbing at her face with her handkerchief. "Always have. Why do they have to happen?"

"Maybe this one is the river's way of telling us it wants you to stay the night," Sophie offered. "We're going to have to find another shelter here tonight – we can't walk back in this and my tent is definitely not going to cut it in this storm."

Another peal of thunder cracked open the sky. Steaming rain, even more violent than before, shuddered down. Ellen started shaking a little and Sophie awkwardly put her dripping arms around her.

"Oh, I do not like this at all," Ellen cried. "Reminds me of when we were kids and the power would go out. The darkest dark you've ever seen. It happened one summer on the river too, down in Mulgoa. We all thought we saw our grandmother sitting by the fire with us. Even my mother couldn't sleep a wink from the fright of it."

There was a moment of respite when the rain softened just a little. Sophie clutched her arm around her mother's waist and ran with her back out under the trees. As they ran, their eyes scanned the sandstone cliffs for signs of a cave. It was almost completely dark now — if they didn't find one soon, they would have no hope of finding one when the sun went down.

As they ran, Sophie whispered a little something to the river under her breath. A sort of prayer or wish to the river that they would be safe, that they would make it through the night. She felt foolish as she did it but that feeling soon faded when Ellen also started doing some murmuring of her own; only she said the words to her mother and grandmother and to Great-Aunt Eliza, praying that they were watching over them.

Lightning illuminated a void in the cliff face just a little further on. They hesitated, waiting for another lightning flash to confirm it. And yes, there it was: a shadowed hollow, not too far up within the sandstone.

"A cave!" they shouted simultaneously.

They let go of each other and concentrated on moving through the last clutch of trees until they reached the rock face again. They would have to climb up a few metres over the rock to make it inside. First, Sophie threw the backpack up and onto the rock shelf, then grabbed everything her mother was carrying and threw that up there too. Ellen was doing her best to get herself up the rock but her eyes kept distracting her. She kept looking back over her shoulder fearfully to the lightning strikes edging closer. Sophie gave her a leg-up and they both strained, scraping exposed skin over the rough sandstone, until finally Ellen was up and rolling over the ledge. Then it was Sophie's turn. She clambered up, fingers and toes straining against the rain-wet sandstone, her shins getting skinned as she misjudged the angles. Another crack of thunder almost had her falling backwards, but she clung on with one hand and grabbed her mum's outstretched arm with the other. Success. As the rain continued ripping down, they gathered themselves and their sodden belongings and ran deep into the cave.

As soon as they entered, there was a hush, as if they had entered a cathedral. The ambient light around the lips of the cave suddenly felt like the only light left in the world. Looking inside, all was completely black — there was no way of knowing how deep the cave went, except for the pattern of echoes from their breathing and footsteps. Finding a hollow away from the rain and wind, but not too far from the remaining light, they finally sat down and rested. The storm still raged through the trees and across the river, but there in their cave, they felt an immediate calm and stillness. They breathed deeply for a few moments, taking it all in, letting the relief wash over them.

It felt like the warmest blanket of care. Kin at last.

***

Ellen still kept a cigarette lighter in her canvas shoulder bag. A throw-back to her thirty years of smoking.

She passed it to Sophie as she was dutifully gathering as much dry kindling as she could scrape together. Anything from the forest floor would be useless now after the deluge.

Her mother always seemed calmer in a crisis than on your average Tuesday. As if high stakes were her natural state and gave her comfort, made her feel safe. As Sophie arranged the kindling into a neat little thatched-roof structure, Ellen started humming a tune that touched something of Sophie's deepest memories. Something hinting at their Irish ancestry. Sophie started instinctively humming along, remembering more of the tune as she did so, until it finally rippled out into the song.

Her eyes they shone like the diamonds,
You'd think she was queen of the land,
And her hair hung over her shoulders,
Tied up with a black velvet band...

The fire now lit, the cave was cast in the glow and flicker that connected them not just to their early Irish ancestors, but far further back, deep in time. A kinship feeling beyond ideas of bloodlines, family trees or family legends. The two women sat around the fire and suddenly words felt hollow and inept. They could feel the breadth of the human family in their contented silence, just sitting around the fire.

The rain, thunder, and lightning had eased, but the wind continued howling in the trees. One big release to clear the air, a fresh start. No remnants of the oppressive humidity and threat of storm, just clear skies and light air.

A gust blew into the cave then, spiralling all the way to its deepest recesses and curving out again to the entrance, bringing with it old scents of earth that had not been disturbed in a very long time. The fire wavered for a moment, then raged back to life with fresh oxygen. The intensified light illuminated the furrowed walls, emphasising all the centuries they had weathered.

***

Tonight was the night that Ellen's decades of overzealous packing for the absolute worst-case scenario really came to fruition. All those times she'd been laughed at for bringing a lifejacket with a whistle and a flare to a picnic, or for bringing a water desalination kit to a fishing trip on the lake, or those three extra jerry cans of fuel for a road trip to her sister's across town... well, who was laughing now?

Although she had only planned to hike to the Narrows and be back well in time to serve her husband the roast chicken that she had pre-cooked for dinner, she had packed enough salmon sandwiches, Anzac biscuits, pre-mixed cordial and diced fruit salad to stave off hunger for both of them all night. In a separate compartment of the bag, she'd also packed a week's supply of instant noodles, muesli bars, a compass, and even water-purifying tablets, and had thought to pack a warm change of clothes and even dry, clean socks, which she was now urging Sophie to change into.

"Or you'll catch your death out here," her mother kept repeating.

Sophie saw her mother shivering as she came back to sit with her by the fire, now clean and dry in the tracksuit and socks Ellen had brought.

"Mum, you're cold," Sophie said, taking the tracksuit top back off and urging her mother to put it on.

"No, no," she waved her away, unravelling a rainproof shell jacket from the pocket of the jacket she was wearing. "I have this one."

Sophie's eyes widened. Now she'd seen it all.

"OK, Mum," Sophie grinned, "your generation are definitely better survivors than mine."

"Well, it's not just a generational thing — I mean, I'm not so old that I lived through the Depression or the War... You just have to be organised."

"Speaking of old timers," Sophie laughed, nudging her mum with her elbow, "who do you think Nell was to Aunt Eliza? Why run away together?"

It was the most romantic story Sophie had ever heard, but she was sure, by the gnawing feeling in her gut since her mother had arrived and started on the topic, that Ellen would do all she could to either dissolve or damn whatever romantic theories Sophie might have about the situation.

"Well, no one really knows, do they?" Ellen said carefully, nibbling on pieces of fruit, which were cut into identically sized cubes. The air bristled with silence while her mother chose her next words. "But, what we do know, and what you should remember from school if you kept your head down long enough, is that there was a Stolen Generation in Australia, with Aboriginal babies and children being sent to English Protestant families, later Scots and even Irish when there were more Irish free settlers. The outrageous idea was to erase who they were, try to make them forget — white families were meant to bring them up as good Christians and set them on a path to earning money, having land, having a family in a white world — it was an attempt to wipe them out..."

"Do you think that Nell was one of these, these stolen kids? That our great-great-grandfather was raising her?"

"Oh, look, we really don't know, do we? But if she was an Indigenous girl, living with a white family, then we can just put two and two together..."

"Hmm." Sophie thought on this for a second, chewing slowly on the second-to-last Anzac biscuit, trying to make it last as long as possible.

"OK," Sophie continued, "so if they ran away together, it seems like it must have been a hell of a bad situation there on the family's property? I mean, you told me before that they ran a hotel out there on the edge of the outback — it must have been pretty rough..."

"All I remember," Ellen said with a voice like sun-toughened leather, "is that Eliza's father, my Great-Uncle Jack, he would crack six raw eggs into his mouth every morning, drink most of the day, and by nightfall, hide himself behind doorways with his belt in his hand, ready to wallop whichever unfortunate child happened to cross his path. And he'd make sure he hit you with the buckle end."

"Fuck," Sophie breathed, then caught herself. "I mean, *damn*, Mum, what a monster. I hate to think that he's in our blood..."

Ellen shuddered and kept her eyes on the fire. "They say that kind of thing has been in the bloodline of the men in our family forever, even back to Ireland. Men like *that* and women with their 'love curse,' as you called it."

"So Jack must have done something disgusting to Nell, and Eliza was close with her and somehow they got away together?"

"Must have been hell on earth there if they chose to run into the bush in the middle of the night with nothing but the dresses they had on."

"And Eliza must have really loved Nell if she chose to run with her instead of staying with her family."

At this, Ellen drew breath sharply and started packing away the food again into the bag. Sophie was surprised that the conversation had lasted this long. Here, with only the space of the cave and the warmth by the fire, with the storm still raging through the trees outside, her mother had nowhere to escape to.

Sophie suddenly remembered her little Bacardi Cola can she had been saving in her backpack for a special occasion – she gasped gleefully and pulled it out, opening it for her mum.

"Welcome to my little world out here," she said half-sheepishly, half-cheekily.

A great peal of thunder rocked the cave then, and a gust of wind threatened to blow out the fire. Ellen jumped instinctively closer and clutched Sophie's elbow.

"Oh, I hate storms," she said again, and took a great gulp from the can.

Lightning illuminated the sodden, thrashed trees outside the cave, and it seemed every creature out there had been hushed into trembling silence.

"Well," Ellen said after taking another gulp, her eyes sparkling now. "I'm not driving so..."

Sophie laughed and grabbed the can, taking a sip of her own. She felt the sickly-sweet liquid pouring down her throat, praying for each percentile of its alcohol content to give her courage.

"Mum?" she said after a time, almost too softly to be heard over the wind and rain. She handed back the can now, also praying that the alcohol content would blunt her mother's edges. "I think that the kind of closeness that Nell and Aunt Eliza might've had, or maybe the love they had, is the kind that I would also like, in my own life..."

It came out more vaguely than she had hoped but her mother responded with even more vagueness.

"Well," Ellen said, clearing her throat, "wouldn't we all like that kind of closeness in our lives? You know, if you're very lucky, you can count the number of true friends in your life on one hand."

Her mother had repeated this phrase to her so many times that even Sophie had started using it as advice to her own friends when they came to her after betrayals and disappointments.

"Yes Mum, I agree," she answered carefully, then took a big swig of the Bacardi and steadied herself before blurting out:

"But I mean I think Nell and Eliza were more than friends. They loved each other, like *really* loved each other, and I want that too—"

"But you have that already with Will," Ellen interrupted. "You're both very lucky to have found each other so young. That's a once-in-a-lifetime chance." She shifted herself away from Sophie now, trying to look anywhere except in Sophie's direction but without anything for her eyes to land on in the darkness, she simply clamped her eyelids shut. With her eyes still closed, she kept on at her daughter.

"Sophie, I'm not the idiot you think I am. You might think I don't know the world, but I know a hell of a lot more than you do, OK? And I know how rotten and cruel people can be. Life isn't meant to be easy, you know, but you don't know how easy you've got it. You found a perfectly decent young man with a good family who loves you, would do anything for you, and wants to marry you. Far more than I or any of the other women in our family ever had. And you, look at you, thinking you know it all — you want to throw all that away, for what? Some difficult life with a woman, is that it? That's the kind of hard path you want to walk down for the rest of your life, do you? You've been so sheltered, I've sheltered you, Will's sheltered you, and you don't know how good you've got it. And still you're not happy, you just want to risk it all for some exotic life with some woman in a hovel God knows where…"

At this, Ellen downed the rest of the Bacardi Cola, crushed the can with one of her knuckly hands, then hurled the can in the fire, all in one singular, fluid movement. It conjured images of a wild youth that Sophie was never privy to — one in which she imagined her mother had gone to parties in the bush with boys all night and stood around oil drum fires drinking premix out of cans. Did they even have premix cans in the Seventies? Sophie wondered. Maybe it was just vodka, straight from the bottle, plus plenty of cigarettes, maybe some with weed in them...? Sophie tried to snap herself out of her reverie and deal with her mother here and now.

"Mum, I'm really not taking anything for granted," she mumbled, staring into the fire. "I'm so grateful for you, and Dad, and our whole family, and I'm so grateful that Will... well, seems to love me."

Now Sophie dared to look over to her mother and, ever so slowly, her mother edged herself back around towards the fire, and towards her daughter.

"But I can't just get married because it's a nice story," Sophie continued carefully. "Or just because it would make other people happy."

"Why not?" her mother snapped. "That's what generations of us have done before you."

"Exactly," Sophie said, a wry smile creeping onto her face, belying her almost complete state of panic. "And now we don't have to. And I mean, look at Nell and Eliza, they also didn't..."

"Don't be making assumptions about my Aunt Eliza," her mother cut her off. "By all accounts she was a very nice girl and she did the right thing trying to help her friend get away from Uncle Jack."

Sophie brightened at this and turned fully to face her mum. "So you do admire her then, for taking off like she did?"

"Of course I do," said Ellen, feeling the knot in her stomach unclench a little; also grateful to find some point of connection. "Most of the family shamed her, but my mother and grandmother told us great stories about her. And we've been trying to work out for the longest time where she might have ended up — but you know that already—"

"Yes, but—"

"But don't go spoiling it all thinking that she was some kind of..."

"Lesbian? Queer? Gay?"

Her mother stood and visibly shuddered again.

"Oh Sophie," she muttered, "you already know my opinion of all of those... lifestyles."

Ellen busied herself in the far corner of the cave, packing, then re-packing what was left of the food, then taking a curt sip from the thermos of water. Sophie watched her, suddenly feeling sympathy with what she could now see in her hunched form were the constant burdens her mother carried with her: fear of not doing things perfectly, not being the perfect mother, wife, sister, or *anything* she could be judged for, and then blamed for, and then abandoned because of. It must have been a huge source of loneliness, Sophie thought, especially after her mother passed away — someone who would have carried and understood the same kind of burdens. Maybe this was one reason Mum was so close to her brothers and sisters. They must have also inherited these heavy ghosts on their backs.

"Mum?"

"Yes Sophie." This through gritted teeth, only answering because they were stuck together in the same cave.

"I genuinely wish that I could take that 'easy path,' as you call it. Get married, be loved, make everyone happy. But it's gonna catch up with me eventually."

Sophie had never had any experiences other than with Will, but she'd known for a long time that who she was wasn't a "lifestyle choice." It was as deep in her blood and in her bones as it probably had been for Nell and Eliza.

"What is going to catch up with you?" Ellen asked quietly, and immediately wished she hadn't.

Sophie knew, of course, that it wasn't a matter of it "catching up with her." But it was a phrase she might have a hope of her mother understanding.

What she really felt was more like the flow of liquids through her body, transforming her body into a body of water, much like her beloved river or a pond or an ocean: just as natural and uncontrollable and uncontainable.

"That I'm gay."

The wind seemed to die down at that moment, making Sophie's voice echo around the cave far louder and far longer than she had intended. *Note to self*, thought Sophie, *never "come out" in a cave with an echo.*

Ellen smouldered silently, eyeing the can of rum she had thrown in the fire too hastily. Her cheeks burned red, and then redder.

Sophie eventually lay herself down on the bare stone by the fire, hugging her knees to her chest. Ellen stayed as she was, silent and staring at the fire, until sleep finally caught the both of them in its fitful arms.

CHAPTER VIII

Morning heat and sunlight woke them gently. The fire was long out but the two women felt wonderfully cocooned and cosy. Sophie was first to open her eyes, catching the distant dazzle of the sun on the river below the cave, then smiling instinctively. The river. She had wanted to spend a night out on its great banks with her mum since childhood, and last night the storm finally gave her that chance.

The morning air was now completely clear of all the tension of the storm the night before, as if it had never happened. The only evidence of its wildness were the branches that had been wrenched from some of the ghost gums and the weedy debris thrown up onto some of the Narrows's sandy shores.

A black swan, now rare in this stretch of the river, swooped its way along the treeline over the water, curving for a moment towards the cave and revealing its scarlet beak, then diving back away again, to disappear in the shimmer of water and sunlight.

With a hopeful feeling, Sophie looked over to her mother, wondering if her period of silent treatment might have reached its conclusion yet. But before she could wonder too long, her attention was captured by something else entirely.

Her mother had been carefully wrapped in sheaths of soft paperbark. Looking down at herself, Sophie realised she had been, too. She had simply felt this safe, warm feeling through her skin and not questioned it.

Sophie immediately startled and wrestled herself out of the cocoon.

At the commotion, her mother's eyes then swam into focus, and, after rubbing them a little, Ellen too shook herself out of the paperbark and rose unsteadily to her feet.

"I mean, thanks for keeping us warm, Mum," Sophie started, "but where on earth did you find all this paperbark?"

Ellen shook her head. Her hair was the most unkempt Sophie had ever seen it — usually it was styled into a perfect bob.

"No, I mean, I didn't—"

"You didn't wrap us in paperbark in the night?"

"No, did you?"

"No...?"

Ellen sank back down to her feet and sat on her haunches by the embers. She smoothed her hair and ran her fingers over her face, inspecting it, judging it. She let out a long sigh.

"Look," she said wearily, "there's that black swan again." Then she sighed even more deeply, this time with a heaviness that Sophie didn't understand.

Sophie felt suddenly self-conscious and started smoothing her own hair and combing it through with her fingers. She was reminded of how hard her mother used to brush her hair as a child and how the pigtails and ponytails and buns her mother would fashion her hair into would be so tight that she would go to bed with headaches most nights.

"I dreamed of the black swan last night," Ellen said with a sense of awe that Sophie wasn't expecting. And then, even less expected, her mother reached out and twisted a strand of Sophie's long, unruly hair around her finger. "And I dreamed of our ancestors. They kept me so busy all night that I don't know how I'll have the energy to make it back to the house."

"I can help give you a leg-up over the first cliffs if you get tired..." Sophie offered, grateful for this sudden softness in her mother this morning, and also grateful she had gone to all that trouble in the night to wrap them up. Sophie guessed that her mother just didn't want to admit to her kindness after the conversation they'd had.

"It really wasn't me, you know," Ellen said, still not letting go of her daughter's hair. "And I think you know as well as I do who it was who paid us a visit last night."

Her mother speaking something unexplainable aloud was new to Sophie. Sure, she had told the ghost stories from her youthful summers at Winbourne, near the river at Mulgoa. Those nights that she and her four siblings were kept awake at night from the mournful cries coming from a locked room upstairs and from the sounds of chains rattling and dragging heavily across the wooden floorboards. But it was always easier to tell ghost stories involving a time long ago, and something all Australians should know from the shared past — Aboriginal people enslaved and dehumanised, and convicts treated cruelly on settlers' properties. But speaking openly about something that they were experiencing in the here and now, this confrontation with the unexplained seemed like a breakthrough.

"And Sophie, I'll make it back to the house just fine by myself — I'm not geriatric just yet."

"What do you mean by yourself?" Sophie was genuinely spooked by this, and, well, everything that was unfolding this morning.

Ellen sighed heavily again, smoothed the clothes she had slept in and double-checked that the bag was packed. "Sophie, remember I said that my mother and my grandmother thought that Aunt Eliza ended up at Mulgoa? How they would bring us there to the river as kids, and all those ghost stories there, and... well, they weren't wrong.

And we weren't wrong either. Do you know what Mulgoa means?"

Sophie stood now too. This was all such an about-face after the silent treatment of last night.

The black swan came swooping back in that moment, drinking in the crystalline blue of the morning sky and calling out, as if looking for someone.

The women watched it for a few moments, silenced.

"See? She's calling you."

Now Sophie was beginning to wonder if her mother had squirrelled away some extra grog in that bag of hers. "Um, calling me?"

"The Mulgoa tribe was named for the black swans here on the river. Too many legends to count about the birds and what they meant for the area, and for the first people here. You'll have plenty of time to find out all about that—"

"Plenty of time?"

"But Nell did warn me that you need to be wary of which black swans you trust — some are shapeshifters, you know, some were humans who did wrong by their country or their people and were transformed into black swans... you can tell which ones after the sun has gone down, Nell told me, because they are able to speak in their human voices again under the cover of darkness — gotta steer right away from those ones..."

"Mum? Was this your dream last night?" Sophie almost couldn't believe her ears. She flung her shoes on and took the bag from her mother. "Let's get going back and have some breakfast. Dad might be worried by now."

"Sophie, you know you can't come back. Not right now. I know that was something else you wanted to tell me last night but I didn't let you. Or, at least, I didn't make it easy for you."

Sophie burned red and lumped the backpack onto her shoulder.

"Let's go, Mum."

"You know I'll always be here when you get back," her mother breathed. "Go to Berlin, make your film, do what you have to do. Just be careful of that black swan."

Sophie had also been wanting to tell her mother of the film scholarship opportunity she had in Berlin. She had always gotten herself tangled in knots with these kinds of things, but this time around she knew she had really fucked up.

"Just go and be Sophie," her mother said tenderly, handing her the bag she'd packed. "I'll be here when you decide to come back."

The black swan circled overhead again and called out three times. A beckoning? Its wings seemed to curve out seductively, drawing her whole being towards it.

When Sophie looked back into the cave again, it was empty except for the ashes of the fire and the sheath of paperbark that had kept her warm. Her mother was gone.

***

Sophie blinked open her eyes to the morning sunlight and the calling of waterbirds.

The fire was long since out, but she had been kept warm and cosy by the sheath of paperbark that was wrapped around her.

She sat suddenly upright, head swimming. *What is happening?*

Her mother was indeed gone but she had left the bag and a terse note.

Gone back to Dad.
Do what you have to do.
Be safe.
Mum.

She must have dreamed the whole damn thing.

Fuck, Sophie moaned, her head aching in confusion. *I knew it was too good to be true.*

Details from what her mother had said to her in the dream came back to her in fragments. Something about ghost stories, her mother, her grandmother, how Mulgoa was the place of the black swans, how she was meant to go there. That all seemed so much more in the realms of reality than the last part of the dream: her mother giving her a blessing to go into the world and just "be Sophie." In any case, she certainly didn't want to go back home to silent treatment from her mother and coming out by proxy to her father. Her brother and sister were away on summer trips with their friends so they wouldn't be there to buffer things. Her stomach churned audibly, and she realised she had been clenching the note from her mother so hard in her fist that she had almost sweated through the paper.

The black swan swooped and dove around the treetops of the Narrows, scarlet beak triumphantly contrasting the grey-green of the bush and the mud churn of the river's water after the storm. The colour almost seemed painted on, like lipstick, with the edges upturned into a mysterious smile.

Sophie threw the crumpled note into the ashes of the fire, kicked the bag aside and stripped off her clothes and all the trinkety jewellery she was wearing. She left it all in a heap on the cave floor and clambered down the rock face to the understory. She looked up again, blocking the sun from her eyes with her arm until her fingers traced the curved shadow of the swan again, circling above. The swan veered hard west then, in the same direction as the river's flow, and Sophie took off, running, after it.

The heat of the sun hit her naked skin as she swerved and dodged the trees and brush in her way. She could hear the skitter of goannas and snakes in the dry leaves as she ran, and the low hum of the cicadas rising up in their stinging chorus for another day. Her chest heaved as she ran faster and faster, not caring when the stray twigs pierced her bare feet or the low branches scraped across her skin. Her eyes remained staring upwards, following the path of the swan, until she reached a sandstone rock ledge, with the river's flow beneath her.

The swan called once then swooped onwards, diving down to fly just metres above the river's surface, then continuing on westwards.

Sophie shrugged then jumped with a scream that was part terror, part exhilaration, into the river.

The shock of the cool after the burn of the sun took her breath away for a moment down there in the deep green quiet. But when she bobbed up again, flicking her long hair out of her face, she laughed again, then called out a long and clear "cooooeeee," just like they used to do as kids, willing the river to flow her the right way.

CHAPTER IX

"She could not rise. But there she lay content. The scent of the bog myrtle and the meadow-sweet was in her nostrils. The rooks' hoarse laughter was in her ears. 'I have found my mate,' she murmured. 'It is the moor. I am nature's bride,' she whispered, giving herself in rapture to the cold embraces of the grass as she lay folded in her cloak in the hollow by the pool. 'Here I will lie.' (A feather fell upon her brow.)"

– Virginia Woolf, *Orlando*

Even though Sophie was swimming downstream, and the river's flow was indeed helping her along, there was no chance she could keep up with the swan's flight. The bird did hesitate a few times, and swooped back around to check on her feeble human follower, but it seemed the swan had other things to occupy her and she eventually flew on, westwards, calling a few times to her mates in the distance.

When Sophie tired of swimming, she let the river take her in its murmuring flow, and simply floated for a while. In these moments, the conversation of the night before swam out of focus and all the hard edges of it blurred. It became simply a talk, mother and daughter, with some emotions attached to it, no more detail necessary. She wondered what her dad was going to say, then ducked her head under the water to clear her mind of such thoughts.

But then every time the black swan caught Sophie's attention again, last night's dream would come rushing back, and, along with it, the deep pain of remembering that it had only been a dream. Her mind's game of wishful thinking, in which her coming out had actually softened her mother, had both drawn them closer together, and opened them both up to the stories of their ancestors, which coursed through both of their bodies in equal measure.

"Mulgoa," Sophie said aloud to the river as she floated. "Mulgoa means *black swan* – that's what my mum said, in the dream at least."

She floated through some tangled reeds and kicked her ankles free of them. Her parents had always warned them of the river reeds when they were kids, and the deep holes in some parts of the river's bed that could suck a person inside. Her father had mentioned once that the original tribes of the area knew the placement of every one of these "devil's holes" and kept themselves and their children well away from them. The white settlers, even now, generations after taking over the land, had no such knowledge. Instead of trying to glean the knowledge, and doing some research, however, they opted instead for jet skis and power boats that roared right over the river's surface and scared the local birds away and caused massive erosion to the river's banks. The loss for these white newcomers was missing out on all the pleasures and adventures that could be had by simply swimming and drifting and diving and floating in the rich waters and letting the river teach and coax them in its own way.

"Maybe you're floating me to Mulgoa? Retracing where Nell and Eliza were, from where they ended up to where they began?"

As she floated on, eyes level with dragonflies skimming the river's surface, the occasional floating tree branch, sickly green algal blooms, and a few frogs kicking with all their might upstream, Sophie tried to piece together what else she had learned from last night's dream (if anything at all, aside from disappointment).

There was something her mother had said about black swans being shapeshifters, or at least some of them who had done ill of some kind and then been confined to a swan's form. Remembering the grace of freedom pulsing through the swan's body as she swooped and dove, Sophie wasn't so sure that becoming a black swan was any kind of punishment at all.

After a whole day of swimming and floating, floating and swimming, the sun began to turn the river golden, along with Sophie's aching arms and her hair, all tangled up with the river's debris. It must have been the way the warm light hit the muddy water, and the high temperature it had reached over the long, bright day, but a scent now rose on the wind that startled Sophie out of her exhaustion. The scent of swamp; the nether-lands of nature.

As she swam on, the scent grew more intense and the plant life in the water grew thicker, more strangling. There was an anomaly in the undergrowth ahead on the banks. Breaking all the green was a track leading up from a small muddy beach to the forest beyond. But Sophie could also tell that the track could only be seen from a certain vantage point in the river — down low, at water level. From any higher, like the head height of the average human, the track would be all but concealed by the undergrowth. It made Sophie feel as if the track had only revealed itself to her and the other river creatures.

Sophie swam her way from the centre of the river's flow over to the little beach the track seemed to lead from. Her muscles ached like they had never ached before, but she barely noticed it in the presence of such a scent. She followed her nose, still naked as she had been when she jumped down from the cave in the morning, and trod her way along the track until she reached a circular clearing in the ironbarks. The clearing was filled with deep, black mud, scattered river reeds, and rotting eucalyptus litter. There were two circular, sunken depressions in the middle of the clearing where the earth was even darker and more damp.

If her nose could be believed, it seemed as if the most intense elements of it were coming from those two circular sinkholes. Standing there dripping, Sophie breathed in the scent, and the life coursed back into her veins.

The ancient stagnant moistness, sealed in by the rotting wood and gum leaves; the resin released as the decaying branches were slowly cracked and crafted to the water's ends; and the mud itself, warmed and engorged by the summer sun and imbibed by the summer rains.

Sophie wanted the smell in her body forever. She wanted more than just to drink it in through her nose. She wanted, greedily, to breathe in more than her lungs could take. Then she was immediately struck with a panic that if she breathed in too much too quickly, the smell might lose its potency.

She lay down, prone, in that late summer sun, right in the wet mud, coiling her body into the foetal position around the two depressions. She felt it all, drank the scent in with her skin and with her entire body. Lying there, loving it, Sophie realised she was incapable of letting the sensory bliss of the moment fully take her over, for fear of that moment being over, at any breath. Is it over now? Or now? What about now?

Are you still there?

When she opened her eyes, the sun was down and the moon was high. There was a chill to the air and the cicadas had finally let the night sounds dominate. There were distant calls of waterbirds spiralling overhead and frogs that were rousing themselves out of the mud and singing their way into the river's lap.

The hours of sleep had not been enough to restore Sophie's muscles after all that swimming. That lost, jet-lagged feeling that comes after going to sleep at sunset and waking up in darkness started to creep through her body, spooking her a little, then crashing down on her all at once when she remembered her mother's abandonment of her that morning.

"It shall forever now be known as the Coming Out Cave," Sophie laughed ruefully. Her laughter might have sounded full of anger to someone who didn't know her well, echoing out across the river in the night air, but she had not yet arrived there in that fiery place — she was still in that softer hollow of sadness.

"Don't let her get to you," a voice said back, jolting Sophie bolt upright from the mud. Had she just imagined it?

"Hello...?" Sophie called, her voice trembling with dread. All laughter had drained from her.

"You did so well, doing what you did. I'm so proud of you."

"Who are you?"

Sophie stood up shakily in the mud, both arms bent at the elbow, raised defensively. The voice sounded achingly familiar, but she could not place it.

"You know who I am, you've been following me all day." The voice started to sound a little irritated now.

Sophie slowly started creeping back down the track, towards the beach, on tiptoe, as if she could catch the bearer of the voice unawares. Her mind immediately jumped to the conclusion that the voice was coming from the river itself. All this time, all this love she had poured into it, it somehow made sense to Sophie that the river had finally given in to a human form of communication, out of pure impatience with her.

As she fought her way out of the last stand of trees and arrived back at the beach, Sophie stopped suddenly. There was the shadowy form of something there.

She took one slight, slow step forwards and saw the naked arch of a back, slick with river water, gleaming in the moonlight. The figure was hunched over, sitting on the riverbank, facing the water. Sophie took another step forward to glean more details. She could see now that it had short, black, spiky hair and long languid limbs. Behind it, crumpled on the bank, was a black-feathered outer skin. It seemed the figure had just shed it like a feathery chrysalis. When the figure sensed Sophie's proximity, it swivelled its head around, impossibly, 180 degrees, to look upon her.

The grey, pained eyes. The sharp scarlet mouth, opening now in her presence. The noble nose. A small, quiet smile now, beckoning her closer. That kinship feeling again. That want of closeness, and that deep fear of closeness.

Sophie's mind was flooded with fragments of overlapping and contradictory stories she had read about black swans... Some tribes' attitudes towards them were guarded and wary — believing black swans were shapeshifters and that some took back their human voice and form at night in their purgatory here. Hard to trust them at face value. So many parables, so many shapeshifters, so much black-and-white binary.

As Sophie met the grey eyes of the figure at the edge of the river, the moon disappeared behind a cloud, plunging everything into darkness. She took a step backwards in fright. She could no longer see anything beyond her feet in the mud or her hands, now outstretched hesitantly ahead of her. The whole world seemed eerily silent for a moment — she could only hear the sounds of her own heavy breathing.

Then a great wind picked up over the water and the voice, now disembodied, rang out:

"A sudden blow: the great wings beating still..."

Sophie instinctively huddled herself down on the muddy bank, cowering at the sound.

"Above the staggering girl, her thighs caressed
By the dark webs..."

The voice was directly above her now, circling her, taunting her. It moved over her then disappeared and came ringing out from a distant tree, all within a few seconds.

"How can those terrified vague fingers push
The feathered glory from her loosening thighs?"

The voice swooped over her with a rush of hot, sweaty air as if a door to elsewhere opened up. At the same time, she felt her legs pressed open and long, sweat-slick, eager fingers run along them from her knees, all the way along her trembling inner thighs. When she tried to push them away, there was nothing there to push. She felt her head being thrown back and her breasts caressed by something slight, quick, feathery. She shivered and delighted in the sensation, despite herself, despite her fear. Her heart beat faster and faster, and she found her hands now reaching out for more, for more pressure along her thighs, for more caresses. The wind made her shiver and when she opened her eyes, she saw a white flash of something like lightning, but it had the constant rhythm of something unnatural.

"And how can body, laid in that white rush,
But feel the strange heart beating where it lies?"

There was a pressure on her chest now, a warm body on top of her body, but all she could feel with her senses was the sound of the disembodied voice — everything else seemed to come from within.

Another white flash illuminated the riverbank on which she lay. She could see something had been written in the sandy mud — huge, hastily written letters, which said, unmistakably:

GO

Sophie immediately leapt from the bank, pushing that warm pressure from her chest and trying to ignore that hot pulse between her legs.

She now felt the warmth from her chest slink slowly around her neck as she stood, shaking breathlessly, seeing the words illuminated over and over again by white, strobing light. The warmth was tightening slowly around her neck, turning her on and petrifying her all at once. The voice again, right behind her:

"Being so caught up,
So mastered by the brute blood of the air,
Did she put on his knowledge with his power
Before the indifferent beak could let her drop?"

Something swooped right at her now and she instinctively closed her eyes and covered her face with her hands. When she opened her eyes again she was treading water in the middle of the river, arms and legs kicking against a powerful flow. A different voice started making itself heard now, but this time it seemed to echo from within Sophie's head.

"For days they argued, until finally, the men of the Mull'goh clan said that they would take matters into their own hands, and began to hunt down the white skinned children and kill them."

She could feel the flow trying to spin her in circles and pull her downwards, but for now she had the strength to resist. The voice continued, calmly. It was a very old voice and its candour was like a well-seasoned storyteller.

"The mothers and grandmothers of the white skinned children ran to warn them that they must flee, telling them about the decision of the men. The white skinned children fled, but the angry men followed them, hunting them down, one by one."

In the flash of light, the water became searingly clear. Sophie could look down as she swam and see all the details of her young flesh in the water which would, she knew, soon bear a lot more scars. Right at that moment it was pale and flawless, growing sinewy from all this swimming, but completely untainted by the world and all its pain, lying in wait. She saw the pain now in serpent form, in the shape of the great eel-being Gurangatch, ready and waiting to pounce.

She slipped underwater and held her breath, releasing nothing, for as long as she could. Down there, the world had a bassy pulse, a steady, beating, watery heart that seemed to synchronise with all the river-borne bodies around her.

Come up for air and you choose to stay in your comfort zone: go back home, stay warm and comfortable, get married, and live in a world of bubble baths, mid-century Danish furniture, third-wave coffee, and a steady, constant love.

Stay underwater and go down into the terrifying spiral of the river hole, towards a life ahead of queer love, loss, absolute uncertainty, and *truth*. Truth of who you are.

Just as her lungs and heart were at bursting point, Sophie opened her eyes down there. At first, all she could see was the brown blur of the river and her own skin. Then she saw a darker shape, moving slowly into her field of vision. She flinched at first, thinking it was the serpent coming closer. Then she followed it with her eyes, straining into focus. She reached for it in the swirling water and tried to grasp it. When she did, she realised it was a feather — a large, shiny black feather.

As she clutched it tightly in her hands down there underwater, something suddenly released with an unearthly squeal — like a bath plug on a gigantic scale. The water spiralled harder, faster, sucking everything into a whirlpool, Sophie along with it. She kept on clutching that black feather as she was sucked like a piece of debris into the water's swirl and tossed around and around in circles.

The water kept squealing, higher and higher, as it spun faster and faster. Sophie swallowed great gulps of it, and it tasted salty as tears.

As she heaved through the water, Sophie thought about all the decisions that she had made that had led her here, naked and blindly spinning in a river hole after a shape-shifting swan. She felt like an utterly lost, misguided child, and all the things she had valued for her whole life, she was now running away from.

With one last almighty squeal of the river, Sophie was pulled right into the river hole, sucked down through the depths of the river, still clutching the feather, until she was spat on through to the other side of the world, into the darkness.

PART THREE:

LEDA & THE SWAN

"*These trees are magnificent, but even more magnificent is the sublime and moving space between them, as though with their growth it too increased.*"

– Rainer Maria Rilke

CHAPTER X

My eyes pulled focus and I was seated, dripping subterranean water, at a desk made entirely from onyx. It was sleek as an oil slick on top, and raw as a cave underneath, as my bare knees soon found out. It made me shiver.

There was nothing on top of the desk, except my hands, curved directly in the centre, in prayer position: a submissive criss-cross of patient, ever-waiting fingers. Waiting for what, I did not yet know. As moments went by, I restrained my fingers from drumming on this shiny black surface. That would have indicated impatience, and I was not yet aware if there was someone or something that would be put out if I displayed impatience.

After untold moments, my eyes dared to travel. They ventured outwards from my desk-bound hands, to the polished concrete floor hosting the desk, ahead to the void in the centre that spiralled down to a lower level, then to the endless parallel shelves of books extending into the furthest distance — a polished concrete floor lined with boundless shelves of books, with black wrought-iron steps to punctuate them. These steps were the only indication that these bookshelves might ever be ventured to, that these books might ever be read.

My eyes then travelled all the way up these walls to the glass roof above, dusted with snow and twisted with iron spiralled staircases for those not bound by gravity. They inferred that the most valuable, the most sought-after books would be found at the top of these impossible spirals, through the glass to the icy sky that lay beyond.

Sitting at my onyx desk, I felt I had been here many times before, or, for so much time already, but had no detailed memory of former occasions, or for how long I had been here this time, only the sensation that I was here yet again, keeping my hands patient and my eyes curious.

The only way of knowing that time was passing was that the snow was growing thicker overhead on the glass. Less light was let in with each passing moment. Soon, the only light that was still able to penetrate the snow was tinged with the gold of dusk. In this golden half-light, my eyes traced the whirling of dust above my head, moving with the rhythm of my breath. My first childhood memory came back in a rush, when my baby eyes watched dust spiralling in sunlight around my cot. This creaked ajar, in a distant chamber of my mind, a far more recent memory of being seated exactly here at this onyx desk and seeing this dust spiralling in the same golden half-light. The freshly-opened memory smelled of stale milk. I shivered.

As I continued trying to exercise patience, following the rhythmic particles with my eyes and searching the memories of sunlit dust in my mind's eye, something else caught my attention. Some shadowed form, fleeting in the far shelves.

I startled and sat up even more rigidly.

Then another dark, distant movement. This time I heard it too. A forceful footfall.

Now another glimpse — it was suddenly far closer, edging closer between the stacks, just beyond the void leading downstairs.

A stoop, a shuffle.

It was now close enough for me to see a black hood pulled down over a stooped head, and then a stride long enough to reach the spiral staircase in the middle of the library — which should have taken half a minute — in just half a second. The shadow disappeared down the stairs.

We know each other, we have met before.

The sentence appeared fully formed in my head, in a voice that was not speaking.

This brought on the night. The quiet sunlight, which had been softened by snow, was now entirely suffocated. The glow down here now was mine-like, subterranean. There was a deeper quiet that blanketed everything, and the smell became overwhelmingly dank: old earth, old moss, the decayed air of a forever of wet autumns.

As if to echo the smell, a slow sub-bass began to groan from beneath the spiral stairs. At first it was almost imperceptible, like the shadow figure's presence, then it shuddered louder and louder until the liquid of my insides started to vibrate. I held a hand against my pulsing stomach to try to still the commotion.

The groaning then crescendoed, bringing forth colossal, twisting tendrils heaving from deep down in the spiral staircase upwards into the library. The tendrils writhed like the tentacles of a deep-sea creature, but their texture was woody and earthy like the roots of a tree. It was as if the ocean had spewed forth its own underwater root system, sprawling upwards into the world, instead of downwards into the hidden undersea landscapes that humans are usually not privy to. I ducked instinctively for cover beneath my desk.

When I ventured to peer out again, I saw hundreds of these tendrils now, forcing their earthy aquatic chaos up from below, onto the polished concrete floor. They crept out along its surface, serpentine, twisting and turning this way and that, through the library's shelves, scattering dirt and debris, but careful not to disturb anything from the shelves. Instead, the tendrils twisted decoratively around the books, like parental arms nestling their literary babies to sleep.

The straining and shaking and groaning finally came to an end. I slowly peered around the library, as dirt and some stray pieces of bark and a translucent substance, like bits of jellyfish, continued to flutter around in the aftermath. The entire library was now cocooned by this giant, achingly ancient root system, coiling and twisting its way down every corridor, along every set of shelves, caressing every book. The smell was suffocatingly dank, peaty, salty, heavy.

One slender new tendril now slid towards me from a far corner. As it moved, it sounded like a moistened finger trying to turn over a stubborn page. It slid ever closer until it was near enough that I saw that it was carrying a book. As it reached my desk, I stood slowly from my cowering position.

The tendril slid up the black surface of the desk, along its top, until it reached where I was standing. It unfurled its grip and let the book rest gently on the desk.

It was an old cloth-bound volume, deep-sea green, and the title had been embossed in gold.

Leda and the Swan, it read.

The tendril opened it to the first page. It contained an archaic borrowing card, with only one entry, stamped "Berlin, April 2009," alongside the handwritten name of the one and only borrower. My name.

The tendril wrapped itself deftly back around the book, and slid it with a dull thud to the floor. It carried the book across the floor and I rushed to keep up with it, running behind like a hapless Gretel. The tendril kept on pulling it along, winding through the roots, into hollows, crunching and squelching through dank debris and tracts of sand, through shelves this way and that, until I was hopelessly lost.

In the darkness and blur, I realised there were words carved into the root system to indicate which section we were running through. I almost tripped over a slimy tendril as I looked up to read the roughly carved words, *Dead Letters*, and saw that I was surrounded by acres of archives of all the undelivered letters, the returned-to-sender letters, the didn't-have-enough-postage letters. There were heaving stacks and stacks of the things, arching off further than I could see. All the lost love letters, the misaddressed postcards, the rejected letters from prisons... As I ran, a continuous stream of more letters fluttered in and landed on the shelves like flocks of nesting birds.

The tendril then made a sharp turn and we entered another section, *Dead Languages*. The shelves here were not so burdened with quantity, but with the weighty dreadfulness of the thick volumes upon the shelves. Each volume was mighty, leather-bound, proud; sitting regally, with their spines stuck out over the edge of their shelves as if hinting, hopefully, to be once again picked up, read, learned, and brought back to life. As we passed, three more volumes dropped bodily onto the shelves, reverberating out into the rest of the tangled library; like the heaviest of heartbeats. How many human languages are lost each year? And how many more-than-human languages are lost, like the language of the permafrost to the reindeer?

The tendril kept on, now through a gloomy archway, and downwards along a wide corridor, lined with darkened archways and glass enclosures within each of them. I couldn't yet see what was displayed, only the name of the library section we were now in: *Dead Names*.

As I moved closer, I could see that in each glass enclosure there was an old, worn, discarded library card with a borrower's name and identity. One by one as I watched, the cards spontaneously burst into flames and burned away into piles of ashes, eddying gently in spirals and dissipating into the gathering wind. I was overcome with a rush of feeling as I witnessed this, realising this section of the library had nothing to do with death — it was an archive for people who were still very much alive; more alive than they had been as these former selves.

The floor continued declining in a long, sweeping curve. We began sinking down and around in a constant circle, as if we were treading the coil of an immense python. I could feel the air pressure changing — we must have gone very deep underground.

As we went even deeper, the only source of light was coming from further down the spiral: a rich, red, artificial glow, and the occasional flash of a strobe light. And then came that bass-heavy rhythm again. As the tendril drew me down deeper, the musicality of the sound swam into focus. It became grinding, almost danceable. The beats became distinct, steady, forceful, and drew me closer, as fast as possible. I was sweating but I couldn't stop my feet from rushing forward in time with the beat. It was intoxicating.

But just as soon as I had established a pace and rhythm, moving with the sound and light, we reached a dead end. The tendril and I were surrounded on all sides by the ancient wall system. It slithered upwards, towards the source of the red light, then stopped abruptly, coiled around the rungs of a metal ladder. As soon as it had stopped its slithering, it hung limply from above, now motionless, as if it had been just a regular, static tree root all along. The book dropped from its grasp and landed in a puddle of liquid on the ground at the bottom rung. In the meagre red light I could see the sheen of oil coagulating over the beautiful cover. It smelled of burned engine oil. I picked up the book protectively and shook off the excess liquid, feeling the slight burn of the gasoline on my skin.

With the oily book still in my hand, I hoisted myself out of the tunnel system and onto the metal ladder. I climbed higher and higher, getting warmer and warmer as I went. The tendril stayed coiled around the ladder, as if waiting for the next one to show the way.

As I climbed, the subterranean tunnels of the library of the dead gave way to a natural landscape: the chaotic mutability of an underground swamp. The ladder was subsumed with all the give and overwhelm of this landscape, which had to be fought through to keep climbing.

I wormed my way up through layers of uneasy marshland, shifting wetlands, and all the shades and wetnesses of mud imaginable: from greyish, firmer clays, to viscous, plunging, deep loam. All felt very uncertain and ever-changing in this landscape: solid ground kept instantly giving way to waterways, and bodies of water drained at any moment and became undrinkable. Freshness became brackish, and brackishness got rained out and diluted. Nothing was fixed or predictable here; and so it was for anything built on top of it, trying to make a life on this shiftiness.

Finally, a ring of meagre red light revealed a kind of manhole through the swamp, which I twisted ajar — but then I hesitated. I was still shaky, uncertain of whether I wanted to pull myself up and out of this swampiness cocooning me, to plunge into even greater uncertainty of whatever this new space was. A new space that smelt old.

As I hesitated, finally having a moment's pause, it hit me that I had literally nothing to show for my life before.

I birthed twin feelings, in that moment: that I was worth nothing, but also that I had nothing to prove.

I forced the manhole completely open, and was hit by the monstrosity of bass and driving beats that seemed to be coming from the very structure of the building I was climbing up into. As I got to my feet, naked, trembling, and probably smelling subterranean, I looked around me to see that I had entered a kind of turbine hall. The entranceway I was standing in was open to the ceiling, three stories above, with a metal staircase off to the right. It seemed to have been partly modernised since it was last operational, sometime in the nineteenth century, but hints at this industrial past were left here and there in the form of great pieces of hulking machinery dotted about the space as if they had resigned themselves to becoming pieces of art, devoid of their factory-floor function, and lay splayed and prone like nude models.

Walking through the darkened space, my eyes and other senses started adjusting. I could smell sweat, cigarette smoke, poppers, old leather, latex, and a faint whiff of sewage. As I got closer to the metal staircase, I saw that there were other people in here too, some flowing in the same direction as me, towards the stairs, and some coming in the other direction, downstairs. I tried to discern what might be going on upstairs by studying the looks on people's faces coming towards me. Some were starry-eyed and glistening, others haggard with eyes sunken into their skulls, some were excitedly stroking each other's flesh and playing with each other's hair, others had to be carried downstairs on legs that had all but given up.

Growing nearer the stairs, the beats swam into focus: ultra-heavy, thrashing, thriving. It sent flutters through my limbs, like tickles from little feathers. I let the book drop from my grasp, leaving it behind at the bottom of the stairs. I climbed, up, up, up, in this state of expectation: my whole body swarmed with adrenaline.

As I reached the top of the stairs I felt as if I had entered a great temple. The ceiling soared hundreds of metres above, and on one side, Doric columns loomed, lit dramatically from beneath. There was a buzzing bar behind the columns, with a swinging platform filled with people in various states of undress, chatting. Another small staircase disappeared beyond that, heading to a hidden space upstairs.

But the pulse of it all came from the dancefloor: a steaming heave of bodies, writhing as if fighting the call of the swamp beneath them. Some of these night creatures gave off a light of abandonment to the aliveness of their bodies; others felt more like voids, driven to decay. Others seemed as if they had stumbled there by accident, much like me, and were mere observers of the whole spectacle from a non-committal space; others still were simply lost, wandering, and flickering between light and darkness, depending on who they were near.

I felt as if I had danced here for a thousand days and nights already, but that now (was it day or night or something in between?) was all that mattered. I felt ancient, as if this whole spectacle and I were just an unending human ritual since the moment our species learned how to dance. I felt newly born, wide-eyed at what was to come.

Dancing alone, in the centre of the sweaty throng, with that dominant red light punctuated by flashes of white strobe, I sensed a creature up ahead to my left who seemed both ancient and new. She wasn't she, he wasn't he; they were more of a landscape shuddering between periphery and focus. Between forest and swamp, mountain and glacier. A place all their own.

A landscape of pleasure. A landscape of pain.

Simultaneously, in a flash of strobe, we moved towards each other, until our bare skin almost touched. This fluttering landscape creature looked up at me from their boots shuffling the filthy dancefloor, and I kept my gaze fixed on them. They were wearing a black bra and black jeans and black leather riding boots, and their shoulders were hunched in, with their forearms crossed over their torso like a pair of wings drawn in protectively.

They had tattooed black feathers all across their back, along their shoulders, and down their arms. When they danced, the tattoos came alive, a kind of living armour against the outside world. I imagined how much pain this armour must have caused the body. And I wondered if this pain vaccine was working.

Then we both spoke simultaneously: *We know each other, have we met before.*

We both phrased it like a question, but we both said it as a statement.

We continued dancing together wordlessly, careful not to make contact with each other's skin, as if one might cause the other to burst into flames.

As we danced, I noticed something drop out of their jeans pocket and fall to the floor. I stooped down to pick it up for them, from the sticky mess of broken glass and cigarette butts. As I went to hand it back, I could see it was an old library card, with a dead name printed there and a picture of someone they no longer resembled.

The card spontaneously combusted in my hand.

They looked at me and shrugged, lit a cigarette, and took a long, deep drag.

There was a moment where we might have spoken, where our eyes searched each other for what to say. But instead we continued dancing, eyes following the whirl of dust from that old library card that was subsumed into the dancefloor around us.

A great shadow passed over us, watching, waiting.

Sniffing the smoke in the air.

CHAPTER XI

We had been in over our heads, undulating in the swamp of Berlin together for untold nights. The sun hadn't come up the whole time.

Of course the moonlight of the long night was ravishing: it lifted us, dripping, into the Euro-tropical air. Slick with sweat, we bent and folded in and through each other's bodies endlessly, coiling into more-than-human shapes.

Directly after we met in that cavernous, heaving place, the Swan made a deal with a demon (let's call him Zeus) who was loitering outside the club that Sunday morning in the wee hours. He had done many a deal with the other club frequenters, particularly on Sunday mornings, a few hours before closing, when everything was coming down, and the sun, before the deal was struck, was coming up. But the deal he made with the Swan was his most powerful work in a long while, as he usually preferred to stay more covert. It was usually along the lines of, say, "Give me your soul and you'll immediately find a fresh gram on the toilet floor," or "Give me your soul for the best sex of your life in the darkroom tonight," etc., etc. That sort of thing. But for his progeny, it seems he made an exception.

The deal was that the Swan would sell their soul to him, along with their ability to shapeshift, in exchange for earthly success as a DJ, and for our mortal passion to transform into love. Once Zeus decided to cast the love spell, the Swan would stay frozen in human form. And when the Swan would start to find their success as a DJ, the city would stay frozen in one unending night.

In the European fairy tales I'd read, being written before the white invasion of Australia when the existence of black swans was "discovered" by the Dutch, the black swan represented impossibility, non-being, *rara avis in terris nigroque simillima cygno* ("a bird as rare upon the earth as a black swan") as a second-century Roman poet phrased it. Their appearance in stories or ballets, or any other form of European mythology, carried a kind of sinister wisdom, coming from an unearthly place, and yet people were fascinated and drawn to them — they represented the rarity of finding your soulmate, or falling in love at first sight, or descending to the underworld and surviving. The possibility of the impossible. The swans in these European tales, whether pagan or Christian, were also often shapeshifters, with many tales describing how six brothers, or sometimes a lost princess, or sometimes a new bride, were transformed into swans by an evil jealous monarch, and could only assume human form again when the spell was broken, or for fifteen minutes after sundown.

Beyond Europe, the "swan wife" was a mythological figure that went as far back as stories have been told, with many cultures retelling more or less the same story of the male hero falling in love with the beautiful maiden bathing in the water with her "feathered suit" on the bank, only to realise after consummating their love that he has fallen in love with a creature who can shapeshift between female form and swan form. Somehow over centuries of storying and re-storying, the Greeks started telling it in reverse: the maiden bathing in the water is a fully human girl and the swan is a lust-fuelled god in the "innocent" guise of a swan.

The Swan wife. The possibility of the impossible. All of these things at once and yet unnameable.

Not long after the pact, the time came upon us when the sludge and reeds and broken glass of the Landwehr Canal parted in a place we had both passed many times without ever noticing each other, at an old stone bridge called the Admiral. But that night, in the instant Zeus commanded, we both saw past the polluted canal sludge and crossed the old bridge from our opposite sides — the north star and the south star crisscrossing the sky — and we met in the middle. This was how we came into each other's lives again for the first time since that fateful meeting in the swampland of dancing bodies.

We stood facing each other on the bridge, unable to move or speak, only able to meet eyes for whatever Zeus proclaimed was the duration it takes to feel a "real" connection. Wordlessly, the Swan shared their headphones with me and I climbed onto their black feathered back.

With their music in my ears, we flew over the locked gates and barbed-wire fences of the Prinzenbad, the swimming pool complex, glowing white in the overhead security lights and saturated by a mist that curled my hair and my eyelashes and gave an unearthly sheen to the Swan's feathers.

I blinked up at the black Swan and stroked their long neck as we sat at the top of one of the defunct waterslides. We shared our first embrace as we slid down it. At the bottom, in the glinting, slime-and-algae-covered water, we chattered like children, then sank, kissing, beneath the green.

The spell had been cast.

When we opened our eyes, we found ourselves in the Swan's steaming bathtub in their Kreuzberg loft. They had shed their feathers into the bathwater and had now been frozen in human form. They slunk down into the hot water with their fresh skin reddening, gleaming. A baptism with bubbles. They cradled me, slippery, against their breast and we were smoking and satiated.

I was blissfully ignorant of any deal being done at that time, having wandered for so long in that subterranean Library of the Dead and, in the first few years, experienced nothing of life, only reading and researching everything I could to transform myself into my New Self.

Key topics: desire, "female" sexuality, the "feminine" body, hysteria, hauntings, being haunted by one's own latent sexuality, transforming bodily and psychic pain into pleasure, the "dark continent" of the female body, getting lost on purpose, getting lost in dark forests, little wooden houses in dark forests, religious indoctrination, Catholic iconography and aesthetics, Flagellantism, longing, rage... the list went on.

Once in the swamplands for several years, the research transformed into field research, field recordings, auto-ethnographies, ethnographies, psychogeographies, until my brain finally admitted to my body that what I was doing no longer resembled research whatsoever. Finally, I was directly, fleshly, living out what I had been so reluctant to allow to come to life before. Out of fear of being a Very Bad Person. Now I had let go of that fear, I was free to live as a Very Bad Person, or a Very Good Person, depending on my level of Catholic guilt on any given day.

New key topics: flirting, making out, touch, queerness, lesbianism, open relationship, threesome, cuddle puddle, polyamory, butch identity, femme identity, non-binary identity, pansexuality, cunnilingus, strap-on, vibrator, BDSM, enthusiastic consent, sex party, and finally, that faraway, exotic continent — Love With a Partner I'm Sexually Attracted To. I had finally decided I wanted to explore that last continent around the time the Swan and I crossed paths again that night on the bridge. Zeus had timed things perfectly.

It seemed this was my second watershed moment. The first was in the midst of that push and pull of the river.

I had always been confused by the contradictory meanings of the landscape of a "watershed": being both the area that drains into a single river, and also a ridge formed by a chain of mountains which sends water to two different rivers on either side. I knew, even in the midst of the chaos back then, that I was literally and figuratively at a "watershed" — I just hadn't worked out yet whether it was a convergence of many things in my life finally finding a defined course ahead or it was a moment of divergence where two paths of my life would be ultimately defined.

So many cautionary tales had been told about the deep holes in the river, like the one that had sucked me in and spat me out; they were said to be the dwelling places of the powerful eel beings that threaten to pull swimmers into their underworld. Some of these river holes have been considered sacred for so long, and some have been considered so dangerous, as portals to other worlds for so long, that only the most powerful *karadji*, the seers who could commune with spirits, could venture near them. Some of these river holes had ancient spirits locked inside of them, deep under the water, some had serpents hiding in lairs deep within them. One was Gurangatch, the giant eel-being who had dived, burrowed, and twisted through Country to create these treacherous holes, one of which was Gulguer, one of the deepest holes in the entire Yandhai. According to the legend, Gurangatch would lurk in the deepest of river holes and drag and drown any passing human.

Now, in this second watershed moment, I felt a gratefulness towards Gurangatch.

The Swan's bathtub was candlelit and surrounded by framed, black-and-white photographic prints of their past sexual exploits. Countless sexual encounters, all going on in this very tub. As I wondered how long it had been since the last one had happened, my eyes landed on a used pair of black latex gloves hanging from the waste bin. Not very long, then. There were exactly sixteen toothbrushes crammed around the bathroom sink, and the basin itself was clogged with what seemed to be black latex paint. (Later, I would spot hundreds of pairs of sunglasses by the front door, which I learned was the "entry fee" for guests coming to the loft for an afterhour. And much later I would find forty or so plastic-wrapped locks of hair in the freezer and a couple of pairs of jeans that had been cut off of whoever was last wearing them.)

But for now we simply melted and melded in the bath together.

They made me come that night. And when I say "made" I mean *forced*. Have you ever been forced by someone to have an orgasm? It's an infuriating push/pull of hot/cold, hate/love, pain/pleasure, until you just stop analysing and resenting it and let your body go off and forget the resentment, and love what it loves. The most confusing pleasure I had ever experienced at that point.

CHAPTER XII

There had been a grace period of about three weeks in which we stayed away from the club because the black Swan had fucked people other than me there — one, two, three times. (This was not counting the time there was the enforced foursome in the toilet stall with one of the Swan's most recent ex-lovers and her boyfriend, who still had a set of keys to the apartment. I say "enforced" because I was encouraged to join the three of them or otherwise wait outside the toilet stall until it was over. The thought of seeing their three sets of feet shifting and shuffling underneath the gap in the door...)

Now that the three weeks had passed and all the apologies and trips to the STI clinic were over with, the Swan wanted back in: to the dancefloor, to the chaos, to all the networking they had to do as a burgeoning DJ. I just wanted to dance it all out and try to avoid fits of jealousy from the very frequent collisions with their former flames.

It was the dead of winter, but when we got inside the club that Sunday, it felt like summer — the heat rising from bodies was sunlight through that dense swampland: wet, rank, intoxicating.

We took several rounds of the dancefloor, the bar, then to the upstairs dancefloor and the upstairs bar, arm-in-arm the entire time, no matter the jostled resistance from elbow-angled dancers and the heavy thumps from the sloppy head-nodders. It was our ritual, every time we arrived: take our turn in the space like a pair of courting aristocrats striding around the palace gardens. Our pride in being out together, and being in love, showed in the way we held our heads tall, looking up over the crowd, and in the way we placed our hands elegantly over each other's forearms, as if they were gloved in silk. Instead, our hands were already drenched in smoke and sweat and had a good deal of white powder under the fingernails. The black Swan called me "my Empress" and I called them "my Highness."

We hit the red-lit backstairs and found the usual crowd to catch up on three weeks' worth of gossip. Benjamin had gotten Lucas a custom-made cock ring for his birthday to wear around his neck. Jenn had officially registered her "cleaning" business so she could bulk buy the chemical that street cleaners use to get rid of graffiti but which she dealt to her friends as GHB or "G." Dionysis was just back from another trip to Brazil to try to cure himself of his secret lovesickness for Lucas. Odile had finally found a name for the "male presence" that took over her petite, balletic body when she was high in the club. Valentine was his name and he was a gay male bottom who slept with gay guys who had never had any experience with a cis female body before (but somehow they were attracted to this one elegant duplicity when Valentine inhabited Odile in the club). Shoulder to sweaty shoulder against the cool concrete wall, Odile showed the Swan and me some pictures of these encounters on her phone. They were so detailed and graphic, I found myself getting giddy. I stood suddenly and declared that I needed "a ski trip."

The Swan smiled deviously, stood up, and took my hand. With their other hand they patted the front of their crotch. It might have looked like bravado to the passing crowd, but they were just checking that their drug stash was still in place.

"Be right back cuties," the Swan said and turned on their boot heel with a flourish.

After a long queue in the bathroom, with the Swan punctuating the wait by kicking the toilet doors one after the other, which did nothing to speed up the people inside, we finally scored the biggest cubicle. The Swan declared this was the very cubicle they had cheated on me in, three weeks earlier, then laughed loudly saying, "Ha, LOL, don't know why I told you that!"

"I have a pretty good idea why," I muttered with a knife in my guts, and pointedly took the biggest line the Swan had prepared on the screen of their phone.

"*Guten Rutsch!*" the Swan cried. "Enjoy the slopes!"

The "soup" (the colourful concoction of crushed-up ecstasy pills, speed, cocaine, and ketamine) rushed through my body — faster than usual since my heart was already racing after this latest information drop — and it took almost my entire mental capacity to stop myself from picturing what had gone on between my Swan and the other girl, right here in this very cubicle. How was it possible to be in love with someone, love the way I felt in the black Swan's orbit, and yet also utterly despise them and everything they stood for?

The Swan suddenly drew the little sock out of their underwear again, and this time they produced a small brown glass bottle and pipette. My heart sank. G. Every time the Swan took it, things ended in tears — usually my tears. It was the main excuse they had used for cheating so many times. "I'm not myself when I'm on G — no one is. You can't think of what I do as coming from me, it's all just coming from the G bottle." I didn't believe a word of it but it did help me rationalise things; make the wound less deep.

"And this time," the Swan said sternly, measuring out their dosage with the tiny pipette inside the bottle, squinting into the overhead fluorescent light, "you're coming with me."

The Swan's smile was full of sex, and they ran a G-soaked finger over my lips. It was so foul it burned — and yet, coming from the Swan's finger, I lapped it up. Maybe it was a good way to blank out the whole infidelity thing, I rationalised to myself.

"Let's start you on 0.7 and see where it takes you."

The Swan measured the dose, and at that point, (Berlin cliche time!) I knew there was no turning back. I kind of didn't want to turn back. Where would I turn anyway? I couldn't even remember what I was doing last week, let alone where or who I had been before these swamplands.

"And remember that now we can't drink alcohol. Otherwise it's KO, OD..."

I opened my mouth like a baby bird, tilting my head back trustingly and accepting the burning liquid into my mouth.

"Don't get it on your gums... or your teeth," the Swan warned with another grin. "*Einfach* swallow."

I did what I was told, mostly because I had no idea what to expect from this drug. No sooner had I swallowed than the Swan kicked the door open into a group of waiting goths. One had a long, expensive-looking leather whip. The Swan took one look at it and grabbed it as we exited the toilet. They ran to the very rear of the bathroom, to a shadowy corner and pulled me there with them. I could already feel myself coming up on the G. Hot and heavy and light and dark all at once.

"I'll bring it back in a sec, babe," the Swan called to the owner of the whip, who just nodded, passively, ketamine glassing over her ashen face.

The Swan stood seductively in the corner, with the whip in one hand and the other resting above their head on the greasy wall. They strummed their black-painted nails on the wall as they regarded me before them. Beneath them. The Swan towered over me, even in flat leather boots, and the fluorescent lighting bounced from every harsh angle of them, from their cheekbones to their collarbones to their hip bones clad in shiny black latex. They smiled a wide hungry smile and in that instant I felt a crackle of something else with us in the bathroom that was no longer entirely the Swan, or me, or any other humans. There was a flicker of the lights. Something had joined us and was now throbbing from the Swan's grin.

"OK, Sophie," said that throbbing thing, "now's the time for my punishment. For all the pain I caused you. Now you get to cause me pain. As much pain as you want me to feel. To release your pain."

I heard that crackle again and felt a prickle in my fingertips. Something like pins and needles rushed through the veins in my arms, upwards, upwards towards my heart. Like the blood had started running in reverse. Something without boundaries, without guilt, without fear of any consequences opened up in me. Something both pure and void. Something that was now seeping through all of me. It felt dead but with a life all its own. Was this what G felt like? Or did the G crack an opening in me that wasn't meant to be open?

It coursed its way now from my heart back to my extremities. Once it reached my fingertips again, I felt my hand reaching for the whip. Once the whip was clenched in my fist, it felt familiar and warm, like the door handle of my childhood home, twisting deftly in my palm.

My eyes opened anew and I saw the Swan now only as flesh, fresh flesh, deserving of pain. These new eyes watched my hand make the first strike with the whip, and then the next. Then my ears heard the Swan's laughter.

"Harder," they mocked, "so much harder."

I gladly obliged.

The Swan removed their shirt so the flesh was exposed to as much impact as possible.

My hand became a blur. All I knew was the whip; and that the whip was coming down onto eager flesh, over and over, until I was the whip and I shivered with the pleasure of my force.

I came down on that flesh so many times, and so hard, that it was not until someone in the bathroom shouted, "They're bleeding!" that I was finally able to relinquish the indulgence and stop myself. To separate myself from the object in my hand.

I looked up to see that a concerned crowd had started to form around us at the back of the bathroom, open-mouthed at what I had done: the Swan's torso cut all over, bleeding in chaotic lines. The Swan's face, smiling through deep pain.

I felt the whip leave my hand; heard it clatter to the bathroom floor.

The Swan, quietly wincing, put their shirt back on and grabbed hold of my waist. I wrapped my trembling arm around them. We staggered like this from the bathroom and remained non-verbal for the rest of that long night.

CHAPTER XIII

They said they could glimpse their black Swan form that day on Good Friday, as we rode the train from Berlin to Poland. They could see them in the reflection of the forest that shrouded the windows just enough to get a glimpse as we hurtled through. While the moon was still bright, we could only see the Swan in these furtive silhouettes of the trees, splintered and skeletal in these last death-throes of winter.

We sat next to each other, both travelling backwards, leaving the two-seater opposite us empty. I realised they'd left the seat opposite empty for this other version of themselves to occupy, and not because they'd particularly wanted to sit close to me. I sank a little deeper into my winter coat and tried not to look at what they were transfixed by on their phone.

We rushed backwards like this, east, accompanied by these glimpses. I had learned well enough by now not to ask direct questions about things like this, or about how exactly the pact with Zeus worked (which was no longer a secret since we'd taken acid together one night and it all came out in a rushed "funeral" for the black Swan, accompanied by a eulogy and a symbolic burial involving bananas. I could go into more detail but it would only bring flashbacks, and let's just say I will never again eat a banana.)

Travelling backwards towards Poland with them, I wanted so much to believe in their own brand of madness or genius, which helped me explain to myself the palpable darkness seeping from them, and into me, and into the atmosphere around us wherever we were. It helped me to justify just how much of an extension of them I had become; losing, forgetting, foregoing everything of my own former self. And at the same time forging my new self.

They were more jittery than usual, and kept getting up out of their seat to pace the train aisles, while we rattled towards their hometown on the Warta River. We were visiting Poland for Easter with their very Catholic grandparents. It would be the first time I met their family, and the first time the Swan had attended a family gathering in a very long time.

Everything I knew about their hometown I had gleaned from the little snippets of English that the Swan and their friends and exes sometimes spoke on the phone when they knew they were on speaker and wanted me to know some basic politics or some old highschool gossip. What I gathered was that it was one of those towns that the Polish president used as a shining example of the possibilities for the "resurrection" of the country after the war, mostly because it was the town he was born in. The first few post-war generations, with their alcoholism and violence and unemployment, were essentially deleted from historical records according to the president, but their grandkids, the generation of the Swan, were the ones the president used as the poster children for his re-election speeches. The town's greatest pride was its speedway track, with its prize-winning motorcycle team, and of course the riotous celebrations and commiserations that happened in town every time the team raced. Their one major rival had almost burnt the clubhouse down and sent much of the team (and the town's biggest fans) to hospital after one heavy loss. That summed up the new generation: loud, fast, violent, and macho. The old generation, the Swan's parents' generation, were still part of the more classical image of Poland, keeping the old music halls, the cinemas, the local restaurants and the love of the arts alive — but these didn't pay the bills or bring the crowds, so much of that world either lay in ruins or was demolished to make way for the speedway.

We changed trains at Kostrzyn, our breath pluming into the frigid air as we stumbled along the platform that looked as if it hadn't been touched since the war times. We made the next train just as it started pulling away from the station. We were lucky that it was one of these older trains with manual doors so the Swan could keep them open for me as I hurled the bags inside and they pulled me up.

We sat down gasping for breath, and this time they sat opposite me, so only I was travelling backwards. Now that the moon had disappeared, we could clearly see each other reflected in the glass.

"In complete darkness," the black Swan told our reflections in the glass, "it's different. See, look at the change in my face—"

I looked at them opposite me, and then I looked at their reflection. It was like looking into the future — a terrible one. The version of them in the glass was gaunt, grinning to the point of baring their teeth back at me. Their skin appeared greenish and verging on the end. I looked back at them opposite me, shaking. What had I just seen? It certainly wasn't the black Swan I had expected to see.

"That's what will happen," they explained darkly, "if I stay in this human form too long."

They sighed and started scrolling idly through their phone again like nothing at all had just happened. In the reflection of their phone in the train windows, I could see there were some more nudes that other girls had sent recently, but that was the least of my worries at that moment.

I was silent for some time, trying not to look at the reflection again, shivering a little. They noticed my discomfort and stroked my knee seductively.

"Let's do some ketamine!" they said, and immediately drew a little baggie out of their wallet in full view of the other passengers. They came to sit next to me and made a small huddled effort to conceal what we were doing as we snorted, then they sat back, satisfied, and said as loudly as possible:

"God I love drugs."

CHAPTER XIV

Easter Sunday was soon upon us, and since we were now well and truly outside Berlin, we were beyond the reach of Zeus' night spell. The spring sunshine was a wonder, and I could see it was working wonders on the Swan as well. Sweetness and light were flowing through our veins.

We had arrived in the sunny fields on the edge of the forest, on the outskirts of town. We had taken our shoes off outside for the first time in the endless neverland of winter, and dropped them under some trees at the edge of the yellow field. My black Swan was ahead of me, half-singing, half-teaching me Polish words as they came to them... *las* for forest, which I called back to them that I loved, my favourite Polish word so far...

Their impossibly long legs always carried them so much faster than I could keep up with, always keeping me breathless, whether I was chasing them across the dancefloor, sliding along the parquet hall of their loft, dashing along the train platform towards another adventure, along the vomit-bright carpet of that hotel foyer before we snuck up to the rooftop... Now they were hurling off their leather jacket and the hoodie underneath, and opening their pale, tattooed arms to the forest of their childhood before us.

They had already explained, as we ran abruptly from the breakfast table of their Catholic grandparents that morning, that they had to show me where they used to run away as a child, from the little house their father had built on the other side of this yellow field. This forest was their safe place, full of their only friends at that time — the trees, the mosses, the sound of the wind, the sixteen kittens running around that they had saved from being killed and tried to nurse from their own nipples.

Las, I called to them happily.

Yes, they screamed back. *Pretty good accent.*

I had almost caught up with them as they rid themself of the last layer — they were now just in a tank top and jeans. I saw them look up to the small wooden hunter's hut that was overlooking the field.

They hesitated, suddenly not wanting to take a single step closer to the forest.

I could well understand why they didn't want to face it. As much as they talked of it as the only hiding place from the drunken screams and hands of their father, and the drunken mind games of their mother, it also had a longer history in their family, which their cousin had explained to me the night before.

He was not much of a storyteller, this round, sweaty-faced cousin, fancying himself as the only true artist of the family, with his mild success as a trumpet player, and he never missed a moment, when the Swan was out of earshot, to place a hand on my leg and tell me that the whole family thought of the Swan as a child of the devil, with a birthmark to prove it.

The cousin told me that during World War II, the father of their great-grandmother was a forester, so he, his wife, his seven sons, and one daughter all lived a modest, hard but happy life right there in the forest. Hidden away, their house was the last one raided by the Nazis in the area. The Nazis killed each family member in the little forest house one by one, oldest to youngest. But because the youngest member, their great-grandmother, was called Adolfa, the family legend goes that they spared her life because she shared the name of the Führer. Adolfa had gone on to have a son of her own who seemed to have inherited a very misplaced sense of revenge and took his anger at the violence inflicted on his ancestors out on his own family. As did his son, the Swan's father.

If this story was engraved in my mind as I stared across the field to the forest, I can only imagine how deeply, fleshly, carved it must have been in the Swan's — their embodied inheritance of pain over generations.

Barefoot, they climbed up the little wooden ladder to get to the hunter's hut. As they looked back, I saw them for everything they were in that present moment, and all the stories that made them, and I saw the little child with the same crooked smile that might have looked back to their family of kittens, decades earlier. And the feeling that filled me then outshone any of the pain that had come before or that I knew would come in the future — to them, to me, to us, if we continued being an "us."

I saw them look back at me from up on that sunny wooden ladder, and, in that little moment, everything was as complex as reality is, as well as how simple. I could feel the clarity and beauty in that paradox: accepting incomprehensible complexity, as well as warm simplicity into my body simultaneously.

I realised I loved them. The most complex and the most simple feeling all at once. Nothing to do with any pact. Not because I willed it to be or even because I wanted it to be. It just was.

CHAPTER XV

"When we saw the little wooden house buried deep in the trees,
Our hearts leapt to our mouths.
We could not speak.
We were silenced by it;
Not choked, but so warmed in our mouths,
So caressed and comforted in our mouths."
                    – Our Little Wooden House in the Forest, 2017

We could feel the little wooden house buried deep in the trees, as we waded through the first light of the morning, shining with dew.

It was Easter Monday and the Swan and I had gathered the courage to come back to the forest, to make our way to the haunted house that refused to keep its ghosts contained. We had a plan.

The freshness of the pine warming as the sun rose was darkened by the lingering smell of fire. It made such a strong presence that we could almost taste it in our mouths. Some long-burning fires, some long-buried fires, some fires raging anew. Each fire had a different texture and depth on the tongue that spoke volumes of how it first caught alight, and the stories it then burned.

It was 2017, and I had just published my first book. As we walked, that morning, through the forest, a lot of the book felt like a premonition. Lives and loves wrapped up in the proverbial space of the little wooden house in the forest. All of it was written years before I had ever encountered the

Swan, or heard any of their ancestral little-wooden-house-in-the-forest stories.

I glanced over to my Swan as we kept on through the forest. Neither of us had slept at all the previous night in anticipation of today. The Swan's young face was careworn, with heavy dark rings around their eyes. They saw me watching and smiled back, first a half-smile, sweet with the promise of the day ahead, which then, true to form, expanded into the hungry grin of Red Riding Hood's forest wolf. They bared their teeth playfully and tickled me as they pretended to eat me alive. My laughter rang high out into the trees and startled some owls. Their flutter and hoots brought back the creepiness of what we were about to do, and gloom settled back over the forest.

The previous night we had huddled together in their grandmother's heavy yak-wool blankets on a couch in the family room, where we had sat to eat Easter Sunday dinner together. The smell of the pierogi with caramelised onions and borscht and cream sauce with lots of dill had seeped into the brown satin curtains and the beige, patchy carpet.

Later, Pope John Paul II, the pride and joy of Poland, oversaw the feverish fingering we did on the couch, after everyone had gone to bed, from his framed photograph over the doorway. The two-room apartment was tiny, so it was probably not just the Pope who knew what we were doing. When we were finished, we snuck to the fridge and midnight-snacked on some leftover dumplings, washed down with swigs of vodka. We stayed up smoking and talking with the kitchen window open. The same window that was directly above one from which the Swan's childhood best friend was thrown by some local older boys. Those boys thought of themselves as gangsters and pranksters, but they had ended up murdering the boy. He didn't survive the fall. The Swan barely survived the grief. But the boys got away with it. "It was just a joke," "Boys will be boys..."

That was the first dead body the Swan had seen, and there was a lot to be said about it that only the dead hours of the night allow room for.

Creeping through the forest, we were both in that state when the adrenaline kicks through your body to make up for the lack of sleep. Our muscles were tensed and our eyes were wide, seeing anything and everything in the trees – especially things that weren't there.

The Swan was sweating visibly. I could see it forming little pearls on their brow and above their top lip. It was still quite cool at such an early hour of the morning, and we were in the deep shade of the trees. They weren't sweating from the walking or the morning air, of course — they were sweating from the old and new fires burning in their bones.

Myself, I was shivering, feverish, hot and cold at once. I could smell the waves of my own salty sweat pouring from me in empathy. These fires were not born from my blood, but theirs – but at this point it didn't make any difference. We were already bound to each other so acutely. I could feel every pounding of their blood, and the blood of their ancestors before them, deep in my own veins.

I had become trauma-bonded to my Swan.

We trod carefully through the fallen pine needles and decaying birch bark, towards the little house. I realised, at that moment, that apart from the two owls that had flown off just now in fright, no other birds were calling. There was no birdsong at all, although dawn had long since broken and it was their cue to begin their Matins. If birdsong in a forest is a sign that all is safe, that there are no predators lurking about in the trees, then what does it mean when the birds are silent? Phrases I had written years ago were coming in hot and heavy:

What would it sound like
If sweat, caused by all these warm,

Pulsing feelings in our mouths,
Came pouring forth from our lips? Would that suffice?
Would the little house feel that this is sufficient?
And what would happen if, through all this excitement,
One of us would bite down a little too hard on her heart in her
mouth?
Momentarily halt its pulsing,
Hurt its feelings through this piercing of its materiality?

We two had also grown silent as we made our way closer, and as the sun rose higher. My eyes were stinging from tiredness, but I noticed the sting was almost identical to that from woodsmoke. The smoke engulfs your vision and for some time you are forced to shut your eyes, as tightly as you can, to make sure more smoke doesn't seep in. You stumble around, with your hands over your eyes, wincing in pain and trying to make sure you don't stumble into the fire itself. Then finally the wind changes, or you can get far enough away from the flames, and the pain subsides, and you can open your eyes again. Your vision still stays cloudy for a while, and your eyes are red and watery as if you had been sobbing.

I looked over to the Swan as they walked, long-legged, their riding boots crunching the undergrowth, the pale sunlight flickering through the branches onto their dark hair and proud pale throat, arched skywards and steady as they dared as they prepared themselves for this meeting with the house.

There stood a little wooden house
— its angles, its squarenesses,
All neatly intact.
The last remaining house of the family.
The first view of it strained the eyes
After so many wavering trees and shadows

Dancing across dirt and heavenly bodies.
There was a glow from it and again, like an oasis,
The eyes did not trust it,
The mind did not trust its scents,
Threatening to churn both it and the guts
With so many different types of hunger,
So many different types of memories.
All these types of longings thrown upon with damp earth,
Calming their fires.

This was the house of dreams that the Swan's great-great-grandfather built. Where the surviving family lived until they abandoned the forest for the city apartment when the Swan was in their late teens. This was their childhood home.

Listening to the Swan's recollections of their childhood was like flipping through the ripped-out newspaper clippings of a hoarder with amnesia. Clippings of twelve different obituaries glued together, a photograph of a flooded house fragmented across various pages until the image no longer made sense, obsessive collections of clippings about one crime and just a few disconnected syllables from the report of another, then a paragraph about a piano concerto. I could feel the mess of it all, and felt I understood it all in my bones, but had no linear chronological sense of it.

When they asked me to come out here to see the little wooden house of the family's dreams, I said yes for many reasons. Out of support, out of wanting to understand better, and out of wanting to help put these ghosts to rest. The house that stood before us was an archive of intergenerational pain.

The sun was warmer now and almost directly above us in the sky. Was it a reflection from the sun's aureate or was that a glow from within the little house? No one had lived here for a decade.

As we approached, the glow flickered and faded, as if someone had blown out a candle. And the smell of fire was more and more palpable the closer we trod. I drew my phone from my pocket and started recording some video of the house, holding it steady and just letting the atmosphere of the house and the trees cowering around it take space in the frame.

As I filmed, I began to hear sounds in the forest behind us. Running footsteps criss-crossing each other. Some were light and airy, like the sound of children running barefoot, and some were heavy and rhythmic, like soldiers marching in line, steadily approaching. I heard faint trickles of laughter, or was it crying? I could see out of the corner of my eye, as I kept filming, that the Swan was hearing it all too.

The little house had two small windows on the ground floor, symmetrically on either side of the front door. It had a pitched roof with a small attic window, also with its own pitched eaves, but this window was disconcertingly left of centre, like an afterthought. There was a chimney off to the right of the roof, and, through the lens of my phone, I thought I saw a tiny wisp of smoke for a moment. The weatherboard facade of the house had been painted a pale mint green, which was now coming off in sheaths, revealing the original ash-grey wood beneath. The roof was black slate and overgrown with swaying grasses and dandelions, brightly out of place. We walked a little closer, down the gravel path, which had long since mossed over and was now a highway for slugs. I must have stumbled over many of their vulnerable bodies as I kept my eyes on the screen and kept tiptoeing forward as I filmed. Through the downstairs window on the right, we could hear faint clatters of dishes and glasses, which sometimes sounded like someone was putting them away in cupboards but would then escalate into cracks and clashes like they were being flung across the kitchen. I took my eyes off the screen momentarily to look over at the Swan. I could see them snapping a black rubber band around their right wrist as they walked – once, twice, three times, then double-time with the rhythm of their steps.

I brought my eyes back to the screen as we moved left now and caught a glimpse of the family room. There was still a rotting, green velvet couch in there, staring mindlessly at a smashed television from the '90s. The sunlight creeping in showed us the glint of the floor – it was carpeted in bottles: mostly beer bottles, a lot of wine bottles, and some vodka bottles. There was no longer any place left to stand on the floor; it was all bottles. We heard them clink like a whole family raising a toast. And then we heard them smash into a thousand pieces. The camera caught a shadow pass across their gleaming surface. The Swan started, and, as I kept filming, I watched out of the corner of my eye as they traced a path from the family room, deeper into the house down the hallway.

We were almost at the front door. There were children whispering and laughing around us and I felt a heavy weight around my waist and lower back as if a small child was dangling from my hips. As the Swan reached out for the front door handle, I tried to get a closeup of their hand turning the knob — finally opening the door to this place so long buried. They jumped back suddenly, pulling their hand away in pain.

"It's burning!" they said, and showed their reddened palm to the camera. "Did you get that?"

"Yes," I replied, looking in shock from their hand back to the phone screen. I managed to catch one glimpse of the screen and the low battery warning before the phone completely shut off.

"Damn," I muttered, "I had a full battery. There's no way that it should be shutting off like that."

The Swan looked visibly furious for a moment, then managed to calm themselves enough to say, "Yeah, that tends to happen in places like this. Not your fault."

I sighed and put the phone back in my pocket. It was burning hot.

The Swan kicked the door open, and we were in.

Instantly, all was quiet. The air was thick.

Walking into the kitchen, crunching through the smashed plates on the floor, it felt like wading across flood plains. Everything was viscous, draining, threatening to pull us under.

We walked together towards the kitchen sink, slowly opening cupboards and finding cobwebs and families of mice. The kitchen window looked back towards the forest from where we'd come.

"My grandmother, Adolfa, was doing the washing up when the soldiers came to the house, so she saw them first," the Swan said as they gazed out. "She screamed out to the whole family but because she was only five, and her father was already drunk, he just laughed and yelled at her. They shot him first as soon as they came through the door — apparently the last words he said were 'Stop whining like a little girl, Adolfa.'"

The Swan put their hands in the empty sink and swirled them around, as if through dishwashing water.

"I had to do the washing up after every single meal," the Swan was murmuring as we stood at the sink together. "Even if it was the middle of the night, if the father finished eating something, he would drag me from bed and force me to wash the plates and stuff right then. And if I didn't do it perfectly, because my eyes kept closing because I was so tired, he'd smash the plate or the bowl or whatever into my head. Weird, because my parents didn't have any money back then, but they kept having to buy new bowls and things..."

Now that we were inhabiting the interior space of the little wooden house, no longer just treading the fringes, lurking at the proverbial edges, the flashbacks from my fiction writing faded out. What took over now, far more visceral and treacherous, were the flashbacks from our own Berlin home. The all-too-real stories that we had written into the walls, the floors, the air, the *flesh* of our Berlin "Dream House." Things I had been denying were real for far too long. Because... surely when you loved someone, these things just *weren't* real. Were they?

In our kitchen you threw a full glass bottle of water at me when you thought I had gone and done something behind your back. You rushed up at me, cornered me, screamed in my face, pressed me hard against that brick wall. Told me never to speak to or see my ex ever again.

I thought of putting my arm around them there at the sink — still in denial of what they had done to me, that what was coming back to me were *real memories*. So I hesitated and they turned away, walking towards the living room.

We couldn't get further than the doorway because of all the bottles. The Swan tried to push through a couple and ended up stranded in the sea of all the green, white, and brown glass.

"There was a piano when we still lived here but my mother sold it. My great-great-grandmother was playing it when the soldiers came. Adolfa said she couldn't remember what it was her mother was playing, but anyway, maybe that's one reason I got into music? But they shot her in the back as she played, which sounds bad, but really, you've got to hear all the other stories, also what the Russians were doing to women at the time. So it was pretty quick and easy, you know, when you compare."

It was not hard to imagine the piano music echoing out from the room through the open window and shimmering over the glass and into the forest air. If I strained my ears enough, I thought I could even hear "The Swan," that piece by Saint-Saëns, lifting us up, out of the chaos of broken glass and lighting up the imitation chandelier swaying from the ceiling. The Swan started moving their fingers out in front of them as if playing something in their mind, something upbeat and something to dance to. And I was transported right back to our living room.

We danced so much, sometimes completely on the floor, rolling all over each other. Once another couple, former lovers of yours, joined us and I didn't want them to but I thought you did and I let them make out with me and touch me because I thought it was what you wanted. You were smiling lasciviously as it all happened but the next day, I thought I would die from your anger. You screamed in my face for hours that I was a liar and a cheater. You wouldn't stop until I said, over and over again, "Yes, I am a liar and a cheater." Those words were the only things that would calm your rage at me. I felt sick at myself.

"My mother played all the time — right here," they said, swaying a little now so that the bottles around their ankles twinkled. "She taught me piano, she taught me singing... although I could never get those high notes like her. But man, her scream though, the sound would make you wanna die. She would scream and she would scream late at night, when they were up drinking. She'd be playing and singing, all drunk and happy, then he'd get to that point, too drunk, and he'd try to rape her there against the piano. And she'd scream for me to come and save her and I would — I'd get up from my bed and stand in between them."

You threw me back on the bed so many times and would lie over me, holding my wrists above my head, saying I was pathetic, disgusting. And other times, in that same configuration, you would say that I was the most beautiful creature on the planet. Some nights there would be so much screaming coming from our bedroom and then it would be like it never happened the next morning. You would always tell me I exaggerated, that I was

imagining it. I was a drama queen. That I should be thankful for
what we have. And yet, I was.

I followed the Swan down the darkened hallway, lined
with deep scratches, paint colour tests, and a height marker
that stopped at age five ("the age my parents got over me,"
the Swan had told me a few times before).

Peering through the first doorway, we could see a toilet
right next to a small bath with an old-fashioned shower
head above it. Looking at the bathtub gave me deja-vu, but
I didn't know at the time where that feeling was coming
from. The Swan was shaking their head, smiling ruefully.

"So many baths I had in there," they muttered, "and
almost every time the father would come in because he
had something so important to tell me that it couldn't wait
until I got out. Or he would have to suddenly pee urgently...
making comments while he looked at my chest about how I
was becoming a woman so soon..."

· I would eventually become suicidal, letting all the things you
called me and all the things you said to me sink in. So many
nights in the bathtub thinking of how I could just quietly slip
under the warm water, drown, and you would finally feel love
for me again after I was gone.

They slammed the bathroom door and we got out of
there. There was more to tell about bathrooms but that
would come later.

We reached the bedroom — there was no door, just
broken hinges. The Swan let out a laugh that sounded like
it came from a nightmare.

"Adolfa, great-grandmother, used to always tell me I
was such a spoiled brat," they laughed, "because I got this
room all to myself and back in her day, all the kids had to
share."

We moved inside the room and I immediately wanted
to be sick. There was no obvious reason for it; the room
just smelled of damp and dust and the only things left were

schoolbooks and kids' books piled up around the edges of the room and a hand-knitted, brightly coloured blanket in the middle of the carpeted floor.

"Ha, I kept that there in case my cat family ever came back and needed something cosy," the Swan explained, bending down to run their long fingers over it. "Grandmother knitted that for me one time I stayed with them in their apartment. It was around the time they caught me on the street with those boys, remember I told you?"

I remembered the story. The Swan had turned twelve and started sniffing bulbs with much older boys who skated, tagged, smoked, and asked the Swan for headjobs. The grandparents found the Swan at it one day, giving a headjob to a twenty-year-old, and kept them away from the house in the forest for a while. They thought they'd be better supervised at their apartment, rather than with their parents.

Our bedroom was meant to be our sanctuary. Over time, it became my most feared place. And yet, I just kept hoping. Kept painting pictures in my mind as I lay on our bed of what it should be. Our bedroom was meant to be my longed-for continent of Love With A Partner I Am Sexually Attracted To, but it was also the place I feared like I never had before in my life. How could one place be both at once?

"This room was where Adolfa hid from the soldiers. All her brothers ran out the back, but she could see them from this window. The men lined up all her brothers and shot them one by one. She saw the whole thing from this window."

We turned to the other side of the room where an antique wooden wardrobe stood watch.

"They found her here, in this wardrobe," the Swan continued. "And you know the rest of the story, right?"

"The soldiers asked her what her name was?"

"Haha that's right," the Swan laughed breathily, lighting a cigarette and dragging deeply before continuing. "And they spared her because she had the name of the Führer."

The Swan got their bottle of G from their pocket and dropped a dose in their mouth, smiling broadly. "So many nights my mother climbed into bed with me in this room. She'd come in here when she didn't want sex with him, and she'd put me in between her and the father."

"*The* father?"

"I'm never going to say *my*."

One physical bruise you gave me was on the inside of my left arm. You created that bruise on purpose during an argument, but the context was that you were trying to explain how it was a common method the father used to use on you. The most pain in a not-so-visible spot. Why did I need to experience that?

The Swan laughed loudly then and swung open the window, letting the sound bellow out to the trees and the river beyond. "I got out this window so many times…"

Their voice drifted outside, dissipating into what I realised at that moment was the night. Somehow an entire day had passed us. Hours upon hours had passed as we ventured through the house.

"OK, so let's do it one last time — escape out that window and put this behind us," I said softly, trying to stop their fingers from twisting open the G bottle again. They pulled away from me roughly and smiled that jagged smile again, now barely visible in the dying light.

They bent down to pick up the hand-knitted blanket and flung it around their broad shoulders like a cape. They laughed again, and saluted me cheekily before rushing out the bedroom door to the last remaining room — their parents' bedroom.

"One last thing to do before our museum tour of hell is over, kids," they called over their shoulder with a Disneyland Tour Guide twang.

In the dark master bedroom, I could just make out the shape of an old mattress in the middle of the floor. It seemed to be heaped with a few old clothes or a blanket.

"Alrighty!" the Swan cried and emptied the entire G bottle over the heap on the mattress. Then they drew two more G bottles from their hip bag and poured those over the curtains and the carpet.

"Stand back, kids," they announced, still with their chirpy Disney accent, then promptly flicked match after match on the heap until it ignited. The flames grew and I jumped back in fright, out of the doorway. The Swan erupted into the happy laughter of a child admiring their birthday candles.

I took one more look then grabbed them by the waist with both hands and wrestled them out the bedroom door. We ran across the hall, the Swan still giggling, into their childhood bedroom, then barrel-rolled out the open window.

We took a breath or two there on what used to be the back lawn with its single apple tree, and which was now a jungle of junk and towering weeds and vines twisting high up into the old, bare branches.

The fire was spreading rapidly. It had already leapt to the other bedroom and had started to lick its way up the peeling paint of the exterior walls.

"*Kurwa*," was all the Swan said, before I wrapped an arm around their back and ushered them through the grass and down to the riverbank.

The moon was already trying to peek through the clouds as the smoke grew thick enough to obscure it anyway. The darkness surrounded us with its simplicity as we let our feet be caressed by the river. The body of water that had flowed endlessly through all of this, and had flowed before all of it and would continue flowing long after all of these cycles had ended. My own stories started flooding back to me; fiction and fact blurred beyond the point they could ever be separated again.

A fire threatened within that smell,
Burning as if with the potential that
Anything in its reach could catch alight.
The sound of their voices
The smell of their fire.

CHAPTER XVI

There's a lot I don't understand about the laws of thermodynamics but one thing I do understand is that energy never disappears, it only changes form.

After the fire, we flung ourselves in the river. Let all that fire in our bones turn to ash.

"We're alchemists!" I shouted to the Swan as we splashed around in the dark, rushing current, toes clinging to the slimy rocks beneath us as best we could.

"We transformed all that shit, like a century of it," I continued gleefully, my arms pulling me through the river's embrace, "into something new."

The Swan howled, loud and wolfish, into the fiery air. Then they disappeared underwater, picked me up by the waist, and flipped me backwards. I felt like a dolphin in tropical sunshine.

We both squealed with release and let the river take us downstream, letting us be whims of its will, turning us over and over like stones in a lapidary tumbler. We were a long way from becoming the polished stones of our dreams — I knew we would still have some rough edges after all this — but I truly believed in that moment that we had double-handedly burned all those generational cycles of abuse to the ground.

Of course, I was also aware, even then, that I had my own selfish (or survivalist) motivations for being part of this burning ritual. I wanted to stop the cycle before I became more entrapped in it.

"Hey, did you know that First Nations people from my country would use fire to sort of regenerate parts of the bush? The fire would help some of the seeds burst open and regenerate parts of the forest, you know... Did farmers here in Poland do that sort of thing too, or is it just an Australian thing?"

I asked this breathlessly as we kept swimming, weaving around boulders, dodging logs, and often colliding with them in the dark.

"Hm, I have no clue," the Swan panted back. "But that's why I love being a fire sign — I'm not afraid of it like most people are. Burn it all down and start over is basically the story of my life."

Remembering this natural cycle of destruction, creation, destruction helped me to wrap my drowning head around why, a short time later, when we were back in the swamp of Berlin, I found myself watching another fire burning.

I was woken by a video message from the Swan late in the midst of Zeus' night spell, after another period of violent fighting during which I'd escaped to a friend's place.

I'd been too fearful to return to our apartment to pick up my things for a week, so the Swan decided to take the books, clothes, shoes, and other things precious to me that I'd left behind, and burn them all in a bonfire on our rooftop.

They had sent me a gloating video of the spectacle: throwing things I cared deeply about one by one into the flames. I called and asked our neighbour to see if there was anything still salvageable. He called me back to say that there wasn't — it was all ashes.

I headed over there with the police but the flames had died out by the time we arrived.

This fire silenced me. It silenced me more profoundly than anything else that had been done or said up until that point. The violence of it, the fury behind it, the feeling that the Swan would have wished that they could have burned me in the fire: this killed something fluttering and trusting in me – a bright hopeful little creature that hasn't come back to life since.

"You burn me," said Sappho, before plunging into oblivion.

Shortly after the rooftop fire, the Swan's anger flared up again and they decided to plunge me into oblivion in the most twenty-first-century way: they cancelled me online. On several social media platforms, they posted that I was a cheater, a liar, a fraud, a user, and, most gutting of all, that I was an abuser. They claimed publicly that what I had apparently inflicted upon them in our five-year relationship was worse than what they grew up with at the hands of their parents. That I had caused them more pain than their mother or father ever had.

Oblivion.

Days and nights and months and years of laughter and kisses and pillow forts and walls of noise and basslines and backbends and sunshowers and both loud and silent agonies, and so many tears that I have a permanently burst capillary under my left eye, burned into oblivion. I didn't know, for too long, how to fully recognise, admit, and articulate abuse, and even if I had, I was far too fearful at the time to speak up, let alone to speak out publicly.

Writing has been my lifeblood since childhood, my only way to make sense of the world and to make sense of myself. By being publicly cancelled, my ability to write was temporarily taken away from me — I became an unreliable narrator. An untrustworthy source of "truth." An image was created of me as dangerous, a liar, manipulative, someone not to be trusted. And the pain it created lingered long after other forms of pain had faded. It lost me friends, colleagues, and respect. But, as my nearest and dearest reminded me, I only lost those who were never really "with" me in the first place. This was helpful. But the deeper fear lingered when I realised I had started to believe it all about myself. That I *was* the monster all along.

This is what I mean about the unreliable narrator. If I'm Leda in our story and they are the shape-shifting Swan, then that means embracing the reality of all the "Ledas" and all the "Swans" that have been interpreted, cast, reinterpreted, and spoken for, over literally millennia. There is Yeats' poetic form of Leda, the one I was first exposed to. In this version she is overtly raped by the Swan, and yet the poem also suggests some erotic tension. Then there are countless visual depictions: Michelangelo, Leonardo, Correggio, and the ancient sculptural versions found in Corfu, Rome, and Cyprus — where it is far more ambiguous as to the borders between consent, pain and pleasure. Most of the sculptural or fresco versions I've seen present a willing version of Leda who invites the Swan between her legs and is pleasured by the bird. She actively chooses the Swan's form over his original Zeus form.

And here is where I draw the parallel with my own encounters with the black Swan. The intoxication I have with the Leda story is probably in part because of its ambiguity. Whether Leda was abused or if the whole thing was consensual, or whether it started as non-consensual and then she derived pleasure from it or vice versa. My encounters with my own Swan were often like that for me — lines blurred between pain and pleasure, consent or non-consent — until I felt like I was losing my mind. Did I really want them to hold me down in the scalding bathwater and force me to come while surrounded by photographs of past threesomes? No. But did I come in the end anyway? Yes.

This is what I've learned about the dangers of seeing the world in binary oppositions, and instead accepting our own unreliability as narrators, even when it comes to such things as seemingly concrete as the physical sensations of pain and pleasure. There were so many moments where I could no longer distinguish one from the other — not even on a visceral level. I justified it for too long by thinking it was pushing me towards realising my own death-drive and overcoming my "symptoms" through pain. A daily, nightly, looping *sinthome*.

When I told the Swan they hadn't been loved like this before, I truly meant it in the way that I, as this person, in this body, loved them. That my version of loving them was safe, they could trust it, and that it was real and unprecedented in that precise, singular way I was offering it. That love can exist and persist, and co-exist with pain. The two are not mutually exclusive and, most confronting of all: that each can ignite the other.

Maybe, like in the little wooden house in the forest in Poland, the echoes of this energy still circle the walls of our old apartment like ghosts. Maybe it also lives trapped in my right shoulder, which is still in chronic pain, even as I write this. Maybe it also lives, energetically, in these words on these pages, which, once read by you or anyone else, can now never be burned into oblivion.

CHAPTER XVII

A SUICIDE SURVIVAL NOTE

When I think back to the Berlin "Dream House" of ours, I forget the polished parquet floors we would slide across to our favourite music, on all those late nights; I forget the sunny balcony with the long table laden with fresh flowers, where we sat for birthday dinners and afterwards we would have to pick out all the cigarette butts caught between the boards; I forget the bedroom with its vampiric lights and latex outfits strewn everywhere and the bed big enough to fit at least four; I forget about the mezzanine you built as our studio and all the music and films that we created from it; I forget about the open kitchen and how it would fluctuate from looking like the site of an archaeological dig, complete with dirt from the boots you wore out the night before, to a shiny, sparkling culinary kingdom that Julia Child would be proud to cook from; I only think of that bathroom, those black tiles, that immense mirror, and that bathtub, that haunted bathtub, that you tried to take your life in.

Does the half-life of yours still haunt the current occupant now when he takes a bath? Does he feel that part of your soul that must have seeped out a little bit as you slipped away as he soaps up his skin? I wonder if you feel the loss of that slippery part now, or if you feel better off without it?

I also wonder if there's any sense of my own echo there, haunting the place, the mark of psychic pain I've left? My mind still lives there, whether I'm awake or asleep — part of my mind refuses to leave. Does the current occupant still sense that part of me there, drifting in and out, a captive there, in spite of myself?

I'm almost certain that if I do haunt the place, I don't occupy the space of the apartment — not the living space, of the bedroom, the balcony, the mezzanine, the kitchen, or even the bathroom — the space I occupy is that liminal space that rises up from the underworld of pipes carrying water, waste, and all the unspeakable, unseeable things. That dark network of waterways beneath our homes that no one wants to think about. The places that sustain us all but that are too messy, too stinky, too ugly to be acceptable for the land of the living, the civilised, the seen.

You tried to take your life in that big, luxurious bathtub, and when they took you away to the clinic, I scrubbed out the remains of your attempt and your rich, vibrant blood was wasted down those pipes and into the realm of the "unspeakable." I barely spoke of this moment to anyone. What could I say? And what should I say? This was your moment of partial release from this world, not mine; it was not my story to tell. Except that it has become so, to the extent that it has evicted most of the more "speakable" tenants from my mind, from our "Dream House," and left me with just that underground cavern.

It was the first and only apartment I lived in that had heated flooring, and that night, after they took you away to the clinic and I'd cleaned away all your deep red stains, I remember being so grateful for that floor heating as I lay limp and inert on the tiles. The trouble with memory, though, is that the day of your attempt was a sticky summer's day, so there's no chance that the floor heating would have been switched on. But that's how I remember it — the coldness of your absence contrasted by the warmth of that black-tiled bathroom floor against my clammy skin.

We already had our two puppies at that point, one pure black, and one pure white, which matched our slick loft perfectly. And after they took you away and I was lying on what I remember to be the heated tiles, the puppies came and nestled into me as if knowing that their nestling was far more useful than any words could be at that point.

"Just us now, kids," I think I said to them before falling deep asleep on those tiles. And that statement came with some relief. I knew the clinic could take better care of you than I could ever hope to. This all felt like deep failure, but at least that failure came with survival.

But I didn't survive this whole; there were parts of me that didn't make it. Those parts now only exist in those non-spaces beneath that bathroom, squirming along the twisted filthy veins of the city. Some days I feel like most of me is still lurking down there, stilted, stagnated, and coated with murk, so deep that I can't surface again. Some days it feels easier not to surface again because down there feels like home — I'm caved, hidden, camouflaged in the filth — no one and nothing down there will see me as a dark, damaged thing, because we are all in the same state. There's no need to coat my skin in sparkles and smiles and pretend I'm whole and capable of normality. Down there, the more damaged you are, the more you fit in, and the more you feel safe.

Days like that, I wallow in the place and fail to see the point of resurfacing, of getting out of bed and being "productive" and "upstanding" and "useful." On those days, there is so much effort in trying to be good, trying to "make something" of myself. Why try when I can stay warm down there in the sludge and sleep and dream dreams that are more fulfilling than what I wake up to?

When I read Carmen Maria Machado's In the Dream House on the recommendation of a friend who knew our story, I realised that staying subterranean could be a selfish act. That if I didn't tell this story, bring it up from the depths, like Machado did, how could I possibly hope to help the next one who ends up on the bathroom floor?

Staying in the muck, wasted in those twisted pipes, would never have brought anything helpful to anyone else. Even if on most days I still didn't see a point, for myself, in getting unstuck from those pipes, writing all this down has let me see what life I could bring to others.

PART FOUR

THE LADY OF SHALOTT

"I am half sick of shadows."
— Alfred Lord Tennyson, "The Lady of Shalott"

CHAPTER XVIII

Hope, like any muscle, takes practice to use again. The longer it lies dormant, the longer it takes to wake back up again and flex into life.

Buoyed by hope, they came to Lisbon as a patchwork rainbow family: Alex, a Berliner in advertising; Sophie, working on her ongoing horror series; and their two dogs, Virginia Woof and Hildegaard von Barken, from previous relationships.

It was a short hiatus in the middle of two hard lockdowns in the COVID-19 pandemic and they made the most of the hiatus to relocate temporarily from Berlin to Lisbon and work there remotely. They were matched in desires, values, aesthetics, and in how they wanted daily life to be. On the one hand, they lived for the promise of endless youth and hedonism that child-free, urban life offered up on its tempting platter; on the other hand they both longed for domestic stability and being able to do "normal" things together like taking the dogs to the forest, getting out on the open road with the campervan, and diving into as many seas as possible.

But after a few years together, the "tempting platter" became all-encompassing. Even being in love didn't make them immune to letting the long nights of cocaine- and alcohol-fuelled escapism in Berlin take over; which soon transformed into the almost-every-weekend parties, which then became every weekend, and soon enough, it became a few-times-a-week indulgence. They weren't alone in their spirals, of course: the constant lockdowns in Berlin sparked the explosion of coke taxis in the city, with drugs just a quick text and a home-delivery away at almost any time of day or night, seven days a week.

***

They decided, in a "come to Jesus" moment after a particularly heavy week, that relocating to Lisbon for a few months, where they knew no one, and had none of the Berlin triggers, especially while they could still work remotely, would be just the break they needed from it all. A chance to prove to themselves, and their anxious pups, that they could reverse out of those spirals of chemical courage and find that sparkle in a new city.

But as they had driven over the Tagus River into Lisbon, the sensation of beginning a new chapter was muddied for Sophie by the ancient urge she had to jump from the bridge. *Disappear here*, were the words that kept revolving in her mind, bubbling up from the troubling depths of the Tagus itself. The river seemed to be telling her that it was going to take more than a change of city to create a change of heart.

The choice of city was partially accidental. Sophie was booked to write and direct the next instalment of her horror series, and her research had taken her on many twists and turns to find the ultimate figure of feminine fury for the protagonist to summon from the dead. She eventually landed on the Lady of Shalott, the tragic, scorned-by-Lancelot, "little lily" of Arthurian legend. Digging deeper, she'd found the thirteenth-century Italian novella *Donna di Scalotta*, and traced stories upon stories from there, each one piled atop the others in layers of time. She pictured each layer being of a disparate density and colour, like the dermis of the earth, exposing the deep centuries they had weathered. With the lockdown continuing and nothing open or happening to distract her, Sophie continued digging, beyond the shale and further down through the dark, moist, hidden soils.

The Arthurian Lady of Shalott was Elaine of Astolat, with Astolat being widely accepted as a fantastical kingdom from the legendary Arthurian times, rather than a real-world geographical location. But after looking into the Italian version, and following rabbit hole after rabbit hole of PhD papers, scattered articles from Euhemeristic scholars that went beyond classical literature and into folklore of central Europe, with some stories being based on ancient historical events and real people, Sophie finally unearthed a much earlier story. It dated back to around the third century BC, from the tribe of the Astures, Hispano-Celtic inhabitants of the Iberian Peninsula, modern-day Spain and Portugal. The tribe was thought to be named after the River Astura, before the Roman conquest. The Astures became a united tribal federation known for their matrilineal and possibly even matriarchal customs. Rather than a helpless, imprisoned virgin trapped in a tower by the river (who healed Lancelot after a joust and fell hopelessly in love with him before killing herself out of unrequited love in the Anglicised tale), this version of the folklore centred on a woman who had fought battles herself, maybe alongside the warrior who became Lancelot in the later versions. This version of the story told that the warrior-woman escaped a great battle and hid out in a tower by the River Astura to nurse her wounds, not to nurse the wounds of Lancelot like in the Arthurian legend. Her time spent trapped away from the world, receiving news only by way of hearsay and whispers, like the shadows and mirrors from the Lady of Shalott story, was a self-imposed exile in this version, as her body strengthened back to health. But when she emerged from her tower, her battle scars healed, she discovered that her true love had already found another.

The last battle she fought was at the hillfort called Lancet, and it was this battle that marked the final subduing of her people by the Romans. Sophie made a few additional leaps, theorising that "Lancet" was the origin of the name Lancelot, which she thought indicated that perhaps the original story was more about the warrior-woman's love for her Astures' culture and land, and her attempts to hold on dearly to what was left of that — even being prepared to die for it — rather than just being about giving her heart to one particular man.

The Astures managed to keep the Romans busy until the first century AD, never fully giving up their religion and their way of life. Proving themselves to be great fighters, they were eventually enlisted by the Romans to assist the Roman Emperor Claudius' incursion into Great Britain from the year 43 AD until 60 AD. Perhaps, Sophie wondered, this was how the Shalott legend initially spread into Britain and became part of the fabric of their national storytelling — this story and other folklore swept into British legend via its invaders and their hired army? This line of thinking helped concretise for Sophie this Euhemeristic way of understanding mythology — that it could all be based in history.

The whole thing ignited something in Sophie. She wanted to find out if there were any direct descendants of the ancient Astures, which led her, after countless Google searches, to the listing of a crumbling old colonial-era mansion now divided into apartments and run by an ageing Portuguese actress who claimed in the rental listing to be a descendent of the tribe, living in the family mansion called "Astur," in Alfama, the oldest district of Lisbon.

There was very little online that Sophie could find about the Astur mansion itself. There was a scant Wikipedia entry, which gave a detailed account of the woman's family tree and her ancient Iberian ancestors, but the entry seemed predominantly to serve the purpose of proving the family bloodline and their "rightful" claim to the prime piece of Lisbon land, rather than providing the reader with any helpful information. Sophie had wanted *stories*, something to justify it as the blood-drenched setting of her new film, with the tragic, watery female warrior as her heroine. She wanted to feel the mansion's history seeping in through her skin and deep into her bones before she even arrived.

"I basically want it to be haunted," she confessed to Alex as they were navigating the van through the intricate cobblestoned alleyways of Alfama, trying to find the place. The confession only boiled Alex's already simmering blood as she reversed the campervan out of yet another dead end.

Alex blasted the horn at a teenager strolling across the road carrying a heavy school bag, face buried in his phone.

"Really, Sophie?" Alex muttered with her cigarette gripped between her lips. "Do you really want our fresh start in Lisbon to be just us scared out of our faces?"

Sophie concealed a giggle at Alex's Denglish, then immediately felt guilty for it. They almost always spoke English together, even though Alex was German. Alex finally manoeuvred the van out of the alleyway and navigated past a corner crowded with crack dealers.

"Feels just like home," Alex joked.

"Talk about a fresh start," Sophie laughed back and distracted herself and her dog in her lap by looking at the decent-looking dog park they were passing now.

"Anyway," Sophie continued with a sigh, already feeling the weight of her naivety, "even though I couldn't get much info on the house, the family that owns it is one of the oldest in Portugal. The Wikipedia article talks about how the ancestors eventually made their way south down here, from where the tribe was originally from, to where Lisbon now stands. Apparently they travelled mostly by river, trying to stay clear of the Roman armies."

Alex was swearing in German under her breath at the car in front, snailing along and coming to a full stop for every ambling cat. Sophie continued on, knowing she was mostly just talking to herself now.

"I'm sure that if a family has thrived for this long and even had a mansion, they definitely were up to their necks in colonial shit in their time..."

After a few more panicked minutes of wrangling the van, they finally pulled up to the place. Sophie and her little dog peered up out the passenger window. The Astur was an imposing sight.

Protected on three sides by the fortified stone wall behind it, overhanging with wild morning glory and passionfruit vines, the mansion teetered four storeys tall and was painted entirely in blush pink: a muted, dusty shade much-loved by the old aristocrats in Lisbon, as Sophie would soon learn. The paint was badly peeling and faded by the sun, and raw stone was left exposed around the window frames, the French doors, and the pillars on the balconies, but like an ageing Hollywood legend in the spotlight, these textures only added to its glamour. All the shutters were down, completely blocking out the golden-hour sun peaking through the magenta bougainvillea branches framing the mansion to its left. It was positioned at the very end of a tiny cul-de-sac, giving it an air of secrecy, as if it would only allow a few choice eyes to glimpse it, not like the other "grand dame" mansions of Alfama, devoured by the eyes of the endless hordes of tourists plying the district's cobbled thoroughfares.

As Sophie stepped from the van to share the shadowy courtyard with the mansion, however, it took on a completely different mood. Feeling the ground it stood on, without the cocoon of the van to separate them, Sophie felt a shudder rush through her. There was a heaviness and dankness that rose up from the ground through her shoes to her feet, rising up through her legs and her entire body to her head, until it felt as if she had put on dark sunglasses — the world around her was suddenly dimmed. She pulled Virginia in closer to her chest, imagining them looking as wide-eyed as Dorothy and Toto. But when she looked over to Alex, beaming up at the place, and seeing Alex's dog leaping out with a happy bark from the van, Sophie tried on a smile and ran her fingers through her hair, as if that would detangle her dark thoughts.

As she did so, her right hand caught on something in the strands — a slimy river reed all twisted up in there. She glanced furtively over at Alex but she hadn't seen it. Sophie inhaled sharply and tossed the reed to the ground with a flick of her hand.

***

Dragging suitcases, doggy beds, boxes of books, backpacks, and shopping bags full of enough supplies for weeks, they made enough clatter for their elderly neighbours on all the other floors of the building to risk poking their masked faces out from their doors as they heaved past on the stairs. On the first round, the dogs softened their invasion – the dogs' cute factor got them past the neighbours' judging eyes. But after the third or fourth sweat up the stairs, all novelty had worn off and they instead got snappy questions in Portuguese, shrugs, and eventually those slow, incredulous shakes of the head.

The face-obscuring masks made it more difficult for Alex and Sophie to remember their neighbours in much detail, but by the time they had finished all the trips up and down the stairs, and laid themselves out on the old parquet floor of the parlour, they had already resolved to bake something or buy some little succulents as neighbourly gifts to placate them. A sudden death of the third-floor resident, presumably due to COVID (but they hadn't ventured to ask), had meant that there was a last-minute vacancy in the building, which was otherwise inhabited by all the same residents since the mansion had been divided into apartments in the 1970s. Alex and Sophie, although in their early forties, were the youngest in the building by at least thirty years.

On the ground floor was the most elderly resident, a single man whom Alex and Sophie named "Tea Cosy" because of his hair. In the rush of the move, they both mistook his headwear as an off-white woolly tea cosy, but later realised it was an unsavoury nest of white dreadlocks. Passing his doorway, there was a whiff of a sweaty, lambswool lanolin concoction, which presumably came from the dreads.

On the first floor was a tiny, crouched couple they called the Hobbits for obvious reasons, who seemed to use the same shade of orange hair dye. Each time they were seen peering out from their doorway or when they perched out on their balcony, they were clutching onto each other's hands like the end was permanently nigh.

The floor above them, the top floor, was home to the owner, whom Alex and Sophie had not yet caught sight of. All they had seen to identify her so far was her full name carved in large, proud letters on her door, with an intricate gold star on either side: Senhora Navia das Astúrias. The only sign of life was the lavish silk robes they had seen fluttering on her balcony as they came and went from the house: peaches and cream in the morning, royal blue at midday, burgundy at dusk, then gold at night.

It was a last-minute subletting, coming about by the kismet of googling, with all the paperwork and agreements done via email through a local estate agent while they were still in Berlin. They had no direct contact with the owner and Sophie was bursting at the seams with curiosity.

In those first few days wandering the city with their medical masks clamped to their faces, Sophie and Alex learned that the Astur was situated in one of the most historic, crumbling streets in the whole city of Lisbon. With the castle at the top of the hill, and the maze of cobblestoned alleys twisting down to the harbour below, crowded both with aristocrats' pastel-coloured mansions that were long past their colonial "glory days," alongside miniscule bakers' and fishermen's cottages converted into little restaurants with their tables and garlic smells sprawling out into the laneways, they were soon convinced that they had stumbled into another time.

As for the mysterious history of their building, when more days passed and they still hadn't crossed paths with the Senhora, Sophie was on the verge of marching up the stairs to her apartment to introduce herself and invite herself in for a tea, emboldened by the presence of earthy Alex and their two protective dogs, when she noticed something had been slipped under the door. It was a handwritten invitation:

Dear Newcomers,
4:30pm today for afternoon tea, followed by a 6pm aperitivo?
Até breve,
Senhora das Astúrias

Sophie audibly gasped – loud enough for Alex to hear her while she was sitting on the toilet.

"What happened, babe?" she called.

"It's the Senhora!" Sophie squealed. "She wants to invite us over today, like soon!"

The toilet flushed.

"Today?" Alex groaned. "But I wanted to nap."

Sophie rushed and grabbed Alex by both hands as she got out of the bathroom.

"How can you nap at a time like this?!"

Sophie grabbed her nicest pen and responded in turn with her own handwritten reply, which she promptly slipped under the upstairs door:

Myself and my partner Alex, new residents of Apartment 3, are delighted to accept your invitation. We will come with a bottle of red wine to share that we picked up on our journey here. PS. We tested ourselves this morning and neither of us are sick with COVID but we can still wear masks if that's more comfortable for you.

She always wrote too much. Birthday cards, leaving cards, always waffling on and taking up all available space on any given piece of paper.

At precisely 4:30pm, Sophie rang Senhora das Astúrias' bell, which sounded like the foghorn of a vast ship.

Alex speculated in a loud whisper that maybe this militaristic touch meant her late husband was in the navy? "Some kind of high-ranking official, maybe, judging by his widow's airs and graces," Alex whispered.

"How do we even know she was married?" Sophie whispered back.

"Just the times, you know? Everyone was married back then—"

They stopped their whispering and straightened up hurriedly as the door swung open with a flourish of Senhora das Astúrias' champagne glass, which didn't spill a drop.

Sophie felt as if she were standing before a Pre-Raphaelite painting come to life.

The Senhora had opted for a layered silk ensemble: a dusty pink chemise and sage green knee-length pantaloon outfit with cream-stockinged legs, tiny, delicate high heels, and a transparent cream robe to add an airiness to her flourishes. She wasn't wearing a mask, which indicated that she either accepted that they weren't sick or was living in an alternate reality in which she had moved beyond caring about the pandemic.

She glided towards them, Alex first, then Sophie, and stood on tiptoe to kiss them on both cheeks, with the familiarity of an aunt who knew them long ago as little children and was now wide-eyed at the shock of seeing them all grown up before her. She smelled of a musk and magnolia perfume, which brought back memories for Sophie of a house with a sprawling garden that she was sure she had never actually visited.

"My, my," she breathed, with a voice smoother than her well-sunned décolletage. "Look at you!"

She said this last part pointedly at Sophie, who nodded smilingly along, as if she knew exactly why the Senhora had said that.

"Thank you for the invitation, Senhora. Das Astúrias," Alex said with unusual politeness.

"Senhora," she corrected, and downed whatever was in her champagne glass.

"Senor—" Alex attempted to right the mistake.

"Senorrra," she said again, rolling her r's with a clenched smile. "By the gods, I hate the way foreigners use my language in their mouths."

Alex blushed slightly and bent down to untie her bootlaces. It took a lot to embarrass her, so I shrugged sympathetically as Senhora grabbed our bottle of wine limply between her thumb and forefinger and spun to lead us inside with another flourish of her gown.

As her eyes adjusted to the darkness, Sophie noticed that on Senhora's gown were tiny, intricate skeletons, embroidered presumably by hand, in a haphazard pattern all over the fragile fabric. She looked back to Alex to see if she had noticed, but after she had bent down to untie her boots she'd become distracted by the leaves of a very exotic-looking plant that looked as though it definitely did not belong in Europe. Sophie slipped off her black platform sandals and focused on following Senhora through her velvet curtain-lined hallway and out into the parlour. She tried to shrug off the imagery that the little skeletons had set off in her imagination.

As they entered the parlour, lit by the dying embers of the day and a few haphazardly melted candles, they let their eyes wander from the French doors piled with cloth-bound books, indicating that Senhora never set foot on her balcony, to the upright piano with its lid shut and more books stacked upon it, making playing impossible, to the lovely green velvet chaise longue with plants crowded on it, making lounging impossible, and to the many framed pictures lining the walls covered by old white sheets so that they couldn't be looked upon. The only "functional" feature of the parlour was the low, dark wooden table with the teapot and cups laid out, three green velvet chairs grouped around it, and a large golden-framed mirror, which was now reflecting the bloody glow of the sunset from the French doors.

Senhora ushered them over to the three upright chairs, awkwardly too tall for the coffee table, and promptly began pouring tea. The tea was barely warm and smelled of a sickly-sweet honey or nectar. Sophie realised, as Senhora poured, that there were little flecks of strange petals pouring into their cups. Then she noticed a tarnished metal vase of long-dead curved stems and pink and green cylindrical flowers on top of the piano and realised Senhora must have run out of tea and simply crushed up a bunch of old flowers to steep in place of it.

"Good for the forgetting, for forgetfulness," Senhora nodded encouragingly as Sophie raised the cup uncertainly to her lips. This close, the tea still had its honey nectar aroma, but underneath that was a decaying, myrrh-type of smokiness. She sipped slowly, then looked over to Alex who was sipping hers heartily while flicking through an old magazine that had been left open on the coffee table. It looked to be from the '60s and there was a series of black-and-white studio portraits of a woman in a long dress, lying in a little wooden boat.

"Is this you?" gushed Alex, poring over the pictures. Senhora's face lit up.

"Oh yes," she beamed, and played with some of the curls of bleached hair around her face. "My favourite role."

Sophie leaned in a little closer to the pictures and Senhora's face swam into recognition, along with the narrative being played out in the studio set-up.

"But that's the Lady of Shalott," Sophie blurted out, "from the poem... I mean, you're playing the Lady of Shalott!"

A little shiver came over Sophie. She had thought that the connection with the "real" Lady of Shalott in Lisbon was all about the Astur mansion. She hadn't known or clearly done enough research into whether the "lady of the manor" also had any personal connection of her own to the story.

"We know each other, we have met before," Senhora said flatly — a statement rather than a question. Her glittering grey eyes fixed on Sophie as the last of the sunlight left the parlour. "But you might not have realised that one version of the insipid King Arthur character was derived from the life of a Portuguese aristocratic lady, shut up in a tower overlooking the river during one of the plagues. A lot of the modern scholars keep arguing over a theory that the 'real' Lady of Shalott was holed up in a tower in Tuscany, but our family has always known that the Tuscan version of the story was just a sort of spin-off or an homage to the lady who came from a grand city directly on the Tagus River in one of the westernmost points of Europe. Namely, right here."

Sophie had already grabbed her notebook from her bag and was writing all this down.

Without a pause, the Senhora declared, "Now that you've finished your Nepenthe, it must be high time for our aperitivo, não?"

She rose, knees creaking slightly, and disappeared into the kitchen with her musky magnolia scent trailing behind her.

"That's *quite* the coincidence, don't you think?" Sophie whispered to Alex as they flicked through more of the magazine spread. "I mean..."

Alex smiled wryly. "I thought you said coincidences are just time looping back on itself?"

"Rightly said!" Senhora announced, as she arrived back with three little crystal glasses on a silver tray. The glasses contained a dual-layered liquid, cherry red below and dusk orange on top, with a slice of marinated strawberry on the edge of the glass. "I call it the Astolat, after—"

"—Elaine of Asolat?" Sophie ventured.

"Quite right, the lovesick Lady Elaine of Asolat, the sickly-sweet Arthurian Lady of Shalott," Senhora continued, setting the tray down. "We drink the weak, sweet stuff before the real stuff, eh girls?"

"But what I read, especially from these Euhemeristic researchers—" Sophie began, until Senhora put a stained finger to her lips to quiet her.

"Not now, darling," she purred as she raised her glass, "there will be plenty of time for explanations. Right now, however, is the time for toasting!"

They all raised their glasses to the centre to toast each other, Alex and Sophie darting glances between each other, to the glasses, then to Senhora herself.

"Eye contact, girls!" she scolded merrily. "To the newcomers — my new favourite inhabitants of my Court Astur."

She downed her drink in one and looked around heartily to both of them, lips glinting in the candlelight.

"May we survive the pandemic," Alex joked and gulped hers down too.

Sophie was still too struck, so she drank hers down without a toast — just a forced smile back at Senhora, giddy on the edge of her green velvet couch. The liquid was cooling and burning at the same time, like when your tongue gets scalded by an ice cube straight from the freezer. It tasted of sun-drenched mandarins and chilli-soaked cherries, and a sickening sweet strawberry syrup raging with pink peppercorns.

It was a sweet, sick fire for the mouth.

CHAPTER XIX

Two nights after visiting Navia (or Senhora as she insisted on being addressed) upstairs, Alex and Sophie were celebrating having finally unpacked everything with a couple of bottles of red wine, sitting on the Juliet balcony by candlelight. A gust of wind came up from the harbour and blew all their candles out at once, leaving a birthday-cake haze lingering.

As they sat there in the early Lisbon night, Sophie began to accept that maybe the stable pleasantness she was feeling here could be a lasting feeling. The simple pleasure of the harbour breeze, two happy dogs curled up, her love beside her, and a balcony that was enjoyable for more than two months of the year... She let the feeling wash over her while she chatted to Alex a little drunkenly about heading up to Sintra on the weekend — the fabled nearby town of impossibly romantic blossom-coloured mansions and castles, with a history of the occult and Freemasonry.

In between reading aloud anecdotal snippets of the history of various Sintran buildings and their culty former occupants gleaned from excited online searches, they heard a thin, reedy warble, coming in and out of earshot.

At first, they peered down to the street below, thinking it might have been a drunk woman singing on her way home, but the street was empty except for a few masked tourists and cats. Sophie turned up the volume on the music playing from her laptop, thinking it might be the faint strains of a vocal track, but it wasn't in the music.

The more they tuned in to the high-pitched voice, the harder it was to distinguish. They had both hushed completely now and were squinting into the dark, as if seeing in the dark would help them to listen.

As they did so, the words slowly swam into focus.

"Wait, I recognise those words..." Sophie whispered.

"Shhh," hissed Alex.

Sophie closed her eyes against the Lisbon night, until she couldn't be sure if she was hearing the slow distant rush of traffic or the secrets of the river rushing towards them on the wind. As she tuned in, she caught a few of the words, spiralling to her ears on the breeze:

"On either side the river lie..."

Just as soon as she could make the words out, they disappeared from earshot. The voice was not strong or sweet, rather it was thin, wavering, and had a whispery undertone of malice to it. It made her shiver.

"Isn't that a line from...?" Alex started, taking another gulp of red wine.

"Yes," Sophie stated bluntly, also taking a large mouthful of wine. She looked up at the balcony ceiling, as if it would suddenly become transparent and she could see Navia up there, ballroom-dancing around in her tattered silk negligee. "She's taunting us."

Her voice warbled down to them again, this time louder, clearer, almost seductive:

"Willows whiten, aspens shiver.
The sunbeam showers break and quiver
In the stream that runneth ever
By the island in the river
Flowing down to Camelot..."

Her voice trailed off into the night, but they could still hear her little high heels tap-tapping on her parquet, along with a third tap that sounded like a wooden cane. It sounded like she was twirling all over the floor, but still keeping up the rhythm of the poetry. Despite herself, Sophie finished off the next lines for her, keeping time:

> "Four grey walls, and four grey towers
> Overlook a space of flowers,
> And the silent isle imbowers
> The Lady of Shalott."

Navia stopped her tip-tapping, as if she could hear Sophie's voice. She let out a high, piercing little laugh before something in their apartment shattered. Alex and Sophie stood up, startled, and the dogs started barking like crazy. Alex raced into the sitting room to check what had been broken.

She ran back onto the balcony, out of breath.

"The mirror in the hallway is broken," she panted. "A big jagged slice right down the middle. Maybe there was, like, a mini earthquake or something?"

They heard Navia singing in her warbling little voice again from upstairs.

> "Out flew the web and floated wide –
> The mirror crack'd from side to side..."

Then they heard the abrupt slam of her balcony doors. She turned all her lights off at once and fell silent.

"'The curse has come upon me,' cried the Lady of Shalott," Sophie whispered into the shadowed air.

***

Later that night, they were woken by the sound of slow, steady footsteps along the parquet hallway to their bedroom door.

Step, *step*, step *step*, step *step*, step, *step*.

Step, *step*, step *step*, step *step*, step, *step*.

The same rhythm, the same cadence, over and over.

Step, *step*, step *step*, step *step*, step, *step*.

The footsteps would stop when they got to the door, then begin walking all over again from the furthest point of the hallway.

Six, seven, eight times, step, *step*, step *step*, step *step*, step, *step*.

Alex and Sophie gripped each other, sitting bolt upright in bed. Somehow the dogs could not hear or feel a thing and were sleeping soundly at their feet.

Step, *step*, step *step*, step *step*, step, *step*.

Sophie and Alex gripped each other so hard their nails were embedded in each other's arms.

The footsteps approached once again, only this time, they stopped at the door and the old brass door handle started slowly twisting. It creaked slowly, torturously. They stopped breathing and just waited, gripping each other in terror.

There was a slow metallic rattle as if a key was being tried in the lock, although neither of them had been given a key to the bedroom.

Alex bent down slowly to the floor to grab one of her boots, ready to hurl it at whoever came through the door.

Then the rattling stopped with a slow deep *click*, and the footsteps receded again, in their eightfold rhythm.

Step, *step*, step *step*, step *step*, step, *step*.

After what felt like an eternity, Alex and Sophie finally eased their grip on each other and exhaled. The dogs were still sleeping as if nothing had happened.

They peered at each other in the dark, suddenly feeling foolish. Suddenly feeling as if it could all be explained away easily. But neither could find the words.

Silently, they lay back down and fitfully tried to get back to sleep.

When they woke up the next morning, the fog from the harbour was still bleaching the light and casting the room pale and sickly. Alex got out of bed, hoping to let the dogs go out to pee. She tried the door handle, rattling it hard, then got Sophie to try. No luck. Both of them tried opening it in every way possible, for a good five minutes, but neither of them could manage to budge the door open. It was as if they had been locked in from the outside.

After several minutes of panic-stricken yelping from the dogs, Sophie finally found a little catch on the old-fashioned lock that, when shifted over, gradually unlocked the door from the inside. They breathed a sigh of bashful relief and all four bounded out, free at last.

"One of us must have accidentally clicked the catch on the lock last night?" Sophie suggested in the hallway, as they got the dogs ready to go downstairs and outside. Alex looked up from fixing Hildegaard's collar with an exhausted look in her eye.

"Yeah, probably," was all she said.

***

The outside world seemed impossibly bright and loud once the ground floor door of the apartment building had clicked shut behind them. Sophie tried to retrace her steps in her mind, where she had been and what she had done for the last few days and nights, and found herself drawing a blank. Specifically, she couldn't remember the last time that she had been outside the building in daylight. And yet, despite the lack of exposure to the outside world, she felt as if she had already lived an age since they had moved into the building.

Like many of the ancient neighbourhoods within Alfama, the cul-de-sac they had moved to and its surrounding streets had become transformed by the recent influx of digital nomads, work-from-home expats, academics on sabbatical, self-professed tech/finance/media entrepreneurs, and trust fund artists. Cafes that were allowed to open during lockdown had become co-working spaces, filled with mask-wearing English speakers glued to their laptops. Music venues had become COVID-testing centres, and pharmacies had become the only places with excited queues around the block. Although Sophie was one of the "digital nomads" transforming the city, or maybe because of that fact, she was somehow able to look beyond the shiny new surfaces and still smell the layers of dust the city's past had laid over centuries.

While Alex was busying herself with walking the dogs, getting tangled in their leads and picking up after them, Sophie wafted along, seeing powdered ladies of the 1920s trotting into a shopfront, which had been preserved from their time, but was now, in reality, a closed-down boutique vintage record store. She saw bloodied gangsters of the '30s, muscling their way down the streets, one with a fighting cock flapping under his arm, screeching at each other about debts someone owed, but they were more likely construction workers on the new apartment building rising up on the corner. Alex made a sharp turn into a cosy-looking cafe, dogs in tow, and when they scratched their masks on and ordered, Sophie felt surrounded by 1800s high society, rustling newspapers, smoking cigars, and sipping tea. She shook her head out of this vision, though, as they sat down and started sipping their cappuccinos. She was in the wrong neighbourhood for this kind of scene so whatever her imagination had invented was not historically accurate for the area. These four walls, if they had indeed housed a cafe all this time, was more likely to be filled with fishermen and market stall owners and maybe the odd Fado singer stumbling sleepless from a late show to try to revive themselves with caffeine.

Looking around the empty cafe, Sophie began to wonder how it happened that the grand old mansion they were occupying, with its old money family, had planted itself within such a working-class neighbourhood all that time ago. Wouldn't this "aristocratic" family have considered it risky or even beneath their station to call this address home? There were one or two other stately homes dotted here and there on the twisted streets, but they seemed to be much more recent additions to the area. Navia's home looked to be the only early property built there from a very wealthy family.

"What do you think, Alex?" Sophie asked as they sipped their coffee and the dogs settled at their feet. "Why is Navia's pride-and-joy mansion right here in the middle of an old fishermen's district? Why would her ancestors have decided on this neighbourhood out of all of Lisbon?"

Alex looked up sharply from her phone. "Oh, babe, I've got a meeting in ten minutes — can we make this quick and get back?"

Sophie continued on, sipping slowly and looking around the cafe, with all its old-world trappings: copper kettles hanging from the ceiling, embroidered aprons displayed behind the till, vintage framed photos from the neighbourhood.... "Maybe they were the first ones here and the fishermen's cottages and everything were all built later?"

As Alex stood to leave, eyes still on her phone as she typed an email, the grey-bearded cafe owner at the till handed Sophie a tourist map.

"I also do city walking tours on the side," he winked. "Technically, we're not allowed during COVID, but if it's just you, and you wear a mask, I can tell you all about Alfama."

Sophie took the map and smiled, then gathered Virginia in her arms.

"Are dogs allowed too?" she laughed.

He looked as though he hadn't been in the cafe business very long. His perfectly on-trend beard and rolled up sleeves revealing an expensive penchant for tattoos belied a recent career change.

"Miguel," he said extending a hand with a hefty ring on every finger. "Barista, tour guide, energy healer..."

He noticed Sophie flinch at the last part and tried to ease her scepticism with a laugh and another wink. "Oh, not that kind of energy healer, like tantric energy blah blah," he laughed. "I'm more of an energy healer of places... I'm more in tune with lay lines than auras, let me put it that way."

As Sophie was about to ask him more, she looked up to see Alex fuming at the cafe door, showing her the time on her phone: 9:45am.

"My meeting, babe!"

"OK, thank you, Miguel," Sophie said, rushing with the dog out the door. "I could come back at closing time tonight if you have time for a tour then?"

Deep in script research mode and unable to resist the promise of someone openly calling themselves "in tune with lay lines," Sophie found herself back at the cafe promptly at 6pm. She was dutifully wearing her mask, had a little warm coat on the dog, and had her notebook and pencil in hand.

Miguel looked up and without any hint of surprise on his face to see her, smiled welcomingly. He finished up cleaning the coffee machine, steam wafting up into the quiet, darkened air of the cafe, and took the black apron off from around his waist. He smoothed a few coffee grains from his hands onto his black jeans and extended his hand again to Sophie. This struck her as a little much, another formal handshake, but then the length of the handshake got her to thinking that maybe he wasn't entirely truthful about not being in tune with human energy — he seemed very much to be reading hers as he clasped her hand in his.

"You strike me as a big believer in coincidence, no?" Miguel said as he rolled a cigarette and examined her face with his eyes.

"What makes you think so?"

"Most people wouldn't just spontaneously take a tour with a cafe owner just as they settle into a new city."

"How did you know I'm settling into a new city?" Sophie started stroking Virginia's head a little too vigorously.

"Most of us locals know when there's a big change in the air around these streets. Especially during lockdown when there's nothing to do. And that change was one neighbour dying and you two moving in to take her place."

"Ah, I see."

"It's been a very long time since Senhora allowed anyone new into her little empire there. So you must be something special to her. Either way."

"Either way?"

"Well, I'm sure you've noticed already that she is a creature of extremes," he chuckled as he closed up the cash register. "Still want to go on our little tour?"

The streets of Alfama were already dark and near-empty as Miguel locked up the cafe and they started heading south. Sophie struggled to keep up with Miguel's lumbering strides along the streets he knew so well. Eventually she resorted to scooping up Virginia in her arms and carrying her as she ran along after him, down alleyway after twisted alleyway.

"I thought there'd be time for questions... or something...?" Sophie panted as they hurried down a centuries-old stone staircase with Moorish towers darkening both sides.

"We have to get down to the river first," Miguel panted back over his shoulder. "Then I can answer whatever you want."

Sophie let Virginia down as they left Alfama and reached an expanse of grass. They ran to catch up with Miguel, just as he disappeared down a little set of stairs that led directly to the endless dark expanse of river beyond. The vastness of the Tagus made it appear like an ocean —

As Sophie puffed down the stairs to Miguel on the sandy edge of the water, she caught sight of him drawing an old glass bottle out of his blazer pocket. He walked to the edge of the water, bent down with the bottle outstretched, and allowed the river water to splash into the bottle and fill it up. Once it was done, he stood and twisted the metal cap on the bottle, head raised to the moon rising in the sky.

He turned on his heel in the sand and strode over to Sophie. He handed her the bottle of river water with a smile and beckoned her up the stairs and back in the direction of Alfama.

Sophie clutched the bottle wordlessly and followed, chastising herself for trusting in this so-called tour guide.

She stayed silent as they walked back the way they had come, up the stairs and through the maze of empty alleyways. Then Miguel took an unexpected turn down an even tinier street, lined with laundry hanging from windows and populated only by a skittish black cat. At the street's end, a sharp corner opened up into a hidden courtyard, shadowed by fig trees and the welcoming sight of the doorway to a little bar — completely painted in black and lit with a neon red sign: "cocktails."

Giving up on the idea of the tour but badly needing a strong drink, Sophie gladly followed Miguel through the bar's soundproofing curtain, Virginia in one hand and the murky water bottle in the other.

She was met with the sight of a cavernous round space, low-ceilinged and lit only by the three curved floor lamps stationed at the lounges lining the circular, black-curtained walls. Sophie could see in her peripheral vision that there were people silhouetted in the lounges drinking, but her eyes were drawn to the central bar space: a colossal block of white marble, as significant as a mogul's mausoleum. While this centrepiece evoked a moneyed, religious kind of aura, the rest of the bar was unbridled hedonism. Everything was draped in either black leather or red wine burgundy velvet, with vape smoke as well as dry ice from the theatrical cocktails pervading the air. All the guests spoke in hushed tones, as if the topics of discussion were either illegal, sinister, or salacious — in any case, not to be overheard by anyone not in their inner circle.

Miguel greeted the cocktail waiter with a knowing smile and that annoying wink. He ushered them to a spot in the lounge and promptly whisked the glass water bottle from Sophie's hands and took it to a hidden room in the back. Miguel greeted almost everyone in the bar in Portuguese, most of which Sophie couldn't follow, except that he seemed to be trying hard to give her the message that he was well-known and well-loved in this place. Sophie was swiftly becoming overwhelmed and her mind was already on her exit strategy. It was not just the unexplained side-trip to the river and the water and Miguel's lack of communication: it was also the basic fact that they were still in lockdown and this bar shouldn't be open. Sophie hadn't experienced this level of human contact and interaction for over a year, so the overstimulation was making her tremble a little — like the small dog in her arms.

As Miguel returned to the table, after this show of greeting the entire bar, Sophie stood to leave, and explained she was tired and didn't want to risk getting sick.

"Oh no," Miguel smiled and waved for her to sit down again. "That's why we're here: to make sure you and your little family *don't* get sick."

"What do you mean?" Sophie asked, genuinely feeling exhausted now.

The cocktail waiter returned with a tray holding two spectacular-looking cocktails. They were both decorated with bright green weeds that Sophie couldn't recognise.

"This place," Miguel explained as he took one of the glasses and passed the other to Sophie, "is run by people who appreciate the stuff most people walk all over or throw away. They forage locally, they gather what's important, even the things most people call weeds or waste. They know what's good for each of us."

Sophie's eyes widened with incredulousness, but she took a sip anyway. It tasted like the grass on the little hill near her childhood home — where she would roll down on fine days and the green would get caught up in her laughing mouth. As it slid down her throat, she could feel her trembling subsiding a little.

The cocktail waiter nodded with satisfaction and headed back to the marble bar. Miguel continued with still, quiet eyes watching her sipping her drink. "You'll need to be part of the river to understand what's going to happen to you inside that house," he said calmly.

Sophie stared directly at him, anger surging at herself for her blind trust in coming out with him.

"You have to know that by inhabiting that space, with its specific crisscross of lay lines, it's an act of disappearing."

"*What did you say?*"

Sophie's stomach knotted. Research for the film was one thing, but when it got personal, when it encroached on the spirals in her own mind like this, her gates slammed shut.

"Here is a very easy place to disappear."

She grabbed a hold of Virginia and rose from the lounge.

"What I mean to say, my dear," Miguel implored, clutching her arm and speaking more gently now, "is that the house you have moved into has a funny way of swallowing people up. Some have said that it needs living human energy to enable it to sustain its power. Without your fascination of it, without your... let's say... *lust* to know more about the house and about the Senhora, they would both simply be lost to time."

Miguel attempted a smile and indicated for her to sit back down. Sophie shook his hand off and left the rest of the cocktail on the table.

"Thanks for the drink," Sophie muttered. She grabbed her coat and strode across the darkened floor to the exit.

Sophie was shaking by the time she turned her key in the lock of their front door. She was hoping Alex would already be in bed asleep so she wouldn't have to tell her about her naivety, and the light of day would burn away all the shadows the evening had gathered in her mind.

CHAPTER XX

The Senhora rang the apartment bell three times with the precision of a ship's captain prepping the crew for an oncoming storm. The dogs went nuts at the sound and started barking and howling like the entire house really was capsizing.

As soon as Sophie opened the door, Senhora flung herself inside, laden with a wicker basket full of dusty wine bottles, a silk bag filled to the brim with a powder that exhaled with a little white puff when she moved, a string of hand-painted masks and hats, and two rusty metal buckets, which she left unexplained at the door. One bucket was filled with bubbling fresh water as if it was emanating from a natural spring, and the other with milk that was warm as if it had come straight from the cow.

"My darlings!"

She hugged and kissed the couple profusely, leaving that musky magnolia scent all over them, then continued as they led her down the hall, her high heels clipping along. Sophie took a closer look at them now as she followed behind. They looked to be made from ivory.

"Now, down to business," Senhora said as she clipped along. "Who was it who said: 'My father warned me about men and alcohol but he never said a single word about women and cocaine'? Whoever gets the answer right gets the first party favour."

"No idea in the slightest, but I like her," Alex said, hanging up the very-real-feeling mink coat.

"Ooh," Sophie said, racking her brain. Something about Navia made Sophie want to impress her, and yet she also terrified her to the core. "Someone like Louise Brooks maybe?"

"Warm-ish," Senhora crooned and sat herself down in the centre of the vintage black leather couch. The newcomers were still pretty light on furniture, so they just sat on cushions on the circular Moroccan rug. The glass coffee table, also circular, hovered in between them and Senhora's stockinged knees at the edge of the couch. She crossed her legs and ran her rouge-painted nails up and down the gossamer stockings feverishly. She sure seemed excited about this guessing game of hers.

"Let me give you one hint... We were the greatest of friends back in the old Studio days, or even more than friends, one might speculate..."

At this, she tapped the side of her nose knowingly.

"And," she continued, "she was a childhood friend of none other than Zelda Fitzgerald."

In the dim candlelight, Sophie could have sworn that Senhora looked ten years younger than when they saw her last. Her skin was flushed and dewy and her golden eyes shone with a light that had been dimmed before.

Senhora sank back into the couch and let out a long sigh. "Oh girls, if you could have seen me then..."

As Alex popped a chilled bottle of Crémant on which Sophie spent way too much in an effort to impress Senhora, she did the maths to try to calculate her age. If her heyday had been around those major Hollywood players she was claiming to have partied with, then that would make her no less than one hundred and twenty years old, give or take. Sophie almost choked on her Crémant.

"I don't know for sure, Senhora, but my best guess of who said that was probably you, yourself."

Sophie poured herself another over-full glass, ignoring their guest's empty one waiting for a refill.

Alex raised an eyebrow at Sophie, unsure why she had suddenly changed her tune. She picked up the bottle and politely refilled Navia's glass.

The Senhora fell back into the couch cushions, laughing like a flamingo in heat.

"Oh my dear, you got it!" she exclaimed. "It's often misattributed to that vulgar Southern beast with a trust fund, Tallulah Bankhead, but it was, in fact, moi!"

Alex raised her glass to the centre of the coffee table. "Well that calls for a toast—"

"I'd say that calls for a different kind of toast... after all, I did promise the first party favour to whoever guessed it."

Senhora then unceremoniously plonked the silk bag she had brought with her onto the glass coffee table. With her crimson claws she rattled around in her gold handbag and produced an elegant pewter compact. She opened it and there was a small mirror inside, along with a metal straw, a metal spoon and a razor blade. She grabbed the spoon with her fist and dug around inside the silk bag with it like a child at the beach. The more Sophie observed Navia, the more she realised her physical presence seemed to rollercoaster back and forth between a serene rehearsed elegance, like she was presenting herself on stage, and moments of unselfconsciousness when she devolved into unhinged-teenager mode, not quite in full control of her faculties.

As her staged elegant side took over again, she emptied a heaped spoonful of white powder onto the middle of the glass coffee table. Alex and Sophie exchanged a glance that was equal parts bewilderment and excitement. This was definitely not the direction they were expecting the evening to head in. So much for a fresh start.

Navia proceeded to arrange the mountain of snow into three elegantly proportioned lines.

"You don't need much," she explained, with a Martha Stewart kind of tone. "I've kept this since my Studio days, and carried it all the way back here from the Hollywood Hills to the seven hills of Lisboa."

Alex and Sophie exchanged an incredulous glance. Sophie could see that now Alex was also cottoning on to how much nonsense Senhora was capable of weaving.

"Which is to say girls —" Senhora sang before leaning down limberly and snorting the biggest line with her shining metal straw. "That this stuff here has more purity than I ever did."

She let out a screech of pleasure and trotted her little ivory high heels in place on the floorboards in glee. The dogs started barking in fright at the sound of this tiny horse cavalcade.

"You're next, my dear," she said to Sophie and handed her the straw. "Enjoy the slopes!"

That familiar phrase. Sophie remembered it all too well from Berlin club toilet cubicles. But rather than letting it trigger her back to swampland, Sophie took the straw eagerly and inhaled her magic dust with the gusto of Hunter S. Thompson. Alex was next and took hers with the grin of someone who was already thinking of racking up the next one.

Powder going straight to her head, Sophie immediately jumped up from the rug and slammed on a Grace Jones record. *Nightclubbing*, of course.

"Grace Jones propositioned me in a toilet stall of a London nightclub once," Navia piped up, getting the next lines organised already. "The *nerve* of her!"

Alex and Sophie exploded into laughter — not at Navia but with her — now, one or two more lines down, they'd forgotten their scepticism of Senhora's stories. Suddenly they were all in, buying every word that came out of her mouth.

The French doors were closed to the Lisbon night so the only hints of where their little pleasure island was situated were the occasional drunken shouts in Portuguese penetrating the windows from the cobbled street below, and the moments when the wind blew in their direction from one of the Fado clubs. The deep melancholia of their voices and the music reached them in waves, motioning between the Grace Jones playing on the stereo. The dogs had finally decided to agree to disagree with Navia's presence in their apartment and had curled up in a corner. The candles were ablaze, casting large moving shadows of the few tropical plants and succulents across the as-yet bare walls. Senhora was in her element, still commanding the centre of the black couch, regaling them with glamorous tales, and Alex and Sophie continued sitting like enthralled children at storytime on the floor on the other side of the glass coffee table. The effect of the cocaine was that they melted and mellowed towards her — she had them in the palm of her hands. It gave her this "mother bird" (or perhaps more apt, "golden goose") presence — they trusted everything she poured into their waiting beaks.

The record finished and Sophie got up to put on one of her favourites, one she thought Senhora and her glory days might appreciate: a rare recording of Josephine Baker performing in Sao Paulo in the 1920s. The music began, and within a few seconds of hearing Baker's voice, Senhora had closed her eyes and a shadow passed over her features.

"Oh that witch," Senhora spat, "another one thinking she could turn over the natural order of things."

"The natural order?" Alex piped up after devouring another line. "What on earth does that mean? We're talking musically here, or...?"

Sophie's stomach knotted a little at what Senhora could have meant. She snapped open her golden eyes, sensing the tension, and tried to wave it away by pouring them each another huge glass of decadent French red.

"Oh girls," she sighed, "I remember one night on the liner on the way over to the New Country, and Miss Baker was on board, ready to tour all those smoky little clubs her fans favoured. There was an architect on board, I can't recall which of the many who fawned over her, and he drunkenly offered to design her a house. A house! A townhouse in Paris with its own swimming pool, can you imagine..."

The music played on and Senhora, seeing that her words were giving them pause, got up and started to cavort her way across the living room, swaying expertly. She kept her wine glass in her hand and didn't spill a drop.

"Dance with me, my darlings," she sang and pulled them up from the floor. The dogs started barking as they rose and came to join the messy little circle on the rug.

As they all danced, Sophie noticed the familiar rhythm Navia's ivory heels were making on the wooden floor — this step, *step*, step *step*, step *step*, step, *step*. All of a sudden Sophie felt sick. She excused herself quickly and rushed to the bathroom.

Sophie sat on the toilet lid, swaying, head all over the place. Even through the bathroom door she could still hear her heels clicking away to the music:

Step, *step*, step *step*, step *step*, step, *step*.
Step, *step*, step *step*, step *step*, step, *step*.
"On either side the river lie...
And at the closing of the day..."
Step, *step*, step *step*, step *step*, step, *step*.
step, *step*, step *step*, step *step*, step, *step*.

As Sophie stood, giddy, in front of the mirror, it finally struck her that the poetry and the bumps in the night followed the same rhythmic pattern, the same meter. They were mirrors of each other, as if the poetry had been subsumed into the body of the house — or perhaps vice versa: that the house itself had been built upon the timeless heartbeat of the iambic tetrameter. It left her to wonder whether the architecture of the whole construction was based around this eightfold beat — she had read about these kinds of architectural concepts in nearby Sintra, where one of the most elaborate mansions was constructed around occult rituals and numerology related to the Knights Templar and the Freemasons. One spiral staircase was constructed in such a way that only an inducted member of the mansion's cult, who knew the meter of their organisation's initiation verse, would be able to manage the stairs without stumbling (the short steps represented a short-stressed syllable, and the long ones the opposite) — making the staircase a surefire way to out any imposters on the property.

When Sophie reached the living room doorway, she caught a glimpse of Senhora and Alex dancing together on the rug, the trickery of the candlelight flickering dramatically around them. Alex was holding Senhora by the small of her back and Senhora had one leg extended out and her back arched, tango-style, an arm dramatically flung back with her. In that instant, Senhora was twenty-something, lithe, in her heyday, and Alex was in a velvet tuxedo, cigarette clenched in her teeth. Sophie froze in the bathroom doorway.

The record ended abruptly and the music faded to a repetitive scratching. The candles were snuffed out by a sudden gust and all the trickery of the light was gone.

The two turned to face her and, at least from what she could make out in the gloom, it seemed all was back to how it had been when she left — Alex was Alex and Senhora was their doddering drunk neighbour.

"Oh darling, are you feeling better?" Navia said, coming towards Sophie with her wrist bent, as if to check the temperature on her forehead. "I really should be going and let you two get your beauty sleep — not that you girls need it, of course!"

"Thank you so much for the evening, Senhora," Alex said, putting an arm around Sophie. "I hope we can do it again soon."

Sophie stayed quiet and nervously tucked her hair behind her ear, not sure if she really wanted to do whatever "this" was again soon.

"Oh but my dears, yes!" Senhora exclaimed, making her way down the hall. "Now, I will leave you the wine we didn't drink yet, you can have it with a nice meal tomorrow, and I leave you my little party bag too—"

"No, no that's too much Senhora—"

"Yes Senhora, we appreciate it but it's too much."

"Don't think I'll just leave you to it, mind you," Senhora said, pressing a knowing finger again to her nose, "I'll be back in the blink of an eye so we can enjoy it here together again."

This sent a shiver through Sophie, while at the same time her inner demons were pleased. She wanted more of what Senhora gave them, much more. She wanted more right then and there. Not even just her magic party favours — Sophie realised she wanted this dark glamour and danger she brought to them — the feeling of being at the centre of a deep mystery that only they were privy to. She made them feel wanted, part of a secret society. Even though they weren't sure what that society even was. She invited all of it, even the fear that came with it.

Senhora was only going upstairs, but she ritualistically wrapped herself up in her fur coat and hat before opening the door. Alex turned on the hall light for her, revealing the two metal buckets she had left there on either side of the door.

The water was still bubbling and the milk was still steaming.

"OK, my darlings." She kissed them both on each cheek and whisked herself out the door and up the stairs, waving a white silk handkerchief goodbye and leaving the two buckets there ignored.

"*Beijinhos*."

CHAPTER XXI

The following evening, as they struggled downstairs, still hungover, to take the dogs out for their walk, there was a silhouette of a man standing motionless on their building's landing.

Sophie paused, scanning the figure's back for clues. Alex, on the other hand, rattled along out the door with the dogs and simply brushed past him, as if he was part of the furniture. The figure's left hand darted out and caught Alex's jacket sleeve as she passed. The dogs snarled and jumped at him and Alex wrenched him off, snarling too: "Man, scheisse."

By the time Sophie had rushed to them, the figure had turned around, revealing his grey beard, sleeve tattoos, and a half-full cocktail glass in his right hand. When he caught sight of Sophie, his face broadened into a grin and he bowed and extended the drink towards her.

"Indulge me, will you?" Miguel pressed.

Since Alex was asleep when she crept inside the night of the "tour," Sophie still hadn't enlightened her on the evening's adventures.

"What are you doing?" she hissed and ushered him away from the building and down the cul-de-sac, as Alex followed, bewildered.

"At least finish your drink, Sophie." He smiled through gritted teeth as she continued ushering him down the street.

Alex stopped in her tracks.

"Wait, you two *know* each other?"

The dogs were silent for a moment and stopped pulling on their leads. Some of the nearby Fado clubs had opened their doors and the strains of warm-up music started to entwine their way along the tiny alleyway that led to their cul-de-sac. It was almost dark.

As Sophie began stammering something, Alex slowly broke into a grin.

"Ah yeah," Alex breathed, "now I recognise you — you're the guy who owns that cafe, the one who does the tours?"

Sophie was ready to send him on his way when he thrust the glass into her hand again

"*Saude*," Miguel said, his smile fading as he looked over his shoulder to their building, "to your health."

Sophie waved the drink away but as she did so, he interlaced his fingers with hers, and placed the glass firmly in between their sweating palms. He looked at her unwaveringly and Sophie could see the reflection of Senhora's top floor French doors in the moistness of his eyeballs.

"To your family's health," he muttered, raising the glass to her lips.

Sophie kept her lips firmly shut and darted a helpless glance to Alex, who was observing this spectacle with part bemusement, part impatience.

"Oh for god's sake," Alex laughed, then lunged wildly at them, whisked the glass out of their hands, and downed the cocktail in one gulp. "*Ex-und-hopp!*" Then she threw the empty glass over her shoulder, laughing harder, and it shattered in the overgrown vacant lot next door.

A banging came, like an echo, from the upstairs balcony: Senhora's French doors slammed wide open and hit the iron railings so hard that the glass in them almost shattered. Sophie froze.

"I tried," Miguel muttered softly, before bowing again and disappearing down the little alleyway.

"Ugh that cocktail tasted like a fucking dead body," Alex burped and ambled on ahead with the dogs, muttering in German under her breath.

Funny, Sophie thought as she stumbled along after them, *when I tasted it, I remembered my childhood...*

***

It became hard to count how long had passed before Senhora visited again. It could have been two nights or it could have been two weeks.

They could blame their loss of time on hard lockdown being enforced once again, with the news cycle looping endlessly through warnings of social distancing, PFFP masks, the shutdown of public transport yet again, tighter border restrictions, restrictions on close contact with anyone except your own household, balcony singalongs, families without funerals, ICU emergencies, park raves, no outside time unless you're walking your dog or exercising, the five-kilometre radius... everything converged into a breeding ground for loss. The loss they weren't yet conscious of, however, was the loss of self. The foregoing of the self; drip by drip, inch by inch, night by night.

All was blurring within the ancient walls of the house as they remained distracted by their daily lockdown routine, which became the only proof of life on their social media accounts: the obligatory sourdough baking boasts; tending to photogenic succulents; endless rounds of tarot cards; dancing on the rug to their newly-found queer R'n'B obsessions. And then there were the things they kept off social media, their remaining proof of life to each other: making out and making love to one another; ripping open delivered bargains from online retail therapy; exploding into frustration over the washing up or the laundry or how obscene amounts of mould had already taken over most of the walls, spreading like ominous Rorschach tests. Things began getting blurry in the short minutes they ventured outside the apartment, too — walking the same circles around the cobblestoned neighbourhood with the dogs; nodding and smiling behind masks to the same motionless elderly neighbours. Life became tangled loops of wakefulness in which sunlight and moonlight no longer played any role. They soon started taking "nose coffee" instead of regular morning coffee until morning was dusk and they were dancing again on the rug in the half-light with their bewildered dogs.

The luxury of lazing in bed with Netflix and home-delivered food, which only began during lockdown, soon became the new normal, interspersed with arguments about why the dogs were barking so much, or who was doing too few chores, or laughing uproariously at the drunken expat chatter in the streets that kept on going, even during hard lockdown. In this shapeless, timeless blur, in this drifting absenteeism, their questioning of the bumps in the night that had terrified them when they first moved in had dulled. The night noises had now become so frequent and commonplace that whoever they were coming from began to take up more space in the house, to feel more present than they were. It was as if, inch by inch, they were becoming the house, and whoever was making these noises, maybe the house itself, was beginning to embody them. It became more alive than they were.

One Friday night, the one night of the week that still felt slightly distinct from the others because the "working week" was officially over and they allowed themselves to delve into Navia's silk bag without boundaries, that familiar step, *step*, step *step*, step *step*, step, *step* rhythm approached again. But this time, it was definitively different: it sounded closer, more present than it had ever been.

It now had a tangible, spatial quality to it, and it was making itself heard, even with all the lights on. Usually it waited until they were tucked up in bed and half-asleep, but this time it sounded distinctly as if it was approaching them as they sat on the rug in their usual spots. Ever since Navia had last visited, they had kept her place on the couch empty, ready for her return. Alex and Sophie now sat facing where she had sat, doing lines from her supply and vacantly listening to the steps growing closer. It felt brazen, unhidden.

What had been a palpable fear the first time the sound had approached them now took them over as a generalised anxiety. It had become so present in the apartment, in their pandemic haze, that it had become hard to delineate the added presence of this more direct fear.

Step, *step*, step *step*, step *step*, step, *step*.

Step, *step*, step *step*, step *step*, step, *step*.

As the steps came closer still, Sophie bowed her head and did another line, as if to block it out. Alex sat numbly switching between stroking the dogs and Sophie's hair. The steps now sounded as if they were coming down from above and then through the wall closest to the French doors. There was a heavy green velvet curtain covering that part of the wall — they had presumed it was hanging there to cover up the worst mould spot in the place.

Slowly, inch by inch, the curtain began to open. It moved with the slyness of a snake, undulating spinelessly. As it crept open wider and wider, Sophie and Alex became transfixed, frozen in place in the floor. As they stared with widening eyes, gradually, a dark void was revealed. Silence emanated from it for a few agonising moments.

The Senhora waltzed her way from the void as casually as if she had just returned from powdering her nose. Sophie and Alex exhaled in relief, laughing a little at themselves. Tonight the Senhora was decked out in a gold and cream batwing dress, cinched in at the waist with a dozen golden threads like a spiderweb. She spun and she spun as she emerged, laughing and making Alex and Sophie dizzy just to watch her. She was holding an open bottle of bubbles, from which she took a giant swig before stopping her dance to curtsey and hand Alex the bottle to help herself.

"*Boa tarde*, girls! What a tangled web we've woven."

They both clapped in awe at the sight of her: she was glowing and dewy looked in the prime of her life. Her heavily made up eyes followed the trails of white powder on the glass table. She raised an eyebrow.

"I hope you left some for little old me."

Alex and Sophie exchanged a glance, slightly panicked — they might have overstepped and consumed too much of her stuff? Sophie picked up the bag to arrange a line for her and realised it felt even more full than when Senhora had left it with them.

Navia winked at them. "Just kidding, girls," she said, dipping a little spoon in from around her neck and snorting a big bump. "There's always more where that came from."

They all laughed with relief and settled in: Senhora in pride-of-place on the couch, the couple on the floor, and the dogs in their disgruntled heap in the corner.

"Speaking of where that came from," Senhora announced after what could have been two minutes or two hours, no one could be sure, "I'd like to tell my new favourite inhabitants a little story. Or a big story, depending on who's telling it."

"Sure," Sophie said brightly, expecting another round of wild Hollywood nights in the '20s or '40s, whatever era Senhora decided to transport them to. Alex nodded along eagerly and raised her glass. The liquid fizzled with a volcanic glow in the candlelight and the music shifted to something rumbling and sonorous.

"Not many of us remember the Little Ice Age any longer—"

"The Little what?" Alex snorted.

"You mean from the Middle Ages-ish? You're talking like the fourteenth century?"

"As I said, we're a dying breed, girls."

The hum and hubbub from the street seemed to all but disappear and the streetlights were snuffed out like candles. Sophie and Alex pulled each other a little closer.

"Uh huh." Alex pretended to go along with it and inhaled another massive line. Sophie did the same — standard coping mechanism.

"The Little Ice Age was around the time we realised we wanted more, that we needed more. The bitter cold winters of that moment of our lives meant less grain being produced and less-than-happy peasants. We had so many riots and uprisings on our hands and then the day came that the king's beard froze off, and that was the final straw. So we followed in the footsteps of some intrepid explorers before us and set sail for the New Country."

"Ahh," Sophie said, tapping the side of her nose knowingly, like she'd seen Senhora do so many times before. She was confident that she was putting the pieces of Navia's puzzle together now. Nonchalantly, she opened another bottle of the priceless old wine Senhora had brought. "I get it now. You're speaking like the 'royal we.'" She and Alex laughed, relieved. "Like when you're speaking about the colonial times, you're speaking of 'we' like Portugal invading Brazil and stripping it—"

Senhora looked up sharply from her silk bag with a twinkle in her eye. "Ah so we have a little history buff in the making, do we? Here, darling, relax, it's Friday night after all."

She dumped a massive mountain of powder on the glass and handed Sophie the elegant little spoon from around her neck. Sophie took as much as she dared into her nose and immediately felt some warmth return to her bones and some liquid return to her muscles. Her brain still knew

Navia was talking bullshit, of course, but no one could deny she was a hell of a good time.

"May I continue?" Senhora purred, and the heavy drumbeats in the music thundered louder. "So, with the peasants kicking up a stink at home, it truly felt like the divine was on our side when we discovered the namesake of the Brazil we all know and adore, you know the *pau-brasil*, those redwoods... I mean isn't it a beautiful thought to know that all the grandeur you enjoy here in Lisboa was first built from the splendour of those ancient trees? It's like we're all really forest people here in Lisboa but with dead trees instead of living ones. Everything here is built upon the ghosts of those primordial forests so far away. But ironically, when so many of the trees were taken from Brazil, and then their custodians just kept getting sick, our weather over here just kept getting colder. I mean, that was a climate change we could all agree on, no? Global cooling, it was though, back then... Little Ice Age did not feel so little back in the day."

Despite the cocaine coping mechanism pumping into her body, Sophie's brain could not keep ignoring what Senhora was saying, nor the flippant way she was saying it. She could see that Alex's blood was boiling too.

"But Senhora, what are you saying? That all the destruction and the sickness and death of millions and the loss of their lands was all worth it? All part of God's plan, or some shit?"

"Language, Sophia!" Senhora laughed and clinked her glass in the air to some imaginary ancestor. "You didn't expect all these riches and this beauty you see before you to come from nothing, did you? We weren't content just to sit back and blame the witches for all the bad harvests and birds dropping dead, frozen, from the sky like you Celts and Goths. No, we went out into the world and turned history in our favour—"

"And ended history for millions of other people that you colonised—"

"Ended? Ha!"

At this, Senhora rose and tried a little imitation of sexy South American dancing, hips moving impossibly fast, feet pitter-pattering.

"Just look at them now!" she continued as she trotted, "They're taking their revenge now, immigrating en masse to the streets of our Lisboa. And look at you, girls! My very own little empire here, divided up for you digital nomadic foreigners to colonise for yourselves."

Alex and Sophie sat in a long, disgusted silence. Senhora's feverish dancing slowed to a slow solo tango. Sophie felt the very strong urge to purge her body of all the hedonistic pleasure that had been plied upon them by the Senhora. She swayed to her feet, suddenly giddy with guilt. Alex joined her and they stood awkwardly in their socks with their arms around each other's waists.

"Maybe we should call it a night, Senhora," Alex said firmly.

"And maybe let's take a break from any more visits for a while," Sophie added, still reeling.

"I'll wager that neither of you even took the time to read up on who I am, my family name, the family home you now sleep in."

Her words were harsh but the way she spoke them was lilting and hypnotic. The way an emotionally abusive mother might chastise a very young, slow-learning child.

"You with your fancy freelancing, paying tax to some other rich nation while living off us here; your Uber food deliveries and your Amazon orders — ha, Amazon, what's in a name, eh girls?"

They both hunched their shoulders under the weight of her words and gulped some more red wine. They looked at each other with hangdog expressions. A corner of the privileged cocoon they had been hiding in was starting to tear. They began to smell the smoke from the world literally burning around them.

A soothing Sade song came on the stereo. It transported them back to a time when they were wilfully ignorant teenagers and none of these worries were even thinkable. It gave them a moment to breathe, to release the panic. The streetlights came back on outside and the candlelight seemed suddenly to grow brighter again.

Senhora threw her head back, gold fillings glinting, and laughed with her whole tiny body. She looked even younger again.

"Oh, my little girls!" she exclaimed. "We can't go around living like ghosts, guilty of even existing. We're alive now and we have a right to be alive. Even you digital nomads!" She laughed again.

"Yes but," Alex started, "that still doesn't justify—"

"Doesn't justify what?" Senhora snapped, handing around another bottle of champagne. "None of us on this earth is innocent, yet that doesn't mean we don't deserve to live."

"But it doesn't justify colonialism, or slavery or—"

"How many slaves do you think it took to make that Zara coat I saw hanging by your door? Or the fancy-schmancy Balenciaga shoes you wear?"

"Yes but—"

"Yes but! What of your own 'origin' stories? One of you is a third-generation descendant of an employee of the Nazis, and the other was born on stolen Indigenous land and thinks she's not part of the problem since she owns a few pieces of Indigenous art."

Navia whisked herself out of the living room and backed out towards the hallway with clips of her ivory heels. Then, just as Alex and Sophie thought they had gotten rid of her, she spun around for one last remark:

"Here's a fun fact for my little Australian: did you know that ancient Amazonian Brazilians share some genetic lineage with the Indigenous peoples your ancestors tried to erase? Look at us, how much we have in common!"

At this Sophie and Alex physically shunted her out the door and slammed it hard behind her.

"*Eu te amo* darlings, and we will see us soon," Senhora sang through the closed door.

They stared at each other in the dark, not really seeing anything amid their tangle of thoughts, just breathing there for a while.

CHAPTER XXII

The pandemic continued raging, and the world continued burning. There were still people out drinking on the street under the cover of darkness, and occasionally they could hear the throbbing of house parties nearby, which were not tempting in the slightest. They had become so much a part of the house that the thought of being out in the world for longer than it took to walk the dogs around the block felt threatening and unnatural. When the wind rattled the windows of the house, they trembled with them. When a passing tram shook the house's bones, their bones creaked in solidarity.

One early evening, some unknown time after going into the most recent hard lockdown, Sophie was walking the dogs by herself while Alex continued working, when Sophie had a moment of doubt about this aversion to the outside world.

Perhaps it couldn't hurt, she was thinking as she reached the end of the usual dog-walking loop, *if I go back and ask Miguel to explain what he was going on about?*

She took a sharp turn and had to tug solidly on the leads to coax the dogs out of their routine. She kept on in the direction she remembered the bar to be, hearing and feeling her own breath echoing back to her from the stiff PFFP mask and realising how unfit she had become — this was the furthest she had walked in a long time. She kept her eyes on her feet and relied on muscle-memory to find the way — it was so dark last time, so no landmarks were going to help her.

As Sophie and the dogs began to grow dizzy from all the twists and turns, and the sky grew completely dark, she realised they were getting squeezed into a tighter and tighter space, as if the alleyway was closing in on all sides. She stopped momentarily as the familiarity of that feeling hit her. Sophie smiled into her sweaty mask as she took them round that final sharp turn. She led them, relieved, into that familiar, warmly-lit courtyard.

She approached the little black-painted doorway as before, the two dogs panting behind her, but instead of the red neon sign reading "cocktails," it had been painted over with thick white brushstrokes, reading "COVID Vaccination Centre," along with a little hand-painted *caduceus*.

Sophie poked her head inside the fluorescent-lit room. There was that beautiful white marble bar in the centre as she had remembered it, but this time there were three masked patients seated up on it, dangling their legs, as nurses hovered around with paperwork. A male doctor with a PFFP mask and a long white coat approached one of the patients, the vaccination syringe in hand.

"*Português?* English?" he asked as he pinched the flesh of the patient's arm.

"Oh um, English," she said with an American accent and squeezed her eyes shut as the needle went in.

"There you go, your anti-venom, Miss," the doctor said brightly, already busying himself for the next one.

"Ah what — anti-venom?" she asked, jumping down from the bar.

The doctor chuckled. "Anti-venom, vaccine, same thing — bit of poison to fight the poison, no?"

The patient laughed nervously and gathered her things as the doctor injected the next patient. "If you say so, Doctor... *obrigada, ciao.*"

Sophie checked in at Miguel's cafe on the way back to the apartment. She could eat her "humble pie" and finally ask him what all that was in aid of before. Why he was trying to help her. But when she finally found her way back there, the cafe was closed, dark, and the door was plastered with a handwritten sign:

Fechado devido ao bloqueio rígido/ Closed due to hard lockdown :(

Too late.

Sophie hurried back home with the dogs, now shivering in the damp air and blustery wind. Her outside-world venture a failure, she was ready for the inside-world comforts of Uber-delivered Thai, and watching *True Detective* in bed with Alex.

It had been some unknowable length of time since Navia's last visit, so when the familiar *step, step* rhythm began that night, it felt like an invasion.

Sitting up rigidly in bed, Alex and Sophie were not so much fearful as they were irritated. They had planned to just drift off to sleep after a few episodes but now these sounds seemed to spell another night of the Senhora's slanders, racism, and narcissism. Usually the dogs didn't react to these disturbances, as if they were just part of the fabric of the house, but tonight, with the sounds invading the very air around the bed, they stood to attention, growling.

The rhythm again — this time sounding like knuckles rapping on wood.

Knock, *knock*, knock *knock*, knock *knock*, knock, *knock*.
Knock, *knock*, knock *knock*, knock *knock*, knock, *knock*.
Louder and louder, closer and closer.

More and more like a heartbeat.

Hildegaard started howling and jumped off the bed, sniffing towards where the noise was now distinctly emanating from. She snuck over to the wardrobe, nose to the ground, tail between her legs, and gingerly tried to open one of the old wooden doors.

"Senhora?" Sophie called in a small voice, "Is that you in there?"

Knock, *knock*, knock *knock*, knock *knock*, knock, *knock*.

Alex got up from the bed and followed her dog.

Knock, *knock*, knock *knock*, knock *knock*, knock, *knock*.

Suddenly the smell of very old, swampy mud entered the room from the direction of the wardrobe.

Sophie got up shakily and followed Alex to the wardrobe.

Knock, *knock*, knock *knock*, knock *knock*, knock, *knock*.

Slowly, deathly slowly, they opened the doors of the wardrobe.

They were hit with the intensity of that dank earthy smell.

The knocking stopped.

Inside the wardrobe it was dark as a cave. Sophie looked to Alex, eyes widening in fear, and bent down to her hands and knees. Silently, trembling, she felt her way forwards into the wardrobe.

"And down the river's dim expanse,
Like some bold seer in a trance..."

Sophie felt as if her heart were being strangled.

"S-Senhora?" she called sheepishly, then "Ouch!" as she felt a splinter pierce her hand.

"What is it?" Alex jumped. The dogs started barking in fright.

Alex joined Sophie in the wardrobe on hands and knees, and they both felt their way further into the dark than the depth of the wardrobe should have allowed. As they crawled, they pushed aside the forest of their hanging clothes, which felt more like the foliage of trees, straining to see anything in the pitch darkness.

Knock, *knock*, knock *knock*, knock *knock*, knock, *knock*.

The sound was louder still. Together, they ventured their hands further into the black until their fingers reached the wooden edge of something.

They ran their fingertips over it, feeling its edges, its size.

"It's some kind of box?" Sophie whispered.

They grunted as they dragged the thing out of the wardrobe and onto the bedroom floor, the dogs exploding again into barking.

Alex scrambled around the bed and found her phone. She turned on the torch to see it better, shining the light this way and that.

In the pale, LED glow, they could see it was a wooden chest, specifically redwood or *pau-brasil*. Moving slowly around it, peering close as they dared, they could see it was carved with a different imperialistic scene on each face – one of Indigenous Brazilians paddling canoes piled with chopped down trees, one of a scene from a slave auction by a harbour, one with an Indigenous baby being given to a white mother, and one of an ornate dining scene with a white family being waited on by slaves.

"Surprise!" said a half-familiar voice, and the chest opened.

Out popped a twenty-something-year-old girl in a long white dress drenched in dirty water and mud, with her long, fair hair flowing wet and plaited with river reeds and flowers.

"You like?" the young woman asked, as she flounced around in the dress. "I made a special effort for you tonight, for our last night together."

"Um," Alex said flatly, unable to articulate anything more.

"Yeah, um," Sophie repeated, "I have so many questions. And didn't we say no more visits?"

The young Senhora busied herself by digging into the wooden box, revealing piles of white linen, towels, and ornate cutlery, glassware, and crockery, all dusted ominously by what appeared to be very decomposed human remains. "It's my Hope Chest! I'd forgotten where I'd put the damn thing."

Then a cascade of sound came from her mouth: a sort of pantomime of laughter, stained deeply with malice.

"Tonight is the night we wrapped *Lady of Shalott*, so now we must have a little party, girls. How does that sound?"

She was speaking so quickly, so feverishly, that it was hard to keep up. The girl leapt from the bedroom in a flurry of white fabric and wet hair, leaving muddy footprints behind her. The dogs chased her out of the room.

When they caught up with her in the living room, she was standing on the glass coffee table in a theatrical "orator's" pose. The dogs were leaping up, snapping at her and yapping. Undisturbed, Senhora cried out:

"There are forces beyond nature that can either help us or hurt us. And until we know how these forces work, we will continue to carry around the unnecessary burden of fear. Are you afraid of me, girls?"

"Well, *should* we be afraid of you, Senhora?" Alex asked, sensibly, but then cracked open the first bottle of the night, throwing caution to the wind.

Navia laughed that chilling laugh again then and hopped down onto her spot on the black couch. "Who's afraid of a drowning woman?"

Virginia Woof started barking at Navia, as if on cue, and they all relaxed into laughter, like old times. Could the younger Senhora be blamed for all the atrocities of her older self? At least for tonight, they decided to wipe the slate clean.

The trio settled into more or less their usual routine of Crémant, then red wine and plenty of lines from Navia's party bag, which still wasn't getting any lighter.

"Well, to be frank, they should have been *more* afraid of us when they first invaded," Senhora tittered girlishly and wiped some excess powder from her nose. "After all, we did manage to turn them into pythons."

"Sorry, when who invaded, Navia?" Sophie asked, completely lost now. Gazing at her ageless, exquisite face and dripping muddy hair, her beauty was like quicksand.

"Those original colonisers."

Alex and Sophie exchanged a glance and then both took a very generous line to cope with this fresh onslaught. It tasted sweet and golden and they threw their heads back for a short-lived moment of clarity in this new wave of Navia's tale-telling.

"Sophia, darling, you of all people should know exactly what I'm referring to, what with your expertise. Aren't you meant to be making a film on the topic?"

Sophie didn't remember actually mentioning the script in much detail to Senhora. Or did she?

Senhora sat still now, breathing deeply, patiently, and finally speaking at a more measured pace. She looked at Sophie piercingly, and then suddenly Sophie saw it. The connection.

"It all started with the scorn of our kind, with ignoring us as if we didn't exist, weren't real. Shut up in our towers with our scales and our song, with just the mirrors and shadows of the outside world for company. Doomed only because we loved and longed for our land."

They could see the tears welling in Navia's eyes. Even with all her mighty oration, she suddenly appeared smaller and softer. Her shoulders rounded and her head stooped into vulnerability.

"You already know, Sophia, about the Lady of Shalott, or Elaine of Astolat. Sure, you read all about the Astures, those river-travelling tribes. The Lady of Astures and her Lancet fort, yes, sure, that's the modern version. But I want you to think back, think right back, down, deep as you can go... drink from those ancient waters beneath the trickles up here you land dwellers call rivers. I want you to remember us, the Tágides, or how you call them, the Tides in your language. The original river nymphs of this land."

Sophie and Alex tried to take all this in, not taking their eyes off of the dripping young woman.

"Did you never think to look up the meaning of my name? I'm the namesake of a whole territory, a river that runs through the Land of a Thousand Rivers, flowing to the Astures; the name of the goddess of sacred springs, I could go on, ladies..."

The dogs had calmed and were curled around her feet, which were still just as wet as if she had only just emerged from the water. She continued, in a low, slow, throaty voice.

"Since the 'pacification,' as the Romans called it, we were forced into human, Christianised forms, and colonised by those logical thinkers — they watered our magic down to mortality. Look what they got for their trouble: generations of pythons who colonised and enslaved and brutalised other lands in turn."

At this, Alex piped up, emboldened by the powder.

"Is this some big allegory where you're trying to justify Portuguese colonisation and imperialism again? Or you're saying all men are snakes? Or both?"

Without missing a beat, Navia had an answer.

"The preternatural of one generation becomes the natural of the next. Like us ancients turning the men into pythons — that became the natural order of things. And like their generation colonising and plundering nations on the other side of the globe — that, too, became the natural order of things."

"So what about our generation? What is 'preternatural' to us that will become 'natural' to the younger generation?" Sophie asked, itching her nose and racking up another line.

Navia laughed and twirled her hands in the candle-smoky air like a snake-charmer.

"Just look at all this before you: it might as well be the Body of Christ itself that you're putting up your noses, the depth of your belief in it! You've been putting your faith in it for months now, maybe years, since you've lost all track of time, letting your lives be guided by it... all the while chastising me about colonisation."

Sophie numbly took another line, her eyes glazing over. She was growing more confused by Senhora and her arguments as she got more high, and at the same time caring less about what she was even trying to communicate. Alex was getting exhausted by it all — eyes dulled, except when she focused on the line before her on the glass as it disappeared into her nostril.

And yet, there was still that tiny voice inside them trying to be heard from some unknown beyond: *What has become of you?*

"I wonder, girls," Navia crooned, leaning forward into the candlelight, letting her fragile white dress reveal her pale, mud-stained breasts, "would you even believe me if I told you this magic powder of ours is made from the ashes of the primordial forests and the bones of the Indigenous people you're both so prone to defending? Does it make you enjoy it any less or, on the contrary, does it fire up your little inner demons and help you enjoy it even more?"

In that moment, as the words left her lips, the consistency of the powder on the plate altered. It became ashen and full of lumps. It became exactly as she described: made of ground-up bones and burnt forests.

Alex and Sophie shoved past each other towards the bathroom to be sick. Alex made it to the basin and Sophie heaved into the toilet.

As they finished releasing all the thick poison from their bodies, coming out black as an oil spill, their high crashing and burning, they heard a voice echoing from the bathtub. It was Senhora, but with the scales and hunch from a reptilian era, pre-human. Barely alive.

This incarnation was reclined in the bathtub, mud-encrusted grey hair strewn out behind her, and black mould rising up around the tub and creeping up the bathroom walls.

"Just as that plucky kid Susan Sontag said not so long ago, girls," the ancient Senhora continued as the mould rose higher around them, "telling a story is both perceived as telling a 'tall tale,' or an untruth, just as much as it is telling a whole narrative, or the 'whole truth' of something."

She paused to let the words fully cascade out of her mouth and echo around her in the mouldy bathtub.

Alex looked at the ancient Senhora in the mirror and sighed heavily, resigned to the madness now. All the exhaustion of the past weeks, months, or even years that they had been there were now showing on her face, reflected in the mirror.

"So this is what you're doing, huh?" Alex muttered in the mirror to the ancient Senhora. "You're simultaneously mythmaking and elaborating upon a myth to establish your own form of truth."

"You think of yourself as both a weaver of myths *and* an authority on Absolute Truth?" Sophie added, needing to sit herself back down on the tiles by the toilet — her limbs were suddenly so, so tired. Her head was so unbelievably heavy.

"Whatever you say, mortals!"

This voice now came into the bathroom with a rush of slender limbs and wet hair: the nymphette Navia was now prowling around the bathroom, leaving a trail of muddy water.

All three spoke simultaneously now, charging the atmosphere with so much electric energy that the bathroom lights flickered and died, plunging them all into gloom. The only light source was the candlelight, wavering from the next room.

"Our stories weave the watery threads between our ancient Navia River, to the faithful Tagus, to the place it empties itself into the Atlantic Ocean, then the thread of this body of water is woven into the Mediterranean and then stitches itself into the azure tapestry of the Ionian Sea. It's part of the river, the Okeanos, that circles the whole earth, even all the way to your stolen homeland, Sophia, in an ouroboros, an infinity loop. Our stories take the watery voyage in reverse that Odysseus and his men took all the way to our western edge of Europe from Greece. Where the two eagles of the east and the west landed for the second time to declare the centre of the world. The last known whereabouts of the Great God Pan. The tiny island of Paxos."

"As was prophesied by Zeus," the ancient one continued.

"As was prophesied by Zeus," the younger ones repeated.

The ancient one continued on alone in a hallowed tone, the disembodied voice reverberating through the dark bathroom.

"When Odysseus and his men got to Paxos, it was steeped in witchcraft, protected by Circe's spell to keep the worst of humans away. This was because the Pythias had relocated our most holy of holies, the Temple of Delphi, where the eagles landed, away from the Gaulish, Roman, and all the other invaders on the mainland. If any non-pilgrims still managed to penetrate the island and make it to the Temple, the spell would give them back their non-human innocence by turning them into pythons, unable to continue their raping, pillaging, rampaging — and the destruction even of what it means to call oneself human. That privilege was permanently revoked. After all, pythons can't fight wars."

The three of them let out peals of laughter that echoed around the moistening tiles, now completely darkened with black mould, just visible in the gloom.

"So this is why I was drawn to this house," Sophie thought, feverishly. "This place is a stepping stone..."

"You are a guest in *our* home, remember, and we say who goes and who remains..." the Navias sang, tauntingly.

Now the middle-aged one continued on alone, in the Senhora voice that Alex and Sophie were most familiar with.

"Now my darlings," she purred, "if you want to continue on, do exactly as I say and reach your hands out in front of you, let them be guided by my voice..."

"Yessss," hissed the other Navias.

Alex and Sophie clung to each other on the bathroom floor, with the dogs shivering and whining in their laps.

"Reach for my voice, girls," Senhora's voice continued, "it's your only way out of here."

Sophie squeezed Alex's arm, then let go with a sharp intake of breath, letting her fingertips feel their way in the dark towards the familiar sound of Senhora's voice. She couldn't be sure whether Alex was doing the same.

"That's it. Now slowly, lower your hands down, out in front of you, fingers outstretched... that's it..."

Sophie did as she was told, letting her outstretched arms come down in front of her.

"Now in a moment, you might feel some cold and some heat, but do not remove your hands... it won't hurt you..."

In that instant, Sophie felt her left hand surrounded by cool, gurgling liquid and her right hand immersed in a warm, thicker liquid. It took all her discipline not to jump away in shock.

As both her trembling hands adjusted to the different temperatures, the lights flickered back on and Alex, Sophie, and the dogs yelped in fright. The bathtub was squirming with pythons trying to make their way down the plughole and Sophie's hands were immersed in two rusty metal buckets: one bubbling fresh water and the other steaming milk.

Alex and the dogs were having none of it. They were backing away towards the door, visibly shaking.

Black mould had spread viciously over every surface of the bathroom, and was now spreading from the floor into the buckets and across Sophie's skin until she was completely covered by the fungus.

In the next instant, Sophie disappeared.

"There are forces beyond nature that can either help us or hurt us," the disembodied voices hissed.

But what, exactly, is beyond nature?

PART FIVE

SAPPHO II

In nova fert animus mutatas dicere formas corpora

"My spirit leads me to tell of forms transformed into new bodies."
— Ovid, *Metamorphoses* 1.1

1. Know thyself.
2. Nothing to excess.
3. Surety brings ruin, or "make a pledge and mischief is nigh" [ἐγγύα πάρα δ'ἄτα].

> *Servant of the Delphian Apollo*
> *Go to the Castalian Spring*
> *Wash in its silvery eddies,*
> *And return cleansed to the temple.*
> *Guard your lips from offence*
> *To those who ask for oracles.*
> *Let the God's answer come*
> *Pure from all private fault.*

— Inscriptions found at the Temple of Delphi

CHAPTER XXIII

The golden tripod, mounted within the adyton, the chamber inaccessible to anyone else, looked precarious to perch on. Yet perch on it she did, teetering on the edge of it with long brown legs ominously crossed against her waiting pilgrim, lying prostrate on the marble floor.

The Pythia's gangly assistants, wrapped breezily in white robes, with wreaths of toxic oleander embedded in their hair, entered the space and hovered in dutiful circles. It wasn't customary for the pilgrim to be on the floor, so the assistants were shaken. The Pythia herself felt that this act was verging on being patronising.

Slowly, the Pythia uncrossed her ankles and spread her legs, placing her left foot in the vessel of gurgling spring water waiting on the left side of her tripod, and her right foot in the vessel of warm milk waiting on the right side of her tripod. The liquids of transmutation.

She took a deep inhalation of the sacred vapours snaking up through the chasm in the temple floor, and opened her eyes wide behind her purple veil. After a few moments of the pilgrim remaining motionless on the floor, the Pythia surreptitiously moved her purple veil aside to take in a more detailed glimpse of this humble servant of Delphi.

"False Humility": that will be the crux of my prophesy, the Pythia mused as she eyed this strange flat creature, making itself known that it was from an unknowable, far-flung land, where the smoky, artificial fragrances of its garments could

not be washed away from one single, ritualistic bathing in the Castalian Spring.

As the Pythia sniffed the pilgrim, she noticed the pilgrim doing the same: sniffing and inhaling from the ground up.

This gave the Pythia pause.

She considered this unprecedented behaviour, then cast it from her mind as she focused instead on the next fresh wave of the sacred vapours creeping up from the jagged crevice. Her direct line of communication with the belly of the earth, via its holy navel.

But there it was again: that sniffing, that sharp intake of breath, over and over.

As the vapours overtook the Pythia, and she leaned back on her golden tripod for the divine to enter her, the messages were interrupted by intrusive thoughts about this sniffing pilgrim.

Then it dawned on her. This interloper on her floor, on her inner sanctum, was all the way down there not out of humility (genuine or false), but because it wanted a taste of the vapours.

It wanted to be as close as possible to the gods' passageways, to their orifice; their entranceway to the materiality of the earth, to take in the ether that was reserved for she alone — the Oracle — to commune with the past and with the future. To be in contact with the non-human, with the more-than-human.

"The Mother is trying to talk to us."

This came blasphemously from the mouth of the prostrate pilgrim.

If it wasn't for the pacifying, anaesthetising effects of the holy gases, this blasphemy would have resulted in the first instance of an Oracle of Delphi spilling human blood, from her own hand. At least on the physical plane.

Then it made noise again.

"The rocks, I mean — Mother Earth is speaking to us through the rocks."

Deep in the trance of the gases, all the Pythia could muster to annunciate was:

"Rise, pilgrim, and remove yourself."

The assistants spiralled in before the sentence was even completed, and lifted the degenerate to its feet, swaying and stupefied by the effects of the ethylene.

The Pythia, rising, out of character, from the golden tripod, looked upon the pilgrim's face and the slack, swaying body.

Whether it was the divinity and mercy of the gases, as the Pythia continued her gazing, she was shocked to realise that she found the wretched creature before her beautiful. And, more shocking still, it was a deep experience of beauty; one that put flesh and blood into the concept that had long since nagged her: the concept of existing in another life, in another body, in parallel with this particular time and body in which she was living.

The effect was dizzying.

We know each other. We have met before.

But the realisation came too late, and her assistants were too quick, attentive, protective.

The assistants stood on either side of this dizzying girl, holding her arms outstretched in the shape of a cross.

Their blades had done their best, most precise work.

The pilgrim's robes were already wet with the externalising of her innermost places.

Her liver, her intestines, her kidneys, even her heart, had become part of the outside world, quickly drying into dust, into something that someone would one day inhale into their own body.

She had become a river of herself.

"We relieve you, Pythia," said the assistants.

And as the Pythia's own heart dropped to her feet at the sight of this beauty lost, her dutiful assistants threw the leaking girl into the temple's chasm. Reducing her to ashes in the fires of the belly of the earth.

CHAPTER XXIV

You cut into me softly, deftly, with those talented fingers of yours.

Well-versed in cutting, stitching back up, caressing back to health, then cutting wide open again. And again and over and up and under and through. Tracing lines across my skin of thoughts, memories, feelings — until the dust comes spiralling out of me.

Just slice me entirely this time.

I want the full autopsy now.

I want to finally make you step inside, see me, and feel the full discomforts of this home inside me that we've co-created.

When I say "you," I mean "you" in plural, in all the plurality of you.

This Coroner, this Oracle, this Medium, are all just vessels for each of you: my past loves are the ghosts in her throbbing machine.

I observe your precision as you slice, one line from my clavicle striding down to my navel with the precision of the ancients positioning their holy places in exact parallel with the movements of the stars and the tectonic plates. I would have shivered at your accuracy if I wasn't fully paralysed by you.

This paralysis is so deep, so complete, that the scalpel I see reflected in your eyes, splitting me into twins of myself, feels as gentle as your tongue. If I could close my eyes, and not see you rending me in two, these caresses would bring me back to our past lives together. Warmths upon warmths.

All the ghosts of my loves, long dead, come to life in your deft hands.

Next, you put fresh latex gloves on your hands and hold out your right hand for a new scalpel. You turn your attention completely to my insides. Reverently, you peel back both sides of my flesh, as if drawing open the curtains of a church tabernacle.

I'm not entirely sure what you see in me as you do this. All I can see reflected back at me are the moist colours and shapes of my most private places. The shock of the violet, the dazzle of the crimson, the startle of the frothy whites. All wet, all meat. Devoured by your eyes.

Being gazed at so expertly, so intently, by you makes me burn between my thighs. Your gaze makes my insides wetter still. My mouth salivates, my tongue is ready, my fingers tingle. Impossibly, I feel my inner thighs twitch and you start. As if to control my twitch, you place your left hand there, attempting to steady me. It only makes my heat rise.

How is it that all of your bodies have died for me, long ago, and yet you still make me warm? The heat still rises from our skin.

Now you begin to unburden me. Gracefully, you lift the heft of my small intestines up and out of me and into the stainless steel tray in the waiting hands of your assistant. Then, the weighty mess of my large intestines are heaved out onto a bigger tray. Next my spongy pancreas, up and out as if it couldn't wait to get out of me. And now my wretched, hard-working liver, colours of solstice bonfires. Then the kidneys, bless them (did you kiss them on their way out?), and one by one, each and every one of my organs, up and out of me.

Lastly, you turn your attention towards my heart. It takes some aorta-hacking before it allows itself to be severed from the rest of me.

Perhaps on impulse, or out of habit, you remove your black latex glove from your right hand and slide your naked skin softly around my heart, blood and acid saturating your fingertips. I sigh, deep and full.

Your assistant shoots a glance at you but you simply close your eyes and let my heart rest heavy in your warm palm. You sigh deeply in response, and I feel the resonance from your larynx, down your sinews, all the way to your fingertips, to my heart, until it vibrates me wholly.

In the slippery caverns left behind in the absence of my heart and all my other organs, I feel a light breeze move through me.

You cave me.

You cavern me.

The unburdening is euphoric.

CHAPTER XXV

"You burn me, so I will flood you in slow-moving, liquid retaliation," Sappho breathes in the medium's ear.

She has tied her to the marble chair. The air is limpid with steam, barely breathable, and the heat is rising fast from the stone beneath their bare feet.

The medium tries to appeal to Sappho's wounded ego. "Your noble fierceness, the grace of your muscular lust, I'm melting, Sappho..."

It's the middle of the night, the bath house is closed, doors bolted, and the electricity is not working.

Sappho is wrenching the water pipes from the wall, one by one, and letting the water gush hot over the marble floor.

Everything is illuminated by darting licks of candlelight; the rising water is glinting lasciviously, and Sappho's own features, drenched in sweat, are raging.

"You! You jest at me in your infinite ruthlessness," Sappho is screaming.

The medium's wrists are bleeding now from her attempts to free herself from the heavy rope she's bound with. Her eyes are beginning to moisten with tears.

Sappho, meanwhile, is swanning around the room in her flowing white robes, with indigo sashes emphasising her shoulders and her waist. Her wild curly hair is escaping its clasps and falling in spiralling strands down her long, brown neck.

There's a large circular hot stone in the middle of the room where, by day, women would drape themselves and enjoy the heat rising from the marble. The circular room is punctuated by arched recesses equipped with marble basins and metal buckets where women could sit together and talk while they filled up the buckets with the thermal therapeutic water flowing from the underground hot springs, and pour it over their naked skin.

If only Sappho could have visited during opening hours — the scene of the blissed-out, glistening, chatting, naked women would have satiated her. Instead, she was summoned by the medium alone to the candlelit bathhouse in the middle of the night.

"Sappho, I apologise until the end of time — I just wasn't expecting — you just took me by surprise –"

"Girl please, I am Surprise Incarnate."

"Yes, I know that now... please forgive me... you don't have to do this."

"You get me wet, I get you wet, it's only fair."

At this Sappho laughs uproariously and starts flaunting around the room, letting her robes fly open and reveal her naked body, all the while turning on all the taps in the marble recesses.

Water gushes now from all the broken pipes around the room and from every tap in the archways. The water is rising fast — it is now hovering around their knees and the temperature of it is almost scalding. A thick steam dances upwards from it, curling into the domed glass ceiling, framing the night sky beyond.

"Sappho, fairest, most fiery flame..."

Sappho strides over to the medium now and points a finger at her chest. She makes contact with her skin, then slowly drags the finger down her skin to her navel.

The medium looks up at her, big eyes, trembling. There's a dangerous silence until Sappho breaks it by laughing her head off.

"Girl, cut the poetry goatshit OK, you insult my artform."

She roars again with laughter and starts flinging herself around and around the circular room, leaping from the marble stone in the centre, then splashing down, then back up again and around and around the whole room in circles until she is panting and saturated.

"Sex can be absolutely anything, isn't that wild?" she exclaims, shaking her wet curls. "Sex can be my submerged legs causing friction in all this hot water, until the vibrations of it cause you pleasure..."

She stops her cavorting for a moment to run her fingers from the water over her knees, all the way up her beautiful brown thighs.

"Or sex can be me, bending down to let this warm water lap at my pussy..." she does just that as she continues murmuring and the water continues rising. "Sex can be you watching me while I force the waves of the water to eat me, to devour me, giving pleasure to my whole body..."

She moans a little and arches her back. "It's completely non-consensual. Don't you think that's a bit sexy, forcing the water to fuck me?"

The medium nods — at first out of fear, and then genuinely. The sights, the sounds, the spectacle of it all is genuinely turning her on. She barely notices that the water is now almost up to her waist.

"And you know what else is sex, girl?" Sappho mutters as she lets herself lie back in the water, her dark hair floating out all around her.

Slowly, ever so slowly, she floats around so that her knees are pointing in the girl's direction. With agonising slowness and precision, she parts her thighs for the medium, opening herself wider and wider until the medium can see her whole open pussy, saturated in many ways.

The girl moans in spite of herself — the noise escapes her throat, rasping and wanting — and echoes through the marble room. This spreads a smile across Sappho's lips. Her hands stroke her thighs and her face lights up.

"You didn't answer me..."

The girl squirms to release her hands again, but this time for an entirely different reason. She feels herself motioning her hips back and forth on the marble chair.

"This is also sex..." the medium murmurs.

"Yes, yes it is," Sappho replies, touching herself fully now.

The water has risen now to the medium's chest. But instead of being fearful, she is distracted by the warm buoyancy of her breasts bobbing in the water, now rising and cresting with Sappho's movements. The medium moans again and grinds herself into the chair.

The heat of the water is making her dizzy; she feels as if she could pass out at any moment. But her eyes are not closing for anything — she does not want to miss a second of watching the goddess Sappho, legs completely spread right in front of her, masturbating...

In between sighs and moans of pleasure, Sappho continues talking.

"And you know, girl," she murmurs, casting a glance down over her as the water rises over the girl's shoulders and up to her trembling, flushed throat. "You know what the best part of our sex is...?"

She then goes back to a frenzy of touching and fingering herself deeply and bucking wildly in the water. The medium does not take her eyes away for a second. She's grinding herself harder and harder into the chair until the water reaches her bottom lip. She drinks in the hot water, thinking about how she is also drinking in some of Sappho's juices.

"The best part is..."

Then Sappho comes, explosive, shuddering, the whole lithe statue of her body aflame in the water. The medium comes too, throwing her head back into the hot water and letting go completely. The throbbing lips of her pussy undulate into the warmth of the water — she comes in waves, over and over.

When she is done, the water is almost at her nostrils, but after an orgasm like that, she could almost resign herself to drowning.

She opens her eyes and Sappho is right there, her lips against her ear.

"The best part is that I got you right where I wanted you, you exquisite, feeble thing."

Then she swiftly unties her, grabs one of her hands and swims her out of the bathhouse.

They're red and panting as they lie in puddles of water in the bathhouse foyer. There's a Chinese restaurant next door and the red neon sign, "Dragon's Den," blinks on and off, reflected on their saturated skin.

"OK, where to next?" Sappho asks brightly.

***

"...Aaaaand CUT!" shouted Sophie into the darkened set. "Check the gate!"

Everyone sighed, relaxed — the gate was checked, chat started up again, cigarettes were lit. The actors peeled off of each other, got up off the floor, and gave each other an exhausted hug.

"Oh my god, girls, that was brilliant," Sophie gushed. "This is by far my favourite scene, and, I must say, my favourite film in this whole fucked-up series."

The "devolution" of *The Circle* — as some critics were calling the last season during Sophie's burnout — was now set to be turned around, since the producers had finally placed the creative reins in Sophie's hands. Whether or not anyone else but Sophie and the actors would enjoy Sappho's erotic screen debut was yet to be determined.

The actors, still dripping wet, laughed and hugged her. "Soph, it's all you baby," said the one playing Sappho. "Couldn't do it without you."

"Oh gosh, I'm still turned on," laughed the one playing the medium, "I'mma head back to my hotel room now to, you know..."

They all laughed and wrapped sweaty arms around each other. The film was almost wrapped.

As they were about to call it a night, someone turned the house lights on, and the First AD pulled up her megaphone.

"Hey Sophie, you still on set?"

She shaded her eyes from the bright overhead lights and squinted into the distance. There was a general spinning this way and that and murmurs from the crew "Yeah yeah she's debriefing with the actors..."

Eventually Sophie turned around and frowned back at Aini. She hunched her shoulders then folded forward dramatically.

"Aini, it's been a long day. What is it?"

Aini shouted back into the megaphone, even though Sophie would have heard her perfectly without it.

"Sophie, the police want to speak to you again."

The whole cast and crew stopped what they were doing and plunged into silence. It had been two weeks since she had been at the station, and that had already caused enough gossip. Now it was time for round two. Sophie groaned and ran agitated fingers through her messy hair.

"Really? In the middle of the shoot? We're almost wrapped!"

"Yes Sophie, the police want you to answer more questions." Aini's volume was increasing as the stunned silence of the crew continued. She could no longer hide the little smirk spreading across her lips. "You'd better go with them right away."

Sophie's eyes widened and she shook her head incredulously. "What a clusterfuck..." she breathed and started shoving her laptop and other bits and pieces from the day into her black backpack.

"Alright fine, Aini, I'll go now."

"Good," Aini said curtly then directed her arm like an air hostess towards the exit. "They're waiting outside."

Sophie walked with a feigned confidence across set and out the door, burning from all the eyes on her. Now that it was the second questioning, she seemed to have lost the faith of even the hair and makeup crew, who had reached out to rub her arm or offer a kind word the first time. This time even those softer ones stayed silent, eyes downcast. David and his wine-stained moustache were nowhere to be found.

Her stomach churned with guilt as she walked, even though she was almost sure she was not guilty of anything. She had only found a body, hadn't she?

But she was realising, as she left set and strode down the dark, crumbling hallway of the masseria, that she would be so easy to crack in an interrogation. The veil between what her mind believed and others' suggestions, other worlds, had always been whisper-thin.

"Maybe that's one reason I haven't made it past directing this fucking 'Circle' series?" she muttered as she shunted open the front door. "I've always been too impressionable, bending to other people's wants, to stick to my own vision."

As the door opened, she was illuminated by the pulsating blue lights from the cop car. The siren had been turned off but they seemed to have left their lights on for dramatic effect. Milos, the same officer as before, was leaning up against the side of the vehicle. She nodded and waved at him with the familiarity of how they had left things when they released her. But this time he only responded with a stilted hand gesture to her, indicating the back seat of the car.

"If you'll come with us, Miss."

"OK, sure, Milos," Sophie said, her nervousness rising as she walked towards the car.

"Officer Makris," Milos answered, getting behind the wheel and slamming the door.

As Milos started the car and reversed out, a figure ran towards the car, lit up in the headlights in his dirty trench coat, the fabric flapping about as he ran.

"I believe in you, Sophie!" David called, spilling red wine all over himself from the glass in his hand as he waved them off. "Don't let the man get you down!"

Sophie tried to get the window down to wave to him, then remembered she was in a cop car. She placed her steaming palm melodramatically against the glass instead, suddenly feeling the tears welling. This was definitely not the turn of events she was expecting. She was meant to be flying back to Alex and the dogs in Berlin next week.

"Um, can I make a call?" she asked, as they left the property gates to the dark road ahead. She dug around in her backpack to find her phone.

"No you may not," Milos grunted, and sped them along the dusty unlit road, framed by the ubiquitous stone walls and olive groves with branches gnarled like the hands of a whole generation of grandmothers wrung with grief.

***

Sophie was grateful again for the dim green glow of the imitation banker's lamp. It was set atop a pile of overflowing case files on the inspector's desk, which inexplicably brought tears to Sophie's eyes. The vulnerability of this grown, macho, puffed-up man and his aspirational banker's lamp and all the late nights ahead of him, spent with his head bent over this very spot... "I must be exhausted," she thought, tears welling.

"Hello?" he said impatiently. "Are you still in the land of the living? I asked you a question."

"Sorry, what was the question again?" Sophie stammered, feeling sweat sticking her inner thighs together.

Milos snapped his pen.

"The last statement you gave us, about your discovery of the body: is there anything you would now like to add or modify? We are kindly giving you this opportunity before we proceed to the next stage."

"Next stage?" Sophie's big eyes searched his face.

"Right now, your concern is whether there is anything that you did not inform us of before that you would now like to add to your statement."

Sophie raced back two weeks ago to when she first found the body. The body that looked almost identical to her body. Only dead.

"No," Sophie said carefully, and then, like a knife to her stomach, she remembered she had pulled the ring from the body's finger. She creeped herself out even thinking about it. "No — well..."

Milos loomed over her, all ears. Sophie fumbled around in her hip bag, pulling out loose coins, rolled-up business cards, an old vape, until she found it.

"Sorry, I forgot that I took this ring from the body that night."

She was met with a look of utter confusion. Milos reached over and, with a gloved hand, wrenched the ring from her and placed it in a plastic evidence bag.

"I mean, I took it *back*," Sophie muttered, realising how unbelievable she sounded. "Because it looked just like the ring I lost years ago..."

Milos shook his head and noted something down. "Right, we'll deal with that later."

He sighed self-righteously and buzzed the door unlocked. The wooden door looked more like the entrance to a garden of Grecian earthly delights, which confirmed for Sophie that this dilapidated building must have once been someone's stately country home. The ornate door opened abruptly and in came the coroner.

She glided in, side-eyeing Sophie, and slapped something on the inspector's desk. Sophie flinched in her high-backed wooden chair.

"Want to explain why your DNA is linked to an open case in Australia?"

Sophie was speechless.

"We sampled your DNA on your first questioning, ran some checks, and now we find it's related to a previously unidentified body."

"What?" Sophie asked, feeling as if she was standing in the middle of a highway, traffic bearing down on her. She stood instinctively and peered over, as close as she dared, at the paperwork in front of her.

Milos and the coroner leaned intimidatingly towards her as she slowly shook her head.

"Again, we are asking you, is there anything you would like to add to your previous statement?" Milos barked at her.

Sophie held up her hand for some silence and space while her thoughts raced.

Slowly, painstakingly slowly, something was coming into focus.

"Hang on a second," Sophie began.

They leaned in closer.

"But maybe you're talking about..." Sophie extended a finger towards the papers and traced lines in the air. Something warm and familiar settled over her. She could hear the sounds of cicadas, smell the wattle in the sun.

Sophie picked up the paperwork — scanning to find dates and locations. The inspector grabbed Sophie's wrist and whisked the papers away from her. Sophie felt as if someone was taking away a mass of malformed tissue she had just given birth to.

"But..." Sophie said desperately, wanting that piece of her home warm in her hand once more.

The coroner placed a hand on her hip and sent a hasty text.

"Talk," barked the inspector.

Sophie thought back to the last time she had visited the Narrows all those years ago — before Berlin, before Lisbon, before the whole grand mess of life.

Will had visited her there, then her mother had visited, and they waited out the storm in the cave. Her "coming out" cave. Her long swim in the river. *Disappear here.*

The paradox was that she was here now too, a living body, in the flesh, sweaty hands trying now to still themselves in her lap. It was all beginning to make a sort of alchemical sense to her in her bones, as she grappled with *how* one could forego a version of the self, decades ago, and yet still carry its essence around within the same consciousness that had foregone it, *and* still remember letting go of it. Bodily, it is easier to wrap your head around, because of how the cells regenerate. Her body that day was physically not the same body as the one containing that version of the self she lost. All of her cells had been replaced. All the cells from that body decades ago had died and been replaced, subsumed into the person she was now.

"Is there a reason, that you would care to explain to us, why you failed to inform us that there's an open missing persons case in your family?" Milos cleared his throat expectantly and pulled some more papers out of his file.

"You mean my great-aunt Eliza?" Sophie said her name with reverence.

"Eliza Fowler, yes," the inspector answered with exhaustion rising in his voice. He and the coroner shifted on their feet, exchanging glances.

"Well, she's been missing since the '40s," Sophie continued. "There was a possible sighting of her and Nell in the '60s at a General Store in the Blue Mountains, picking up some supplies, but the family gave up looking for her decades ago. She'll never be found."

"She has now."

Silence filled the room.

"And we can only assume that the second female remains found with her belong to this 'Nell.'"

Noise filled Sophie. A cacophonous mess of questions rattled around her brain. These were words she had been wanting to hear ever since she had heard the family legend as a child. These longed-for words she never thought she'd hear.

She remained silent. Anything she said now would be superfluous — *how, where, who found her?*

What mattered now was that all the stories of Eliza and Nell were no longer just stories: nebulous and porous. They were no longer at the mercy of whoever was the storyteller and their intentions, nor at the mercy of what era the stories were told in. The story now had a body of its own: with weight, flesh, bones, and truth. It was a story with a beginning, middle, and finally an ending.

Or was she getting it backwards? Maybe now that this story had a body, it was only the beginning, and all the twists and turns of the marrow and truth of it were just opening up?

"We have," the inspector continued wearily, "or our Australian counterparts have matched your DNA as a relative of one of these unidentified females in their database. Thanks to that match, one Jane Doe has now been identified as the reported missing person Eliza Fowler."

"But what about the dead body here on Paxos?" Sophie asked.

"All we know now is that the two cases are related."

"How?"

"Because you are the common denominator in both of them," the coroner added.

"Hence, why you are here. Why we are all here."

"Understood?"

"Confused."

"As are we. To say the least."

"We expect your full cooperation."

"But—"

"But? You claim to have found a dead body, which bears some physical resemblance to you. Now DNA tests show you are linked to an old missing persons case, which you failed to mention to us."

"It's in your best interests that you be completely cooperative."

"Am I a suspect?"

"Let's just say you are our main person of interest."

"Should I be worried?"

"Absolutely."

CHAPTER XXVI

Overhead fluorescents flicker on. My eyes are open but I can neither move them, nor my fingers, toes, nor anything else. Complete paralysis again. You and your assistant are back in the room, moving around in your white coats with efficiency, drained of any recognition of me, any memories. You're cleaning up, washing away the last traces of my living body.

I feel again the emptiness of where my organs once warmed me, and the coolness of the slight breeze in the room swirling around the wetness of this empty cavity of mine.

You both remove your gloves and abruptly disappear, chit-chatting brightly to each other like you're at a brunch. I'm left lying there in the bright light alone.

This is a very lonely feeling, this slow draining of myself, of my essence. As I lie here, I wonder if this is how rivers feel when the rain stops coming, when the land is in drought? Slowly, ever so slowly, that moist bed, which had cradled all manner of life, coursing through it season after season, recedes into nothing but a tentacular line ribboning through the land. From a body of water, from a giver of life, to just a line in the land. How lonely.

I can feel the process gradually separating me from my physical body altogether. Soon, I am left to drift alone in the fog of an interstitial place that has begun to flood me.

In this other place, all behaves as if underwater and yet this place consists of neither water nor air, but some other chemical state of matter. All is dimmed with a green-blue glow, and yet there is no light source, no defined edges to the light, no shadows. It is neither warm nor cool, there is no wind, no ambience, no sensations. It just *is*. And I just am. Floating yet formless. My body feels as if it is in this under-place as well as feeling as if it has transmuted into this place itself. I am both floating and the essence I am floating in. Reduced and expanded equally into this disembodied translucence.

Is this the River Styx? Were the ancients right all along about the next place?

All that is "present" here are my own self-critical thoughts: my own shortcomings, regrets, mistakes, all exposed, all out in the open here in the glare of my mind's eye.

There are no sensory stimuli to distract me from myself: no bodily sensations and no worldly pleasures to soften myself from myself. Just the harsh reality of all the things I have done or have failed to do. Every insecurity, every petty revenge, every bizarre fantasy, every time I have done somebody harm. I can't escape it. The formlessness exposes everything...

In the peaks of these maddening spirals where I would've given anything to escape this place and be back in my own body and feel the rain on my skin, I can almost glimpse shadows of the real world again — perhaps the silhouettes of people moving around me in the autopsy room, or maybe feel my own hands against the cool metal table, clenching and unclenching my fingers into fists. Sometimes I can feel the muscles in my legs twitch involuntarily, and once I might have heard the autopsy assistant cry out in surprise.

Then I am flung back into the body-less, formless space again and my mind breaks down all over again in loneliness and hopelessness. Am I being punished? What can I do to make up for this? How can I prove that I will live a life from now on that is worthy of inhabiting a body?

Maybe the formless space is trying to tell me that even lying paralysed on an autopsy table with my organs taken out is better than being unmoored and identity-less in the endless fog. That all my anxieties, fears, spiralling thoughts, pain, regrets — that even all these things that I thought made life *unbearable*, these are at least human, part of life, part of being alive, no matter how painful.

After what seems like weeks of spiralling in this nothing-fog, and then waking up on the autopsy table, and inching towards awareness and learning all these lessons, then falling back again into nothing, one day I wake up again to a bright, overhead light. But this time it is the overhead light the cell warden had switched on to force me into consciousness.

"Fáo," he yells as he passes a tray of food into my cell.

I startle into awakeness, into body-ness. I feel my feet in thin socks on the cold concrete floor, my legs cramped and contorted, my torso wrapped in a musty blanket, shivering but delightfully full again; my arms are tucked in at my sides and my head is arched back against a hard, narrow bed, drool escaping one corner of my mouth.

"Drool!" I croak. "I'm drooling!" I say delightedly to the warden. "That means I'm alive and I have a body again!"

This is too much for him. He slaps shut the little opening in the cell door as quickly as possible and runs off.

***

Some unknown length of time later, Sophie was hauled back to the makeshift interrogation room. This time there was the disturbing sight of a recently-slept-in mattress and sleeping bag on the floor next to them, presumably for

Milos' all-nighters. It looked like a crime scene waiting to happen.

There were no pleasantries this time.

The coroner, her hair pulled back into an even more severe ponytail than usual, cleared her throat.

"We have now determined the time of death of the Jane Doe you found on the beach. You were filming a scene of whatever it is you're making, on a closed set at the time in question — or, in other words, you have an alibi."

Sophie's head was swimming as she gazed up at them. Her knees were twitching up and down and her hands were buzzing with adrenaline. It was impossible to tell from their expressions what the implications of this were for her.

"So, lucky for you," the coroner continued, "that time of death and your solid alibi means that you are now ruled out as a suspect."

Sophie exhaled and let her head rest momentarily on the desk. She raised it up again almost immediately and looked at each of them in turn.

"Oh, thank God," she breathed. "Thank you."

"Well, yeah," Milos muttered and shuffled some papers before closing his folder. "Unfortunately, we have to let you go."

"Oh thank you," she said again, really not understanding anything that was happening except that she could get out of there.

"Stay available in case you're needed for more questioning," Milos commanded, waving her away.

"And the gods know there are a lot of unanswered questions," the coroner muttered darkly, looking skywards.

Sophie jumped into the nearest taxi and sped back towards set, following the golden-lit coastal road that twisted in and out of tiny white-pebbled coves and ancient overhanging trees, and always the turquoise lapping waters, giving way to that expanse of azure that pumped aliveness back through Sophie's entire body.

"I'm no longer a suspect," she whispered to David as she got out of the taxi. He wrapped her up in his scrawny arms. That mouldy couch smell of his couldn't have been more welcome. They walked back to the terrace, arm in arm, and Sophie continued gushing all the details to him. "Whoever she was apparently died while we were filming so they couldn't accuse me of anything anymore."

David nodded enigmatically and handed her a glass of celebratory wine, although it was still morning. They sat on the back terrace again while the crew raced around setting up for some of the final scenes. They could hear splashing in the distance, which probably meant the cast were in the hotel pool, making the most of the downtime before they were needed for more madness. David was the only one who had greeted their director. The rest had averted their eyes and busied themselves, including Aini, who had side-eyed her and gotten on a whispered phone call.

David and Sophie laughed over their glass of wine. Finally, Sophie felt the tension melting and she sighed and put her feet up on the table, letting her legs get some sun. David patted her knee sympathetically.

"You might want to treat yourself to one more glass, honey, soften the blow..."

"Soften the blow of what?"

A couple of the on-set runners came by then, and awkwardly dropped Sophie's luggage at their feet. As Sophie looked at the pile of her belongings, the penny dropped.

"Ohhh," she said, with a nervous giggle. "That's what's happening."

"Yeahhh," David groaned and smiled at her sadly. "They told us last night in what they called a 'Crisis Meeting'..."

Sophie really laughed then. Deep, loud, reverberating relief that echoed out across the terrace and beyond, reaching the burning ears of her cast and crew.

"They think that their horror series director being accused of murder and spending time in jail is a crisis? They could have really milked it... turned it into a great PR story for the next season..."

David laughed now too, relieved that Sophie wasn't going to shoot the messenger.

"Honestly David," she said, her head swimming into more clarity than she had felt since leaving Lisbon, "this couldn't have come at a better time."

Now he grabbed Sophie by the arm. "Really?" he asked, downing the rest of his glass. "Do tell."

"Well," Sophie began, her eyes wandering the distance, out towards the sea, and the cliff edge where she had found the body that night. "For the first time in my life, I finally found a story I want to tell. That story has been begging to be told for decades. And its characters are now begging me to tell the world about them. Loudly."

David put his arm around Sophie and squeezed, as she continued.

"So I'm going home, back to my river, and I'm finally going to tell a story that matters. Something I should have done a long time ago."

PART SIX

THE ANCESTORS

Safeguard;
Yuoli (Yoo.oh.lee)
To protect

Safeguard;
Ngamuru (Ngah.moo.roo)
To guide.

     – Aunty Fran's dictionary of English terms translated into
             the D'harawal language

CHAPTER XXVII

As winter melted into spring, Eliza was spending inordinate amounts of time gazing out to the back lawn from her bedroom window, in the hopes of catching a glimpse of Nell. Perhaps it was the life-affirming tingling feeling that the coming spring was buzzing through her limbs, or plain impatience, but Eliza was growing more reckless and bold.

One spring morning, as she watched Nell traipsing from the scullery to the outhouse, across the back lawn, Eliza noticed that Nell was pointedly refusing to tread upon any of the flannel flowers that were sprouting up in the grass. A patch of sunlight danced across Nell's features as she side-stepped yet another patch of flowers, almost dropping the whole load of crockery to do so.

For Eliza, this was the unmistakable sign from the Heavens she had been waiting for. When the luncheon rush was on and all the servants were busy preparing, Eliza skipped downstairs and plucked one of the tufts of flowers that Nell had been so careful not to ruin. Then she twisted them into a delicate bouquet and whisked them back away upstairs before anyone could catch her at it.

Later that evening, after supper, Eliza placed the flowers, twisted with one of her hair ribbons, outside of the door to Nell's little room.

A week ago, she had noticed Nell's hair growing longer and sweeping into her eyes when she was trying to work, so had offered her the ribbon directly then and there as she passed her in the entrance hall. Nell immediately paused mopping the floor and nodded her head politely, then looked up. Seeing the deep fear in her eyes, Eliza instantly realised her foolishness. Nell taking the ribbon could get her in all kinds of trouble with the Master and with the other servants. So today, after receiving the divine sign she was waiting for, she instead bound the bunch of flowers with her black velvet ribbon and left them softly at Nell's door.

Late that night, when the workday was finally over for Nell, she stumbled over the flowers at her door. She froze. As quick as she could, head darting in all directions to check if anyone had seen, she rushed the bouquet into her room and sat on the bed in the dark with them, hoping to God that no one had seen them. *What was Eliza thinking?*

Once the initial waves of panic had subsided, Nell brought the soft blossoms to her face and breathed in their scent, as subtle and gentle as their pale petals.

In the space that the subtlety of the scent allowed her imagination, she smelled the long-held warm smells of her family. Usually their smells only came back to her in dreams or as sensory phantoms coursing through her body in her darkest moments of solitude. Or sometimes their old, familiar smells would exude unexpectedly from her own skin, like when she would be bent over, grinding the flagstones, or scrubbing dirty sheets, or whatever other exhausting acts would cause her body to break out in a sweat. When she looked down at her own prematurely weathered hands, or in those rare moments when she caught her own reflection as she passed one of the hotel's mirrors, she was certain she must carry physical resemblances to her past in her features, but without many visual memories of them left to compare herself with, it was like looking at pieces of a map with the ink smudged off by rain. Obscured beyond recognition, lost to history.

But their smells and their warmths — she would carry these with her to the day she died. She would carry them, hidden, within the chemistry of her own body; scents and sensations to enjoy the recognition of for herself, and only for herself. No one on earth, or indeed in this hell, could take that away from her.

Tonight, as she nestled her face into the flannel flowers, a warm sensation of a different kind bloomed across her skin, flushing her cheeks. It reminded her that now, not *all* was wrong with her world. An entirely new kind of spring was creeping its way into her.

CHAPTER XXVIII

Nell

There's a patch of scrub, just beyond the outhouses, where no one can see me from the Big House. There in that sorry ring of ghost gums, with the run-off from the outhouses moistening the trees' roots and greening the grass in between them, is my only place of solace. It's there that my fingers transform back into tendrils and my toes turn back into river reeds, longing to find their home within wildness again. Back to how it was in our old Country by the river.

Some nights at the Big House, if the Master's drunk and the Matron's not paying any mind to us staff, I venture further past the ghost gums to the Dahl'wah tree. The tendrils of my fingers reach in the dark to fondle any new seed pods, and ripple through its foliage, straining my ears to hear the ancestral chatter of the old women who must have sat here on days long ago, making string from the trees' bounty. Then my hands traverse curiously across the Dahl'wah's curved trunk, feeling satisfied when the rough bark draws blood across my knuckles. I tell myself that mingling my blood with the sap of the Dahl'wah bonds us forever.

I remember the story of these trees, with their other name, she-oaks, that tells any lost child to sit beneath their boughs and wait until their kin follows the whisperings of their foliage on the wind, and comes to find them. Each time I sit with my bleeding knuckles in my lap, waiting to be found, I try my best not to feel anger that so far, this story has not come true. No one has come for this lost child.

Night after night, year after year, I have listened to the she-elders' whispers for as long as I dared to, while I gave in to the moist, giving green of the moss underneath my feet. It's the only place in this dead end, edge-of-the-desert place that I've ever seen moss survive. Slowly, I allow the tenderness of it to move up my ankles, sending a cool rush up my calves and thighs and finally in between my thighs, which grows as soft and liquid as the green beneath me. It's as if my feet drink in its generous liquid and transport it upwards through my veins, then emanate the liquid out again through the porousness of my body.

Surrendering my feet to the moss, I'm transported back to the river of my kin. Where moss and ferns and slugs and all kinds of watery things were home. And for a few short moments like this, it feels like it's my only safe place left in the world.

Now, for the first time since I lost my river and my kin, I've felt a kind of closeness, a moistness, even a feeling verging on a kind of *safety* with someone in this desert-place. I feel this, all the while knowing she is the *least safe* choice I could possibly have made. The Boss's daughter. A white girl.

My head has known all along that these whisperings I hear in my place of solace are really only the wind through the foliage of the she-oaks, and that the moss beneath my feet only exists because of the run-off from the outhouses. And despite what I feel, I know that there is no such place as a safe place for me, anywhere or with anyone.

Most definitely not in the company of the white girl called Eliza.

And yet I want to be near her every moment.

***

Since I've been feeling like I've got something to lose, I've been living on a knife edge yet again, here at the Royal Hotel. It has always felt like the end of the world to me, especially after they announced to me one day that I was the only survivor left of my family. Some riots had broken out at the Mission, and they said my family were all lost to the violence. But since I've dared to even articulate her name, I feel like I've got a reason to fear death again. The fear opened me up again, to that feeling of loss that defined much of my seventeen years so far. All at once, all the losses drowned me again.

They must have rounded us up for the Mission when I was only about six or seven. That means I only spent the first few years of my life living on Country by the river in Mulgoa, and I don't remember much of our river life, not in any clarity. But deep, colourful feelings, yes. Always. There were still quite a few of us in the Mulgoa Valley then, which was traditionally the meeting place with the neighbouring, much bigger clan, the Dharug. Being near the Yandhai River, or the Nepean, as the whites called it, of course it was prime territory for the whites' farming. Beautiful water source right there — something they could use to irrigate all those fruit trees and potatoes and give their cattle to drink. My grandmother told me there were so many battles back in the early days. Massacres even. Our school books spoke of the valley becoming farmland swiftly and quietly: the whites simply "settled" the land — as if it was an unruly child that just needed a good bit of discipline. But my grandmother said we fought back, good and long, and for some of the time after the invasion, we even lived in the valley while they kept on with their farming ways. whatever scant memories I still carry in my body, and whatever I still carry of my grandmother's tellings of those times, they have all since been named by the Mission as violent, primitive, dirty and against "God."

Us kids, my brothers and sisters, were all pretty dark skinned, so we didn't get shipped off and adopted into white life, like some of the others from Mulgoa. Some time around twelve or thirteen, just before we girls got old enough to get pregnant, they shifted us over to the Brewarrina Aboriginal Station Dormitory, which was just a way for them to force us to learn how to sew, cook, and do any of the other domestic work the rich white girls didn't want to do. It was way out west, over the mountains, on the edge of the outback. Country unrecognisable from our river home. Fast forward a few years and a good proportion of the friends I made there ended up disappearing when their pregnancies started to show.

When I arrived at the Station Dormitory, the "Boss," as we had to call the manager, was the most frightening human being I had ever encountered. He acted like the Lord of the Manor over our Dormitory as well as the neighbouring Brewarrina Mission — apparently it was the oldest Mission in the country, so he thought he was pretty much God's gift to us all. He would barge into families' houses unannounced, take peoples' war pensions and wages, and would beat us — men, women, even kids — with his baton. We thought the worst was over when he got sacked and even charged for some of what he did to us. But then in '36 we got Dalley, who managed the place for the next four years. He wasn't the violent type, so at first we thought we could rest easy. But it wasn't long before he and his lowlife son would come over to our dorms at night. The dorms were only lockable from the outside and only those two bastards and the priest had the key. That was maybe worse than the beatings. Yeah, it was definitely worse.

The Boss of the Station and his wife, the Matron, worked us so hard and so long that we had nothing left of ourselves at the end of the day to dream, to remember, to think, to plan. They exhausted us to nothing. At the end of those hardest, longest days, I could barely picture my parents, my siblings, or my grandparents anymore.

There was one story I really held onto, though, because my grandmother told it over and over in those early days. There was so much power in it, especially now that I know what I know. It's the story of the totem of our Mull'goh mob.

How the Black Swans Came to Be

(Or, at least, the story as I can best remember it)

Long, long ago, when our lands were very, very cold and covered by snow almost every day, our Mull'goh clan lived in the north and to the west of the Yandel'ora. The Yandel'ora was known, as far back as anyone could remember, as the place of Peace between Peoples: where clans from all over would meet without their weapons to settle disputes.

Our clan was known for the great beauty of our long, slender necks, and we would adorn our necks proudly with all kinds of decorations to show off to the other clans. But there came a time when the Bubuk (Owl) clan came to visit, and, instead of admiring our beautiful necks, they commented on how many children in our clan had been born with white skin. So many, in fact, that they became impossible to hide from visiting tribes. The Bubuk remarked that these white-skinned children resembled the people of the Goolay-yari (Pelican) clan who had been banished from walking on these lands due to a terrible crime committed by their Pelican ancestor.

This comparison brought shame to our people, and, after days of arguing, the men of our clan decided to kill all of these white-skinned children. Their mothers and grandmothers warned the children to flee but the men caught up with them and began to hunt them down, one by one.

The children that did manage to escape eventually fell down with exhaustion in the swamps. The kindly Wigan (Raven) clan saw what had happened and, unbeknownst to the men, swooped down to cover the white-skinned children with their black feathered cloaks. The men returned home to tell the rest of the clan that the children had all been killed in the swamplands.

Disguised in their black cloaks, the survivors escaped in two directions: west over the mountains, and north through dense, thorny forests. The black feathered cloaks of the ones who made their way west over the mountains sealed into the skin of the children and they became the Wawaran clan, the People of the Crow. The cloaks of the ones who went north became torn on the thorny plants of the forest, allowing the white skin to show through. These children became the Diri'wun, the People of the Magpie.

The Spirit Woman was angered by how the Mull'goh had driven their children into the swamps to die and made it so that they would only be able to make camp on water, never on the land.

And that's how our people, the Mull'goh Black Swan People, came to remain by the river, and by the swamps, forever.

***

I remember asking my grandmother about only making camp in water, never on land. I asked her to tell me more about how we had come to make the river, the Yandhai, our home. There was so much love in her words, as much love, or even more, than I ever heard when she spoke of my mother, or us kids. The only time that love drained from her voice was when she warned us kids, in no uncertain terms, about staying away from the river holes with ancient spirits locked inside of them, or the ones with serpents hiding in them. She instilled the "fear of God" in us (as those Mission people would say), when she told us the stories of the giant eel-being, Gurangatch, who created these treacherous holes. She drew us a map of the river and made us memorise where each and every one of these holes were, especially the deepest one in the entire Yandhai, which was the hiding place of Gulguer, who had a nasty habit of dragging people in, especially teenage girls, and making them disappear forever.

One day before class, in the midst of the worst of times at the Mission when Dalley and his son were making their night visits every single night, I remember standing by the window in the Mission school room, staring out the window to the vast desert, reaching all the way to the horizon. Such an alien landscape to us river people. Next to me was a globe, which stood dusty and unexplained (since all our lessons were religious or domestic). I remember putting my finger on one side of the globe where I thought Mulgoa Country must be, east of the desert, and, keeping one finger in place, I spun the globe all the way around to find the exact opposite side of the world. The city of Berlin, Germany. In those days, even I knew from our shoddy education that this place was all bombed out and in ruins from the War. But I prayed to that trickster eel, Gulguer, with all my childish might, to take me into his underwater lair and disappear me from this place — suck me all the way through to the other side of the world, to Berlin. Even if it was a smoking ruin, it had to be better than the Mission. All I had to do was get back to my river, remember my grandmother's map, and find Gulguer's lair. I was sure that all my praying would reach him there in my Country and he would grant me my biggest wish.

Please, Gulguer, please… make me disappear to Berlin.

But now, for the last reason I would ever have imagined, I finally have cause to stay here in Brewarrina.

CHAPTER XXIX

Eliza

The first time I felt the slide of the priest's fingertip making the sign of the cross on my forehead, tilted heavenwards, I was surprised by its coolness. The ash he placed there felt more like the satisfyingly viscous icing of a cake, fresh from the icebox.

My immediate and obvious association with ash is fire, and along with that association comes hell and all the flames of damnation. Well, that and the annual bushfires out on the Plains.

So this sensation of cake and coolness was at odds with all the fiery sinfulness I was expecting to feel burned into my skin. The coolness of the ash soothed me with the reassurance that maybe I'm not so sinful after all. Maybe all the minutiae of my miniature life can be forgiven? Wasn't it just the worst of the worst who had their skin burned when it was marked by the sign of the cross? Up until that Ash Wednesday, I had thought that I counted among them, those worst of the worst doomed sinners, as Father McGee described them.

I thought back over everything that I'd said and done that Father would consider fire-worthy — all those things I've carried around my shoulders like a corpse dragged from a swamp. And that dead weight grew infinitely heavier after the "unnaturalness" of my feelings welled up so strongly in my chest I could no longer contain them.

I mean, I've been deliberating long enough about all things sinful. There's obviously no other place I could turn to get these things off my chest. Under no circumstances would I ever dream of bringing these thoughts to the priest himself in confession, and of course no one on the property I would think of confiding in; except her.

So all I have are these outpourings to bear the weight of all that is objectionable about me. All the things that make me the monster I am.

I suspect this line of thinking might run in the family — from my mother's side, of course. The guilt of being monstrous.

My brothers and sisters and I learned that wine is the only thing able to bear the weight of my mother's assumed monstrosity, as it's only when she has an open bottle in front of her that she can speak of herself or her past with any lightness.

She would only dare speak of her jaunts in Sydney, for example, when a bottle was near her (and our father was not). It was a sore topic for our father since he, the Big Man in Brewarrina, was very much a small fish in Sydney, since he had never made it that far east. Only Mum had, which gave her a cultural edge above his that he would never admit to. So she painted the bright lights for us children in the darkened sitting room, in the hopes that her stories might one day inspire at least one of us to pack a suitcase for the city and continue living out what was cut short for her.

Her favourite story to tell was the late night in Kings Cross, when she and her plaid-frocked secretary girlfriends encountered the infamous Witch of Kings Cross, the occult artist Rosaleen Norton. It was around the time Norton was gallivanting around the late-night cocktail bars with a well-respected Symphony Orchestra conductor ("or someone of that ilk, someone posh," as Mum put it), and Rosaleen took a liking to the girls and decided they'd be good for a drink or two. They obliged, paying her tab all night while she predicted their futures and offered to paint them one day. The future she saw for my mother was that she would end up "somewhere sacred, somewhere red hot" but with a tyrant who would make her disappear into dust. At the time, Mum said she put it down to witchy nonsense designed to keep her around for more drinks, but the prediction always gave us hot chills of sinfulness whenever she managed to make it to the end of the tale without nodding off into the empty wine bottle.

Why is it that the very things that we — us kids, my mother, and her mother before her, and on and on as far back as you want to go — are told are the most dreadfully sinful are the very things that make us pulsate all over with life? They're the only things in this dead-end hotel that make my blood keep flowing... These things make me want to see beyond the desert horizon, even to finally see the ocean... they make my fingertips want to tell stories with everything I touch, and they make the spring blooms so intoxicatingly magnetising that it spreads my smile through my entire body. The body electric.

To put it plainly, my most dreadfully sinful thoughts are thoughts of Nell. It's always been her. It's only that now I'm finally grown enough to admit she's the source of it all. All of these bubbling, gurgling, wet, overflowing feelings — she's the wellspring of the whole mess.

It's her power in the way she glides through all the tasks she's forced to do, day in, day out. The way she moves through it all, her muscular form radiating itself beyond this hotel hellhole to the heavenly life she *should* be living. She moves herself like she is commanding all the oceans of the world.

There have been sweltering midsummer days when the head maid allows the staff to tuck their skirts into their aprons and roll down their stockings, and unbutton their blouses a little when they're working out in the yard. I think I fainted at my first glimpse of her lean, elegant calves and ankles as she charged through the grass at sunset. It was enough to keep me dreaming sweetly for weeks.

On one of those suffocating afternoons, I saw her sneaking a peach from one of the trees in the orchard. The sky was burning amber and gleamed from all of her curves. The sheer pleasure in her waiting lips, in her open mouth, in the slow descent of the juice down her chin, sliding down her neck, then pooling in that little recess between her collarbones. If I had been that juice I would have dripped as absolutely slowly as possible, never wanting to leave her skin, unless she licked me off with her pink tongue.

I was watching her from behind one of the sheets on the washing line, thinking I could satisfy my voyeurism without any chance of discovery. I didn't realise though at first that I was silhouetted by the sunset. I must have startled a little at the moment of realisation as she stopped devouring the peach momentarily to look up in my direction. She smiled, quick as lightning, and for that tiny instant I floated on the merging of her eyes with mine. Then, just as quickly, fear clouded her features and she disappeared into the trees, dropping the peach in the grass as she ran. I blushed in the glow of the sun, and my entire body flushed hot and sweaty.

I turned on my heel and hurried noiselessly back to the house with my tail between my legs, muscles and feelings tripping over each other. I skittered upstairs, snuck into my bedroom and locked the door, panting heavily.

I could still smell her heady peach juices as I lay on my bed and promised myself feverishly never to even think of this in the presence of Father. Only God will ever know.

But now after this Ash Wednesday realisation, that my forehead wasn't burned to a sinful crisp by the sign of the cross, rather, it was pleasantly cool, maybe I'm not so bad after all?

She has riven my entire landscape and made the whole world verdant again.

CHAPTER XXX

Eliza was standing up against one of the veranda beams of Winbourne one spring morning; the sun so golden and blinding that her vision was blushed with the blood behind her eyes.

She stood squinting into the light, long auburn plaits, all of six years old, and let her being drink in that morning goldenness. A silhouette crossed her field of vision, and just for one breath of a moment, the figure shadowed her from the sun. She un-squinted her eyes in that very instant, and allowed her eyes to take in the tiny person before her.

Dark, curly, wiry, and tensed like a sugar glider, the diminutive Nell allowed her mind's eye to be burned by Eliza, leaning up against the verandah beam, just as Eliza allowed her mind's eye to be burned by her. All the chaos of the world quietened, and a single word passed between them — aloud or not, neither could be sure — *friend*.

Winbourne was the grand colonial property established in the verdant countryside (one of the first places "land grants" were given to white settlers to cultivate the land into a food basket for the colony) that had been in Eliza's family for generations. It was built upon a picturesque bend in the Nepean River and, as fate would have it, also near a Mission for Indigenous children stolen from local clans of the Mull'goh and Dharug, along with "half-castes" and some of their mothers.

Eliza's family were there in Winbourne ostensibly for a short respite from the "uncultured" west, where the children could be around other white children of their "own standing" (of course all Eliza and the other kids cared about was the river and spending as much time as possible in its cool, liberating water), while Eliza's mother could busy herself enquiring next-door about appropriate domestic help for the family's Royal Hotel. She and the wardens of the Mission were well aware that "appropriate" meant well-trained, obedient and free Indigenous labour, and had meant that since the first Mission was established in the 1860s.

Nell, at eleven years old, was the best contender, but was not yet domestically trained, so it was decided she would be transferred to the Brewarrina Mission, with its associated Aboriginal Station Dormitory for girls. There, she would be directly streamlined from her reading, writing, and arithmetic classes in Mulgoa, into learning only the skills that could be used as a domestic maid in Brewarrina, and she would be local, no longer living directly with any family members that could be a distraction. When she was ready, a few years later, Eliza's mother would take her into her employ.

Once Nell had been stolen from her family and clan and isolated in the girls' dormitory, she was soon informed, matter-of-factly, that all her family members had been killed in inter-tribal skirmishes at the Mission. That level of isolation caused a dependency that left Nell with no reason to escape the property she was now employed on, other than very occasional errands in town when the head housekeeper had a rare day off, or, even more seldom, a soda or milkshake in a segregated section of the milkbar in town with a few of the other dormitory girls she kept in touch with, who were placed in local farmers' homesteads or with one of the wealthy settlers that still existed in the area in those booming river trade days. Those were the days before water-hungry cotton farming and rampant climate change, when the ancient Barwon River (*barwum* or *bawon*, the "great, wide, awful river of muddy water") still flowed all the way from their dusty little town into the Darling River, making trade and transportation of all the produce and bounty out west towards Sydney a very profitable thing indeed — precisely why Brewarrina became a place of note on the white fellas' maps, not, mind you, because of the stone fish traps situated there in the river, which were finally carbon dated to be probably the oldest human-made structures on earth...

The property that the Royal Hotel was situated on was vast: vast on the scale that it was larger than the size of most of the entire new suburbs of Sydney that were home to thousands, so not leaving the property so often shouldn't have felt like being caged, except that it did, for every soul there aside from the Master, Eliza's father. There, surveying his fields and the bush beyond, standing pensively with a clenched jaw like in one of the epic Westerns that were just beginning to reach Australian screens, the Master felt like a pioneer in the Wild West.

There on the banks of the wild Barwon River, on the eastern edge of the outback, the Master had raised his three-storey, wide-veranda "Royal Hotel": the most common name for a hotel in Australia, which said a lot about the Master's lack of both imagination and business prowess. In spite of the Master's shortcomings, which are far too many to mention, the Royal Hotel was doing a roaring trade. The credit, largely, ought to go to the reliable ebb and flow of the river itself, which brought all manner of trade, travellers, and produce to and from the big smoke, along with providing rich alluvial soil along the length of its banks. In almost every respect, the hotel's fortunes, and indeed the whole family's, relied upon the river.

It all began with their first glance in the morning light at Winbourne, and trickled along as the years passed, as

Nell and Eliza exchanged fleeting glances at the Royal Hotel — passing on the stairs, passing in the hallways, rushing out to church, gathering grass for the horses, gathering wood for the fireplace, watching the Queen's Birthday fireworks... Each exchange, drip by drip, gave life to the unspoken language between them.

But it was the first time that their hands met, for longer than could be called accidental, or inconsequential, that provided, in an instant, a translation of all the indecipherabilities they had both endured within all those glances before, since they were six years old.

**

It was a crisp evening, the winter's chill still in the air, so there was no climatic reason for Nell's hands to be so slippery. With seven bowls already stacked upon her forearm, only the slightest tremor of her hand, with the slightest additional lubrication to her palm, was enough to send the bowls on a slow, deadly avalanche down her arm, over her wrist, and beginning down her open, moist palm.

It was this moment that Eliza grabbed Nell's hand instinctively to stop the descent. In the same instant, their eyes met, and this time they held each other's gaze so tightly — not letting go after one moment, then two, then three.

The rest of the family around the dinner table were silenced; their attention turned burningly towards this meeting of hands and eyes. All held their breath in anticipation of the inevitable, almighty crash of eight plates to the floor, but instead came the clasping of two hands together, one a servant, one the Master's daughter. The only sound was a small sigh that escaped one, or both, of their mouths.

Their skin was bonded together long enough for the translation of their unspoken language to be transmitted into both of their heads:

We were right
We're not crazy
Yes I feel this too
No I can't name it
But it's here
It's real
And we both feel it at the same time.

Just as soon as the precision and clarity of those words had rung out in their heads, Nell grabbed the plates with both hands and Eliza folded her hand politely back into her lap. With a sharp breath, Nell continued off into the kitchen as Eliza stood slowly and exited the room mutely, leaving her chair untucked and letting her napkin fall softly to the floor. She trod softly and with purpose upstairs to her bedroom, unblinking eyes fixed ahead.

Even though they were now in separate parts of the house, the connection had been opened, and the invisible thread had been woven that tethered them to each other, no matter how far away from one another they became. There was now a tangibility to it, that only grew more so as Nell stood scrubbing dishes in the kitchen, moving to a lilting melody playing out in her stomach and spreading up in little jitters to her smiling mouth. Eliza sat at her desk and gazed far out the window to the Western Plains beyond. All the ache and the heaviness that had taxed her limbs for so long was lifting from her body, until she found herself raising her arms above her head and twirling her fingers in time to some unknown tune. She felt, on her fingertips, as if she were dancing them through thick, warm, golden honey.

CHAPTER XXXI

The sound of the Master's dining room chair scraping across the floorboards was the servants' nightly signal that the meal was over and it was time to enter and clear the plates.

One night, by the middle of that spring, though, the Master scraped the chair back, and they all cleared the plates, as usual, but this time, the Master lingered. He watched the servants' every move as they worked away, as they made countless trips back and forth to the kitchen, with dinner plates, cutlery, bread baskets, vases full of flowers, candles, and so forth. This night, the Master stood with his chair tucked underneath the table, with one hairy, ruddy hand laid upon the curved wooden top of the chair. The hand was idle, expectant. The hand that had dealt out so much punishment was threatening, menacing even, just sitting there idle. *Who should I strike next?* it seemed to ask.

Nell and all the other servants were keeping a wide berth of him, spying that waiting hand and remembering all the things it was capable of.

As Nell and the others made their last trip to the kitchen, carrying the white tablecloth, Nell saw his index finger twitch then point unmistakably in her direction. She stopped immediately and bowed her head to him, waiting for his orders. The others carried on with their clearing and were soon in the kitchen, leaving her alone in the dining room with him.

She dared now to look in his direction, and, slowly, up to his features, starkly shadowed in the candlelight. She found herself already shaking in anticipation of what his needs might be. One more twitch of that index finger and he pointed to the closed door behind him — the door to his personal study.

Nell had never entered that room — only the head housekeeper was allowed in there to tidy up and clean — and Nell knew nothing of what he could possibly spend his time doing in there. He was certainly no scholar. He could barely string an intelligible sentence together when he gave orders. He was the son of a former British convict, turned "free settler," who was given land and the opportunity to farm it and make something of it. When he inherited his father's cattle station in Brewarrina, the Master saw the business opportunity of providing reasonably priced accommodation and plenty of cheap booze to all the entrepreneurs, gold seekers, travellers, and businessmen passing through the town — and could turn a hearty profit by making use of the free labour of the Indigenous youth he was also "granted." Just another right-time-right-place mediocre white man with all the confidence and cruelty of a Titan.

Nell could barely remember her other life, but that didn't mean she learned from example from her current one. She had always known that if she was ever to escape her situation and the authority of the Master, she would find a world full of other human beings that she knew instinctively must exist: kind ones, gentle ones, one that had no lust for power and no mind for psychological warfare.

Even now, alone with the Master and his stink of wine and the day's sweat, she did not assume the worst yet. She only had in mind that he must trust her enough now to clean his Study. She must have earned that trust, finally, after this long year here in his hotel.

So she obediently walked towards the Study door, turned the ornate knob, and walked briskly in, dust cloth in one hand and kerosene lamp in the other.

The Master closed the door behind them.

CHAPTER XXXII

The Barwon River, which flowed through the eastern edge of the property, was the mutual, immediate thought that came to Nell and Eliza as they tore across the paddocks that night, with the weight of abject horror in their blood.

The moon and stars were thickly clouded, so the only light they had as they ran were the distant headlights of the Master's car. This was a good sign as it meant that he hadn't seen them take off east through the paddocks. He must have assumed they had headed west down the drive and towards the road into town, and he had already started his car to take off after them.

Until he drove off, they could find their way across the dry, rocky ground by the meagre light of his headlights, keeping as low to the ground as they could. Nell was still in her work clothes — her restrictive, starched pinafore and apron keeping her from powering ahead like she was capable of. Eliza had already changed for bed before their escape, so she was barefoot and dressed in a long cotton nightdress, which was snagging and tearing on the dying corn stalks and thistles as they ran. Spending as much of her childhood summers running around barefoot as possible, the soles of her feet were leathered, and her leg muscles were well toned — as if she had been training her whole life for this moment of flight.

"We just have to make it to the treeline," Eliza panted, catching Nell's hand, "then we'll have some cover and they won't be able to see us."

"Yes," Nell panted back, looking over her shoulder to Eliza, her sweaty features caught in the distant headlights, "and it looks like he's going in the wrong direction anyway. Idiot."

They continued running, stumbling, aching, through the paddocks, until the headlights were out of sight completely, and they had to feel their way blindly in the dark.

When it dawned on them that Eliza's father really had driven off in the wrong direction and that no one else was after them, they slowed their pace to a skittish walk. They still hadn't let go of each other's hands.

Hours passed like this, until they finally made it to the cover of the treeline. This first line of introduced variegated pines along the fence eventually gave way to the natural scrubby bushland of grey gums, which continued down a slight decline, until the scrub became a little more nourished, and then opened up gradually like a curtain to the theatre of the river beyond, and all it signified.

It was almost dawn by the time they made it to the final little clearing that led directly to the teeming banks of the river. It was there that the whole sky opened up into the dawn chorus of cockatoos, kookaburras, whipbirds, and bellbirds, all singing their praises to the promise of morning. Eliza had heard this dawn chorus almost every day of her sixteen years, living out here in the bush, and she had often found herself wondering, *what on earth about the day ahead could possibly be so wondrous to inspire such song?* And it was only on this morning, here with Nell, that she heard the dawn chorus and finally understood it; finally feeling full of life and full of hope.

The lag and lull of the river water wallowed by, thick with reeds, happy fish, and wild lilies. Some early-rising frogs paddled tentatively, opening their mouths to the river's flow as if yawning their way out of bed. The spring wildflowers were raging here. Riots of pink gum blossoms, lewd as tutus, tufts of yellow wattle, burning with sweet fragrance, and of course those bunches of gentle flannel flowers, shyly nodding at the water's edge.

These sounds and smells of life, of things thriving despite the monstrosity of last night, soothed the both of them as they simply stood, quietened by so many things, both inside and out. The sight of the flannel flowers especially swarmed both of their insides with butterflies. In their barren home where words and contact were completely forbidden between them, flannel flowers had been their only connective tissue.

The sight of the flowers now by the river, and the sight of Nell standing here right beside her in the dawn light, with nothing and no one to stop her, moved Eliza to take Nell's burning cheek in her palm and press her lips to Nell's. It felt like the most natural and sacred thing she had ever done.

With their feet on the warming earth, the river flowing widely by, the two stood and drank each other in: lips, hands, necks, tongues, fingertips, rippling over and through each other. Eliza felt her body becoming alive for the first time, coursing through with a vitality of pure sensation that had been missing for her entire teenage existence.

When she closed her eyes she could see a sky full of shooting stars and when she opened them she could feel the stars exploding in her chest.

But after a few glorious moments, Nell flinched from Eliza's touch, and cast her eyes down to the mud. Her whole body began trembling, sending shock waves out along the river's surface.

Eliza searched Nell's features for an explanation, desperately wanting Nell to share the elation that was rushing through her. But Nell's face and her entire body had shadowed and numbed, and her gaze had travelled to somewhere far away that Eliza did not recognise. All she could do was hold Nell to her chest.

As they stood there at the river's edge, Nell's trembling turned to shaking, until a shuddering, silent weeping overcame her, reverberating out from the deepest, loneliest place within her.

***

There was so much the river could teach them as they followed its flow. There was so much learning to be felt in its slowness, in its reflectiveness, in its spirals and eddies and its reedy mysteries. There was so much it could say to them about the slippery eagerness of their skin, and about the luminosity of the way they looked at each other as the moon rose.

The river was even older even than the first tribes that drank from it and washed their children in it. Its history was even deeper even than the mythologies of the first people who stood awestruck on its banks as the waterbirds circled it, calling to their lovers, to their young. The river had withstood it all, from the firestorms that ravaged its forests, to the droughts that almost vanquished it.

The escapees were quietened by the feeling of all of this history and knowingness in the water — but they allowed themselves to be buoyed by it, rather than weighted down. They let its wisdom wash over them, every dusk, as they had finished their day's gruelling march eastbound, for the coast, and cooled themselves in the water. They splashed and spun around each other, exploring this new feeling of weightlessness that life had never afforded them before.

Eliza had at least had a childhood, although it was a highly controlled one on the hotel property, but Nell had never even understood the concept of childhood once on the Mission. Life was an endless stream of workdays, and the vitality she was feeling right now, even with all this gruelling walking, was something formerly resigned to her imagination.

After walking seven days like this, following the serpentine teachings of the river, the two were finally able to start speaking more openly to each other — at least more than just asking and responding to the immediate needs of the day like "are these little red berries edible, do you think?" or "do you know how to trap fish?"

What they also learned was that they could unburden each other by throwing, one by one, the hard stones of their past stories off of their chests and into the river's forgiving flow. It happened very slowly at first, with Eliza throwing the topic of "mothers" out into the air, and Nell helping her land it through letting her realise she had gotten to this point in life and had survived without a mother at all, and that Eliza would be strong enough too. The stones then came flying off of their chests with each passing day as they talked, in turn, about both never having gone to a real school, both never really knowing the world outside of the hotel, to Nell having no idea who or where her real family were, or if they were indeed all dead, and finally to the topic of "fathers" — Eliza's father and Nell's "Master" — the ultimate reason for their escape out here in the first place.

One night, after several weeks had passed, they both found an especially slippery stone that was burdening both of their chests, causing them both to choke up even at the mention of the word, precisely because it was a word that was so seldom said or spoken of in either of their lives. They hesitated and then stopped, as the sun was dripping orange through the trees and the cicadas were fading. The sound of the river's flow filled the space around and between them, drawing them closer with currents of warm air.

CHAPTER XXXIII

The forest sang.

Rain had thrust itself upon the thirsty earth for the first time in long enough that the frogs and the cicadas had gone dormant. Now, as the ferns were unfurling back into life, the frogs and cicadas were rising up with them.

Some lines from Deuteronomy rattled around Eliza's skull, dull echoes of Bible study. Wasn't a swarm of frogs, especially the kind that defied death, one of the signs of the coming Apocalypse?

Eliza's feet were still bare, all this time, since their escape from the desert. Nell always said she was too thin-skinned, so this was one way to prove otherwise. This morning, though, was testing her resolve.

At first light, letting her toughed feet sink into the forest floor as she stepped off the splintered veranda of their squatted cottage, she had twirled her best Ginger Rogers numbers in the twigs and leaves, her stained apron spinning out, enjoying this new freedom from the dilapidated kitchen. The sight of the flowers springing up around the cottage gave her a burst of much-needed hope. Spring was coming again, *their season*, meaning better days ahead, more roos and rabbits around to help nourish them.

She went for her usual morning pilgrimage down to the river's edge to draw water for the day. She'd taken her time this morning, relishing the warmer air creeping beneath the starched tunic, and venturing to dip her toes in the river. Not so bad.

By the time she was headed back, carrying a metal bucket heavy with river water in each hand, the forest floor was crawling before her eyes. She dropped the pails with a shriek, then another, much louder wail as the pails came down heavy on the little bodies of the frogs as they were waking up. The final blasphemous roar she uttered came when her startled feet squashed more of the frogs, and then more still as she attempted to dance around them. The slime-flesh squirted obscenely between her toes.

"This is NOT a good omen!" she screamed as she darted around the furiously hopping frogs on the track back to their squatted cottage, buckets abandoned where she'd dropped them.

She was met halfway by a panicked Nell, hair sleep-tousled and only dressed in her shirt. No pants at all to speak of.

"What the devil has happened?" Nell asked, out of breath and reaching for Eliza, crushing her protectively against her chest. "Are you alright?" She pushed her back at arm's length to take a better look at her, eyes travelling all the way down to her frog-encrusted toes. Then she burst into ripples of laughter.

The kind of laughter that the struggles of the long winter in the mountains had robbed them of. The kind of laughter that was unheard of in the past.

***

There must have been a bushfire raging in the mountains overnight, possibly even as far away as the Western Plains.

The smoke that lingered there in the gorge, heady with blackened eucalyptus blossoms, wild grasses and sticky, volatile gum sap, created a blanket around them that seemed to know that what was happening there was secret. As if it wanted to conceal the runaways. The smoke shrouded them, as did the sheaths of paperbark they had set up as a meagre shelter and that they used as blankets in the evening, arranged around the saplings rising up from the pungent tree litter, which had sprouted up from the last time a fire raged in these parts.

They had finally found the perfect spot to rest their aching, sunburned legs. After venturing from the squatted cottage and making it over the Blue Mountains by the end of that spring, they finally settled by the gentle banks of the great Nepean River, or the Yandhai, as it was called in kinder times. So tired had they grown from walking that they had resolved to steal the next little fishing boat or even dinghy that they could, and let the river's current ease them onwards.

But here, now, they found a more urgent need to fulfil. The relief of finally finding the cool, moist bends of the river, after the endless heat of the vast plains, then the bone-biting cold of the mountains, had taken them over, made their bodies feel again that ease is possible and that abundance might be just around the next bend. The relief coursed through their bodies, beginning in their sweaty chests, bared by unbuttoning their calico blouses, then streaming down to their stomachs as they gulped down handful after handful of river water, then moving down as they dried their hands on their torn and filthy skirts, then found those hands making their way up and underneath each other's petticoats.

They gave in to it and fell back together into the beds of fallen gum leaves, hoping to hell no snakes were sleeping there, laughing as they wrenched off their blouses and finally got themselves free of their skirts. Their sweaty thighs now entangled, their lips all over each other, Nell suddenly cried out:

"Let it be decreed that I shall never wear a skirt or a goddamned petticoat ever again!"

"Hear hear! The world needs to see those perfect pins of yours!" agreed Eliza and covered Nell's calves and then her thighs in a frenzy of kisses.

She straddled Nell and swept up a bundle of the gum leaves into her freckled arms, then showered her with them like a bride in a bushland wedding.

"We will be naked like the day we were born from here on in."

"Until wintertime," Nell laughed, holding up a finger, feigning a matronly sternness.

"Oh, yes," Eliza laughed, "until bloody wintertime."

Eliza suddenly sat more upright, still straddling Nell's body. She squinted thoughtfully up to the canopy of eucalypts, and the sheltering Ancestral Tree, silhouetted against the blue sky. Then she looked slowly around the little shady clearing they had found, with the river lolling by.

"Do you think we'll make it to Sydney by winter?"

Nell's wide smile faded momentarily.

For her, Sydney was only a notion that existed through Eliza's words, and even those words were hanging by the thread of her imagination. Eliza had never set eyes on Sydney, had only known it from her mother's hushed regaling of it.

"I'm not sure about Sydney," Nell said quietly, unable to make eye contact. "We definitely don't want to be stuck in the mountains over winter, but Sydney isn't what's calling to me. I'm not a Sydney girl, you're not a Sydney girl..."

Eliza started shivering a little more and searched Nell's face, which had suddenly taken on a faraway look. "I mean, if not the city, where else would we find refuge, two women like us, living, well, *like us*...?"

Nell sat up from her bed of leaves to kiss Eliza, gripping her head vigorously with both hands.

"What if they lied? What if my clan, or some of them, are still alive? Shouldn't we at least try to find out? I used to have a home, I used to have people... and we're so close by..."

Eliza felt all this new information directly in her body. She was hit all at once in the guts with the guilt of her realisation of how little she knew of Nell's history — just the basics, that Nell was an orphan from the Mission, and that her family had taken her in at the hotel. But Eliza had never believed a word of what her father said on any other matters, so why should she believe what he told about Nell? And, as much as she was ashamed to admit it, she had created her own narrative around the patchwork of information she had about Nell's story. So caught up was she, and swept away by their whirlwind elopement and their "honeymoon" out here on the run, she had barely given a thought to even ask Nell what she remembered, where she had come from, and her story in her own words. Mulgoa was all she knew. The place Nell's clan called home; the very same place that her own relatives had built a stately homestead on and taken land to farm and grow prosperous from, where her parents would take her for holiday jaunts.

There was so much more to ask.

Eliza realised for the first time how much her love was limited ignorance, not least ignorance of how very dangerous this love was for Nell; dangerous to her very existence. No amount of listening would alleviate that danger, but acknowledging it could be one step towards loving Nell in her entirety, instead of just the exciting ideas of her that Eliza had been holding so tightly onto.

Since their escape, it had been all about daily survival, and if Nell was honest, she was often struck by the difficult thought that she would be far safer out here on her own, especially if she was caught. A runaway Black servant on her own would be subject to one level of punishment, but a runaway Black servant in tow with the daughter of wealthy white landowners? The punishment was sickening even to think about. She had wondered many times, as they trod through the bush along the riverbank, if Eliza understood how different were the risks they'd taken. Had she realised yet that, were they to be caught, Eliza would simply be seen as an innocent white girl swept up in the whole affair and be whisked back to the safety of the family home?

After a long silence, all Eliza could muster for now was, "You're right."

Nell closed her eyes and let out a sigh that released a tiny portion of her fear.

There was so much more to say. But there would be plenty of time now, out here, just the two of them.

The wind picked up and buffeted heat and the smell of burning trees all the way to their little oasis by the river. It hit their nostrils acridly and went straight to their guts: a reminder of all the danger, destruction, and fear they had run from. It twisted something in their veins.

The scream of the cicadas exited the stage for the day as the bellbirds and whipbirds entered. The soft and cool of their sound helped to ease the knots in the empty stomachs of Nell and Eliza. They built a small fire by the river and warmed some of the remaining damper and cooked a little pot of tea.

That night, Nell dreamed of the river in the future. There were three elegant wood-and-glass houses by it, and the land around them had been completely cleared to allow for an uninterrupted view of the water. The houses looked like no other buildings she had ever seen, and included metallic machines and tools her mind could not bend around. As she walked fearfully around this strange, stark property with its bizarre gardens and artificial pools, she slowly understood that the houses contained rich white couples just lazing around.

Nell followed another rich-looking white woman who walked around like she owned the place, as she was taking her guests on a tour from the property to the banks of the river. She was talking very loudly to them about the history of white settlers and convicts who turned the wild land there into rich farming soils that fed the growing city and even had their own "bush theatre" there on the banks of the river. The guests later sat by the river in baths of mud with flowers over their eyes. Later, it was nighttime and the group was sitting around a fire wrapped in fluffy blankets. The white woman then said they would take a journey into the distant past, when the land was full of deep "mythology" and "unexplained rituals." She mispronounced the names of tribes and clans, and mistold their Dreamtime stories. Nell laughed in her sleep about the irony of a white woman making money from other white people with something they had formerly wanted to erase completely.

Eliza was smiling intently at Nell when she opened her eyes to the morning sun.

"What's so funny, then?" Eliza asked her, grinning, getting the fire going again.

Nell rubbed her eyes and scratched some twigs out of her hair. "Oh," she breathed, "that dream was so real."

"I could tell," Eliza said, stoking the flames, "you were laughing your head off!"

The knot in Nell's stomach eased a little and she allowed herself to rest against Eliza's warm body.

A black swan curved a great arc in the sky above them, and called out melancholically. Its cries echoed from the river's surface, then spiralled back around, and echoed again from the sandstone cliffs, giving the illusion that the cry had come directly from where Eliza and Nell had made camp.

Come home, the black swan seemed to be calling to Nell. *Come home.*

EPILOGUE

CHAPTER XXXIV

Sophie slips in, unnoticed, to the darkened back row of the cinema, carrying Virginia Woof in her arms. She fumbles to the empty seat next to Alex, who grins up at her as she shakily sits down. Her stomach is a riot of butterflies and her new "premiere pants" suddenly feel way too tight.

The film fades into the opening shot: a black-and-white slow-motion love letter to the glimmering surface of the Yandhai.

Sophie feels her cheeks burning in the dark as the circularity of it all hits her. From the Yandhai and the Narrows of her childhood, then the Spree of Berlin and the subterranean swamplands that nourish it, then, briefly, the Tagus River of Lisbon, and then the fabled River Styx that unexpectedly led her to the outback Barwon River, and all the way back around to the Yandhai.

"I've got rivers in my blood," says Nell up on screen.

Sitting there in the darkened theatre, with so many eyes and ears listening to Nell and Eliza's story, lost for so many years, Sophie begins to understand how all the tributaries life has taken her on, even if they felt like singular, disconnected stories at the time, were never singular in the slightest, any more than one river is just a standalone body of water. All of our bodies of water, and all of the stories which flow from us, are interconnected.

And it's the listening, telling, and retelling of our stories, especially the most traumatic ones, from personal traumas of sexual assault, generational traumas of domestic violence, national traumas of war, to genocidal traumas like the Stolen Generation, that hydrates our understanding of our intrinsic interconnectedness.

What we do to each other, we do to all of us.

Sophie exhales loudly as she relaxes into the film, and someone in the row in front shushes her. For the first time in a long time, Sophie allows a small smile to creep across her face.

"I think I'm finally beginning to understand how it feels to just *river*," Eliza says tenderly to Nell up on screen.

CHAPTER XXXV

When the time comes, they take the flood in their stride.

The river gives them no other choice.

It comes in the night, with the worst storm they had experienced in their entire lifetime out in the bush.

They had taken shelter on higher ground in the cave that was usually reserved for their winter dwelling because it was higher up from the cold ground and was protected by the treetops. The cave was deep enough to crawl far inside and forget about the wildness of the outside, and just exist in their warm universe of two.

Tonight, though, the storm and the river takes them completely unawares. It enters their home, up there in their cave, and forces them out of their comfort zone.

The wind should have been warning enough. It had been growling since sundown, low and menacing. Its sound now circles the rocks over and over, pacing and snarling over ancient boulders, wrenching rotted logs from their resting places, ripping over the waterhole and spraying the air like saliva frothing from a dingo's mouth. As the darkness falls, the growl becomes a howl and echoes high up into the clifftops and the treetops, thrashing the branches of the ghost gums without mercy. Even the oldest gum, the Ancestral Tree, is clinging onto life as the wind thrusts it back and forth, back and forth, towards the mouth of the cave. No one but the two of them huddled deep in the cave can hear the cries of the tree, and there is nothing they can do to stop the onslaught of the wind.

Then the thunder begins and overpowers even the wind's fury. Its sound is unleashed first downriver, as if brumbies are running for their lives, then comes roaring all the way down the rushing river, galloping towards them until it is so loud the brumbies might have been right there in the cave with them. Their fire had long since been blown out by the wind and then been destroyed by the rain, unable to be lit again. The cave shakes with the fury of it all.

The lightning, also coming closer and closer with alarming speed, is their only light source now. It is the only way they can look upon each other's faces, pressed wet and cold cheek to cheek as they cling to each other.

When the thunder and lightning coincide above them, there is an almighty flash, first blueish green, then magenta, then a raging flame for a startling moment, before it is extinguished by the lashing rain. The Ancestral Tree has been struck. It stays strong, though — its leaves are scorched and so is its bark, but its sap must still flow inside, and its wet roots are still protected under the earth, sustaining.

That quick smell of fire reaches their nostrils, and their danger instincts are piqued. They both stand immediately, not letting go of each other's hands.

The lightning illuminates their two bodies again.

There they stand, Nell and Eliza, two women in their sixties now. Nell, the taller of the two, her tangled, dark grey hair swept up off her neck in a calico scarf, her form muscular, wiry, bristling with strength. She wears a pair of fitted corduroy pants, tied with string at the waist, and a handmade thick wool coat. Her arm is wrapped protectively around Eliza and she holds Eliza's shaking hand with the other. Eliza is slighter and stands a little stooped. She appears a little emaciated and her skin is freckled and leathery from long years in the sun. She is slender and strong, despite the apparent fragile state of her health, and she wears a pair of green velvet pants and heavy riding boots. Her grey hair is loose and curly around her elfish face. She smiles up at Nell and shrugs a little, trying to shake off her fear. Nell, with her big kind eyes, smiles back at her, resignedly. They are both afraid but they have each other.

The river is flash-flooding. An unprecedented swell that neither of them has seen nor experienced before. There is a fury here that they do not know and cannot predict.

A great roar of thunder hits the cave again, and with it come the waves. The river's banks have broken and it has swollen all the way up to the mouth of their cave.

The women scream. How can this be happening?

"If we stay in here, we'll be trapped," shouts Nell.

"If we leave, we'll drown!" Eliza shouts back.

"I'd rather try my luck swimming, wouldn't you?"

Eliza nods, eyes darting to the rising muddy water.

Quick as they can, they remove their boots, their woollen socks, and all their clothes. They throw them all in a heap in the cave behind them and stand in the darkness shivering.

"It's bloody freezing," laughs Eliza.

"We promised each other we'd go skinny dipping again, remember?" Nell chuckles back.

"Wait..." Eliza says excitedly. "Just a moment..."

She goes over to her discarded trousers and pulls out her knife.

"Oh good idea, yes, we can take that with us..."

Eliza rushes over to the cave wall. "Yes and also..."

Eliza starts carving into the sandstone wall with the knife.

"Dear, what on earth, we haven't got time for that! The water's coming in!"

Nell rushes over to her and tries to grab her hand. "Please, we have to go now!"

Eliza keeps carving. The water begins to trickle into the cave now, and starts to pool around their feet. The cold of it is shocking.

"Eliza, now!"

"OK well, you do it then, Nell, you've always been better with a knife," Eliza says, turning to her with panic in her eyes. "Please, it's very important."

Nell groans exasperatedly and grabs the knife from her.

She expertly continues what Eliza had started, deep, clean cuts into the giving sandstone.

The water is rising past their ankles but the adrenaline rushing through them is warming their skin, their muscles, their bones. Eliza wraps her arms around Nell from behind as she finishes carving, and presses their bodies together.

There is a moment of calm as they stand back and admire their memento.

Nell & Eliza

Now & forever.

Then the moment passes and the reality of the raging storm and the rising river around their knees jolts them out of their reverie.

"Hurry!" Nell shouts. She's clutching the knife in one hand and Eliza's hand in the other. They wade against the rush of the water towards the cave's mouth. The world outside is a chaos of ripped branches, vicious rain, and the undeniable force of the river untethered from its banks.

They push out, as one, from the cave, but have to let go of each other as they hit the current in order to swim.

"We can use the trees as resting spots," shouts Eliza over the wind. "We can swim from one to the next and rest at each one."

"Liza," Nell calls as she forces her way through the fury, "know that I have always loved you and will always love you."

Panic grips Eliza then, more deeply than the panic already coursing through her body from the storm.

"You're strong, stronger than I've ever been," she calls to Nell. "You'll make it through this, even if I don't."

"No," Nell shouts and swims back a way to reach Eliza behind her. "We either both survive this or we both do not. There's no question."

Eliza tries to protest, river water flooding her mouth and her arms hitting rocks and broken logs.

"I have always loved you too, from the moment I saw you. And will for longer than this river will course through this earth..."

"This was our river," Eliza continues, swallowing water and panting hard, "our lifeblood for our whole lives. Why is she so angry with us?"

Nell grins back at Eliza, struggling too as a tree wrenched from its roots hits her face.

"She's not angry at us," Nell replies, arms heaving to stay afloat. "She's calling us home."

Another colossal tree now hits them both hard and knocks them beneath the surface. The water surges and rips them both further down, deep underwater, eddying them into its spirals.

The storm continues raging and the river is unstoppable. The lightning illuminates the surface once, twice, three times, revealing wreckage, debris, and the merciless dark current.

The river surges on.

Fade to black.

This could not have been written without the wellsprings of support and inspiration from:

Astrida Neimanis, my former PhD supervisor within the Gender and Cultural Studies Department at the University of Sydney.

Joanna Eberstein's 'Manifesting from the Beyond' class from Morbid Anatomy.

Holly Rigby and her wonderful writing groups, including fellow Repeater authors.

The Berlin Writers Club, with particular love to Arikia Millikan and Cathy Bijur.

The always-insightful, sensitive, and crucial editorial work from Christopher DeVeau —thank you! — and Tariq Goddard (formerly Repeater), who first took the chance on my book proposal: oceans of gratefulness.

My family and friends for your loving patience, especially during my moments of estrangement from my own story. And my partner Lisa — you always managed to nudge me back into the current.

And my furry familiar Dallas — you stayed warmly by my side for every last word I wrote.

BIBLIOGRAPHY

Acker, K., Eurydice in the Underworld, Arcadia Books, 1998

Alaimo, S., Bodily Natures: Science, Environment, and the Material Self, Indiana, Indiana University Press, 2010

Antichrist, dir. Von Trier, L., Denmark, Zentropa, 2009 (online)

Bachelard, G., The Poetics of Space. Presses Universitaires de France, 1958

Bird-Rose, D., Wild Dog Dreaming: Love and Extinction, UVA, 2011

Bird-Rose, D., Dingo Makes Us Human; Life and Land in an Australian Aboriginal Culture, Cambridge University Press, 2009

Björk, "Hope is a muscle," lyrics from the song "Atopos," as well as the title of the 2022 album

Blom, P., Nature's Mutiny: How the Little Ice Age Transformed the West and Shaped the Present, Picador, 2019

Bodkin, F., and Bodkin-Andrews, G., D'harawal Dreaming Stories

Carson, A., Float, Penguin Random House, 2016

Cixous, H., "Laugh of the Medusa," in D. E. Richter (ed.), The Critical Tradition, Boston, Bedford Books, 1998 & Oxford, Oxford University Press, 2006, pp. 1453 – 1466

De Botton, A., and Armstrong, J., Art as Therapy, London, Phaidon, 2013

Federici, S., Caliban and the Witch: Women, the Body and Primitive Accumulation, Autonomedia, 2004

Find and Connect: https://www.findandconnect.gov.au/entity/brewarrina-aboriginal-station-dormitory/

Gaard, G., "Ecofeminism and Wilderness," in Vance, L (ed.), Women, Ecology, and the Environment, NWSA Journal, Vol. 9, No. 3, The John Hopkins University Press, 1997, pp. 60 – 76

Gaard, G., 'Toward a Queer Ecofeminism', Hypatia: A Journal of Feminist Philosophy, Volume 12, Issue 1, 1997, p.114 – 137

Haraway, D., Simians, Cyborgs and Women: The Reinvention of Nature, FreeAssociation Press, 1991

Haraway, D., How Like a Leaf: An Interview with Thyrza Nichols Goodeve, Routledge, 2000

Haraway, D., 'Tentacular Thinking: Anthropocene, Capitalocene, Chthulucene," e-flux journal, Issue 75, 2016

Healing Foundation, The: https://healingfoundation.org.au/map_marker/brewarrina-aboriginal-station-dormitory/

Heller, C., "For the Love of Nature: Ecology and the Cult of the Romantic," in G. Gaard (ed.), Ecofeminism: Women, Animals, Nature, Temple University Press 1993, pp. 243 – 272

Irigaray, L., This Sex Which is Not One, Cornell University Press, 1985

Karskens, G., People of the River: Lost Worlds of Early Australia, Allen & Unwin, 2020

Kheel, M., "From Heroics to Holistic Ethics: The Ecofeminist Challenge," in G. Gaard (ed.), Ecofeminism: Women, Animals, Nature, Temple University Press, Philadelphia, 1993, p. 243 – 272

Latufeku, Dr. Ruth A. Fink, Recollections of a Brewarrina Aboriginal "Mission" in 1954, Aboriginal Support Group: https://asgmwp.net/recollections-of-brewarrina-aboriginal-mission-in-1954/

Le Guin, U. K., The Carrier Bag Theory of Fiction (with an Introduction by Donna Haraway), Ignota Books, 2019

Lindsay, J., Picnic at Hanging Rock, Penguin Books, 1965

Lorde, A., Zami: A New Spelling of my Name, A Biomythography, Penguin Books, 1982

Machado, C.M., In the Dream House, Graywood Press, 2019

Manathunga, C., Selkrig, M., Baker, A., "Enlivening the senses: engaging sight and sound to (re)consider the hidden narratives of academics in the histories of university education," History of Education: Journal of the History of Education Society, Vol. 47, No. 2, pp. 169 – 189

Merchant, C., The Death of Nature, HarperCollins, 2010

Mulvey, L., Visual and Other Pleasures, Palgrave Macmillan, 2009

Neimanis, A., Bodies of Water: Posthuman Feminist Phenomenology, Bloomsbury Academic, 2017

Nelson, M., The Argonauts, Graywolf Press, 2015

Plumwood, V., Feminism and the Mastery of Nature, Routledge, 2002

Picnic at Hanging Rock, dir, Weir, P., Aus, Australian Film Commision, 1975

Plumwood, V., "Ecofeminism: An Overview and Discussion," Australasian Journal of Philosophy, Vol. 64 (S1), 1986, pp. 120 – 138

Sappho, selected fragments from papyrus, c. 630BC

Sebald, W.G., Rings of Saturn, Eichborn, 2005

Shakespeare, W., The Tragedy of Hamlet, Prince of Denmark, 1603

Schalansky, J., "What We Know of Sappho," The Paris Review, December 8, 2020

Solnit, R., A Field Guide to Getting Lost, Putnam Penguin, 2005

Solnit, N., A Paradise Built in Hell, Penguin Random House, 2019

Sontag, S., On Photography, Penguin Books, 1977

Steyerl, H. (ed.), Beyond Representation, Marius Babias, contributions by Elsässer, T. & Sheik, S., Berlin, Walther König, 2016

Tennyson, A. L., "The Lady of Shalott," in Poems, 1832

Vance, L., "Ecofeminism and the Politics of Reality," in G. Gaard (ed.), Ecofeminism: Women, Animals, Nature, Temple University Press, 1993, p. 118 – 146

Walton, S., Cinema's Baroque Flesh: Film, Phenomenology and the Art of Entanglement, Amsterdam University Press 2016

Wark, M., The Beach Beneath the Street: The Everyday Life and Glorious Times of the Situationist International, Verso, 2011

Wark, M., Raving, Duke University Press, 2023

Warren, K.J., Ecofeminist Philosophy: A Western Perspective on What it is and Why it Matters, Rowman & Littlefield, 2000

Warren, K.J., & Erkal, N., Ecofeminism: Women, Culture, Nature, Indiana University Press, 1997

Watson, I., Aboriginal Peoples, Colonialism and International Law: Raw Law, Routledge, 2015

Winterson, J., Sexing the Cherry, Vintage, 1990

Woolf, V., Orlando, Hogarth Press, 1928

Worms, E.A. (ed.), "The Poetry of the Yaoro and Bad, North-Western Australia," Annali Lateranemse, Vol. 21

Yeats, W.B., Leda and the Swan, The Dial, 1924

Yusoff, K., A Billion Black Anthropocenes or None, University of Minnesota Press, 2019

REPEATER BOOKS

is dedicated to the creation of a new reality. The landscape of twenty-first-century arts and letters is faded and inert, riven by fashionable cynicism, egotistical self-reference and a nostalgia for the recent past. Repeater intends to add its voice to those movements that wish to enter history and assert control over its currents, gathering together scattered and isolated voices with those who have already called for an escape from Capitalist Realism. Our desire is to publish in every sphere and genre, combining vigorous dissent and a pragmatic willingness to succeed where messianic abstraction and quiescent co-option have stalled: abstention is not an option: we are alive and we don't agree.

01 14

✓